Imagine you and your two sisters are off to spend a week at dull, old great-Granny's house while your folks go on vacation. Boring, right? Well, that's exactly what Kari, Leah and Mia thought until Granny, dulled by grief and infirmed by age, forces them into her Caddy for a road trip from Southern California to Oregon. What could possibly go wrong? Well … everything.

Go along with resourceful Kari, impulsive Leah, and adventuresome Mia as they embark on the road trip of their lives. It will be a trip you'll remember for a long time.
—ANGELA MOODY,
Author of *No Safe Haven*

This road trip novel is a story both tender and terrifying about one inexperienced teen driver who must take her family on a journey not of her own choosing.
—CYNTHIA T. TONEY,
Author of the *Bird Face* series

Road Trip to Delusion is a captivating story of the hair-raising adventures of Kari Rose and her sisters, staying with their great-grandma. Faced with a difficult choice, Kari opts for a 500-mile-long trip north from California to Southern Oregon to visit family. Kari's first attempt to drive is jerky at best, but with Granny no longer able to, everyone depends on Kari to survive.

OTHER BOOKS BY JEAN ANN WILLIAMS

Just Claire

God's Mercies after Suicide: Blessings Woven through a Mother's Heart

Road Trip
of
<u>Delusion</u>

Jean Ann Williams

Love Truth

Road Trip of Delusion

ISBN: 978-0997701623

Published by Love Truth
Glendale, Oregon

Cover illustration by Carley Rose Herlihy
Cover design by Nina Newton, Creative Life Publishing
Edited by Nina Newton and Leslie L. McKee
Formatted by Lee Carver, author of *Katie's Quest*
Copy edits and proofed by Barbara Oden
Chapter titles taken from 1 Corinthians 13

TEENS / Literature & Fiction / Action & Adventure / Survival Stories

1

If I Speak

My heart sank to my navel. I left behind my plans for a week of recipe testing as I hugged the cookbook on my lap.

Great-granny's foot went heavy on the gas pedal of her Cadillac Fleetwood. The vehicle backfired with a zoom onto Highway 101. Her ancient hawk-like eyes never seemed to wander from the approaching headlight beams.

I shook my head, trying to dislodge a huge regret—I wasn't able to talk her out of taking this trip.

In the backseat, my sister, Leah Bedeah, two years younger than me at thirteen, jumped on the roadway of reasoning. "Granny, don't you think we should tell someone?"

Great-granny's head barely crested the top of the seat. "Your Grand is gone, so it's just me now." She lifted her chin.

Little sister Mia Babe sat next to Leah. "Kari?"

Twisting in my seat, I faced them. "What?"

"Mom says Grand's in paradise, but where's that?"

Ah, Mia, an old soul at the age of seven. "Well, from what Mom taught me, it's a spiritual place where people go when they die".

"Oh." Mia rubbed her left eye, a sure sign she was sleepy.

A scary notion surfaced, and I slapped my forehead. "Do you even *know* your way to Oregon?"

"Of course." Great-granny flicked her blinker and passed a small car. "Grand and I visited Oregon when your mama was a slip of a teenager."

"But—" Leah counted. "That was around twenty-five years ago. Right, Kari?"

"Right." I rolled my eyes and refocused on the headlight-brightened pavement. "I don't think they moved the state since then, Leah." *But, does Granny remember how to get there?*

"Very funny, Kari." Leah huffed as she threw herself back against the plush seat. "You don't know everything."

I waved her off. "Just hush, and let me think."

"Whatever."

"Would you stop?" I hissed as Great-granny launched into one of her tales.

"I wish you'd known my bigger sister, Doreen." She cackled and slapped the wheel. "When she was Kari Rose's age, we set out on one of many road trips. This trip here is undersized potatoes in comparison." Nodding, she continued. "When we decided to go somewhere, we went—one way or 'nother."

How would I convince my grief-stricken great-granny to turn this once-proud Cadillac around before we traveled farther from home?

A hint of dawn brushed the base of the eastern sky. The Coastal Oaks struggled to peek through the dark. Their branches gnarled like an old woman's fingers.

My lashes fluttered. *Stay awake.* Didn't Granny need two sets of eyes to watch the road? I pictured the drivers' ed manual on my dresser and remembered something about this. Or could it be my distrust for an eighty-year-old driving a vehicle which swayed side to side.

Although it was still too dark to see anything but shapes in the backseat, from the outline of Leah's crossed arms she was ticked-off angry.

"Mama's gonna be mad, Kari." Mia's voice quivered. "I'm on this trip only 'cause you're biggest, and Granny's the oldest."

Leah grumbled. "Just chill, ya little baby."

Granny looked in the rearview mirror. "What's that you say?" The Cadillac swerved.

Gripping the steering wheel, I steadied it. "You drive, and I'll handle the rest."

"A bit bossy, aren't we?" Granny crossed the dotted lines on the road.

Here we go, again. Letting go of the wheel, I then clenched my cookbook as well as my teeth.

"No, she's not bossy." Leah unbuckled and leaned near Granny. "You jerked this bat mobile." I shook my head at Leah, but she didn't take the hint and pointed her index finger at Granny's head. "She's driving reckless."

Beads of sweat dampened my bangs, and I heaved a huge sigh of frustration.

Granny eased her foot off the accelerator. "I didn't mean to scare you, Leah."

In reply, she folded her hands together on Granny's head rest. "Please, dear Lord, keep us safe."

My sister never knew when to quit.

Granny *harrumphed.* "Don't be disrespectful, Leah Bedeah."

"I'm. Not. I'm praying." She squinted. "And thank You, Lord, ahead of time for—"

"You girls don't *have to* take this trip with me."

Mia shuffled in her seat. "Aren't you supposed to be babysitting us?"

"Who's babysitting who is the better question?" Leah snorted.

Was Granny joking? I couldn't imagine her driving five hundred miles to Oregon by her lonesome. In a car older than my mother, even. "You know, Granny … wouldn't it be fun instead to stop at Monterey Bay Aquarium and see the dolphins?"

"Suppose not." Surely she spit the *t* through a space in the steering wheel.

Mia banged her shoes against her seat. "C'mon, Granny, let's go."

I rubbed my palm over the cookbook cover, itching to stare with longing at the fudge brownie recipe. "There's no way we can get to Oregon and home again before our parents get back on Sunday."

"And why *not*?"

There she goes, spitting a whole word.

"Four days is time enough to visit my son."

Leah's chin hugged the top of the front seat between Granny and me. "Granny, you shouldn't take advantage of Mom and Dad on their vacation with no cell phone."

"How come we didn't get to go?" Mia stroked my neck. "I wanna sleep in a tree house and burn marshmallows in a fire."

I waved a hand to shoo off her question. "Kids don't go on second honeymoons."

"Why?" Mia's voice became super whiney.

"It's a celebration of the day they married seventeen years ago." Leah yawned. "That's why."

Mia sighed. "I miss Mama."

"Personally, I agree with Kari." Leah looked down her nose at Granny. "No way will we get this Caddy home in time."

"It's not a *Caddy*." Granny stretched her neck, as the car weaved again. "This gem is a Cadillac."

I touched the wheel to stop the swaying. "Whoa."

"More like a prehistoric beast." Leah muttered.

Granny pinned her eyes on the road. "How do you know we won't get home before your parents?"

Ducking her head, Leah resurfaced seconds later, shaking a large travel map. "Because, Granny, these road directions prove we won't."

Silence filled the car, and I squirmed in the leather seat.

I pointed. "You had time to look at it before we left?"

Leah nodded. "I did."

"I'll look at the map later on." Granny's voice oozed as smooth as hot fudge sauce. "And, girls, I've got a thousand dollars in my purse. You'll be my bodyguards."

A gas bubble shot to my throat. I choked on the burp. That was too much cash to carry, and Leah was right about *prehistoric beast*. The way the car spurted and clunked, we'd need all the money for repairs.

Leah groaned. "It's too dangerous to carry this much money."

Granny shrugged her boney shoulders. "We'll be fine."

I wiggled my fingers at Leah. "Give me the map." Granny must know what she's doing, right? Now it was my turn to talk to God, but in silence. *Please, Lord, change Granny's mind about this trip.*

~*~

As the Cadillac sped along, my eyeballs burned from lack of sleep. I rolled down the window a crack. We passed a huge boulder next to the highway where people can begin to see the beauty of the Pacific Ocean. The view of the sea now was shadowy, and I inhaled. The same aroma ever since I could remember. Yep. Fishy.

Upset plans swirled in my brain like ingredients under a high-speed mixer. Tonight, I was supposed to cook fish and chips in Granny's spacious, fancy kitchen. One like I hoped to have some day. I was going to use the cookbook my grandmother, Granny-Too, gave to me. I even chose a strawberry pie recipe made from the fresh strawberries which would now rot in Granny's refrigerator.

At the thought, I stuck out my tongue.

My pie would not come to fruition. A grin tugged on a corner of my mouth, and I allowed a few moments to admire my clever pun.

Changing gears, I considered my favorite person: Granny-Too. She created the best breads and desserts, so my reason to learn pie making. So far, I specialized in salads and smoothies. And fish. With saliva pooled around my tongue, my taste buds tingled. Dancing my fingers across the glossy cover of the cookbook, I'd learn how to cook just as well as Granny-Too.

The Caddy swerved far to the right and startled me into action. I clutched Granny's wheel. "You're weaving, again."

"Don't I know it? I can't remember the last time I drove my car."

My nerves zinged like an electrical spark from a stove.

Granny yawned. "Now Leah, get back into your seatbelt."

"Wow, your driving is scary." Leah covered her face. Granny gave her a sideways glance, and Leah tapped the back of the seat between Granny and me. "And Mama's right."

"About what?" Granny stretched her neck and peered into the rearview mirror.

"You have eyes that circle your head." Leah shook with the giggles.

Even though Leah had become rude, I hid a grin behind my hand.

"I *beg* your pardon." Granny's voice wavered. "This hurts my feelings, Leah Bedeah. Buckle yourself up and don't worry about how I drive, you hear?" She thumped the dashboard. "Besides, we've got James."

At the mention of Grand, my fingers touched the photo of a much younger Grand in his World War II uniform.

Leah's laughter ended in a sigh. "Yeah, but, he's *not* the driver."

~*~

After miles of silence, the sun topped the eastern foothills. Granny wiggled her hand in my direction. "How about we get a bite to eat?"

Mia kicked her heels against her seat. "I want French toast with powdered sugar."

To stop would be good. With a glance, Leah and I nodded.

Granny steered the Cadillac from the fast lane to an off-ramp. I craned my neck this way and another to watch for vehicles. The car slowed and halted in front of a café.

Mia un-clicked her safety belt. "I'm so, so hungry, Granny, I could eat two plates of food. One of French toast and the other pancakes."

"Oh, yeah, Mia Babe?" Granny switched off the engine. "Just as soon as your sisters help me from this car."

I opened Leah's passenger door. "Get Silver, would you Leah?"

She squinted. "Oh, I forgot, Granny's walker with a built-in seat."

Why didn't I think of Granny's feeble age when she woke me early this morning and said she was leaving? This meant she drove. Our granny couldn't even move across a parking lot without Silver.

My mom and I took Granny and Silver on errands. Granny would sit on Silver once she got tired and someone—usually me—would push her as we finished our shopping.

Now, I groaned. This trip unsettled me more by the mile.

I hurried to the driver's side of the car and stood by Granny's open door. Leah pulled Silver from the trunk with a clatter, clack and pushed it into Granny's outstretched hands.

Before she stood, Granny tested the brakes to make sure they were locked. She clutched the handles until the flesh over her knuckles stretched white and readjusted her whole ninety-five pounds. Once she hovered above Sliver's built-in seat, Granny sat with a plop. "We did it."

With Granny ready to shove off, I swiveled on my heels. "Where's Mia?"

Leah spun round. "Mia Babe!"

No answer. No Mia.

A group of people walked past and made a line at the entrance of the café. "Leah, take Granny to the door." I motioned with my hand. "I'll run ahead and make sure Mia went inside."

Leah wrinkled her nose. "No, you take Granny, and *I'll* look for Mia."

We glared at each other.

Granny tugged Leah's sweater. "Go, Leah, go."

Far too long later, the front door *swoosh*ed closed behind me and Granny. I scanned the crowded room and a waitress met us. "How many in your party?"

I lifted four jittery fingers. "My two sisters are already here. I hope."

She grinned. "Younger girls than you, honey?"

"Yes, ma'am."

"Follow me." She led the way while I wheeled Granny into the dining area.

My sisters sat in a booth. Before them on the table were cups of hot cocoa and whipped cream piled in peaks like meringue on a pie. As I drew closer, their grins were also

15

giggles. I frowned at Leah. "You could have told us you found Mia."

I waited for Granny to agree. But she laughed for the second time this morning. "Cocoa and cream on your lips. It only took one shake of a dog's tail to decide upon your drinks I see."

Tilting her head, Leah murmured, her voice syrupy. "Yeah."

Mia peeked over the rim of her cup. "I sure like my cocoa. But, what do you mean about a dog tail?"

The waitress got a word in edgewise. "What may I get *you* ladies to drink?"

Granny released Silver and plunked her skinny self on the diner's seat. "I'll take water and my coffee black, thank you, ma'am."

I decided to forgive Leah. "Cocoa for me." It was a silly incident compared to what we faced.

I've got to navigate us to the Monterey Bay Aquarium.

2

A Noisy Gong

While we waited for our food, I excused myself to use the ladies' room. Granny knuckle-rapped the table. "Get the map afterward, Kari Rose. I'll take a look at where we go from here."

Ah, thank You, God, an opportunity. I tugged on Leah's arm. "Come with me." I pulled her out of ear shot from Granny. "Let's skip the bathroom for now."

In the backseat of the Caddy, we moved Leah's belongings to give us room. "I've got an idea of how to get Granny to stay on Highway 101 and not cut across to Interstate 5." Our heads bent over the page of California. "If we go to the aquarium she'll be so exhausted. We'll head home before dark." My lips flattened on my teeth.

"Good, 'cause Granny's driving is horrid." Leah squeezed my hand. "She's so fragile. She should be home in her recliner. Not behind the wheel of a car that rocks like a boat."

"I know, huh?" I used my pointer finger to mark our location and dragged it along the route. "If I tell Granny to stay north, which takes us to Monterey, she just might believe me."

"She'll ask for the turn off to Interstate 5." Leah tapped on the city of Paso Robles. "Where we are now."

I followed Leah's nail and studied farther north. "To stay on 101, this is where we would go. Then swing over if Granny catches on."

"But, look, it's into the Bay Area. Remember when Dad took us on a business trip to San Francisco?" Leah shivered. "No way could Granny drive through that big of a city."

"I agree." Heads bowed, we continued to study the areas. "Looky here." I flipped a thatch of hair behind my ear. "We'll lead Granny to Monterey. If she insists on not stopping, she can go farther north. Then, we'll cut across at Gilroy and east toward Los Baños. Even at this point, it's still close enough."

"You mean, by the time we're near Los Baños, we'll have another plan to get us home?"

"Exactly." I pointed. "Once we're there, we'll take the South Bound lane of the freeway. See?"

Leah slapped my hand in a high five. "And, I don't even feel guilty plotting against her." A puff of air escaped between her lips. "Granny thinks only of herself."

"It feels mean to me, but she started this. Not us." I touched Leah's arm. "Besides, Mama would split a temple vein if she knew what Granny has done."

"True." Leah's lashes flickered. "But, Mom will no doubt look at it as what *we've* done as well."

Mia knocked on the Caddy window. "Here you are. You weren't in the bathroom. Food's ready."

We nodded. Leah bent close to my ear. "If turning around at Monterey fails, one of us could pretend we're sick. Granny would surely head the car back home, then."

I didn't want to lie.

Walking across the parking lot to the restaurant, I took Mia's hand. "Did you know there's a place near here where there's dolphins and otters and fancy, bright-colored fish?"

She skipped. "I wanna go."

I jiggled her hand. "Let's ask Granny." And Mia nodded.

Nudging Leah, I whispered, "Show no expression on your face."

When we came to our booth, Granny was munching on a piece of bacon. "Took you long enough."

I settled the bulky map on my lap.

Before we ate, Leah folded her hands. "Granny, do you want to say the blessing?"

She swallowed her food, before bowing her head. "Our gracious, bountiful Father, we thank thee for our food. In Jesus' name. Amen."

Utensils clanked on plates as everyone dove into their breakfast.

Halfway through the meal, Granny laid aside her fork. "When I finish, I'll take a look at the map over another cup of coffee."

Leah and I locked fingers under the table and squeezed. My sister and I hadn't discussed this part. What do I do when Granny asked for the map?

~*~

As the waitress whisked away our empty plates, Granny ordered seconds on our cocoas. When fresh cups arrived, the mounds of whipped cream mirrored the clouds outside the café window.

Leah scooted closer until our knees touched. "Granny, what—"

"I wanna see the dolphins, Granny." Mia's lips pursed.

"Sounds good to me." I straightened my shoulders, grateful for the direction of the conversation.

"Me, too." Leah sucked on the cream. "You know, Granny, the one in Monterey Bay?"

I chimed in. "Not too far from here."

"So *whaaaat?*" Granny's voice grew shrill.

We sisters gave each other the, *uh, oh,* look.

"Now, girls, it's not what I decided, so don't pester."

I slurped a mouthful of the whipped topping. My homemade tasted fresher and better. "But, Granny…" Milk products always made me feel calm and bold. Although, I doubted this stuff had even a smidgen of real dairy. "You changed *our* spring break plans."

"Kari Rose." Granny waggled a finger. "Let me see the map."

I placed it on the table but didn't move to give it to her.

"Yeah, poor us." Leah gripped her hands around the cup. "At three in-the-ridiculously-dark morning, we left like criminals in the dark."

Granny squinted. "Please, give me the map." She sipped her coffee.

I released a sigh, pushed the map toward her, and clutched my hands. She'll see the turn off for Interstate 5 right here in Paso Robles.

We're sunk.

3

Understand All Mysteries

The coffee woke Granny, and the cocoa made us girls kind of hyper. Those drinks did something else. Within an hour along Highway 41, we stopped at a gas station.

Nervous, I picked at the skin around my fingernails. *What if we're not home by Sunday?* Did Granny even care Mom's going to have a meltdown? This must be how my hamster feels, eyes wide, running circles in her cage.

We were headed east for Interstate 5. No Monterey Bay Aquarium. No turning back, yet. No way could my stomach settle and stop its burn.

Why did I go along with Granny's trip idea after she interrupted my sleep at her house? Deep down I knew. I grew fretful. I made a wrong choice.

At yet another stop, we entered the ladies' room. Leah signaled me with a finger tapped to her lips as Granny went inside a bathroom stall. Would we now decide who had to act sick? Not only did I not want to make our mom furious by having left, I didn't want to lie.

After she pressed the hand dryer with an elbow, Leah placed her digits underneath the air flow. "Mia, it's your turn to push Granny in Silver."

"I get to help?" Mia stood at attention, her eyes roved from me to Leah.

"Yes." Leah wiped the rest of the damp from her hands on her jeans. "Are you ready?"

Granny pushed Silver to our huddle. "Mia's not strong enough." The lines on her forehead deepened.

"Oh, but I want to, Granny." Mia raised her shirt sleeve and flexed a flat arm. "See? I'm buffed."

"Where do you get this stuff?" Leah grinned.

"Come on, then, muscle girl." Granny's eyes twinkled. "First, I need to warsh my hands."

We waited for Granny, and Leah's brows rose toward her forehead. She mimicked, *Warsh*? Leaving the bathroom, we sauntered behind Granny and Mia. Leah hooked her arm into mine. "We're never getting to Papa and Granny-Too's at this slug pace." She shrugged. "Whoever thought a great-grandmother could act like a spoiled brat? Or maybe it's worse. Like as in—"

I withdrew my elbow. I halted along the outside wall of the bathroom. "What are you saying?"

"My friend, Ana? Her grandmother has reverted." Leah's eyes dulled. "At first she was really forgetful. Before they knew it, she wandered outside and got lost." She buzz-sighed. "Our great-granny's weaving down the interstate. The only reason she's not lost is because I brought the map."

"But she's lonely." The possibility of her words raised goose bumps along my flesh. "Granny's in mourning, Leah. Besides, the reason doesn't matter." I shrugged. "What can we do?" All my ideas were burned away like rubber on tires.

"We can call the cops." Leah pointed at Granny as Mia wheeled her in Silver. "We could tell them we saw this old lady rob the gas station, just to get them here. Then, we can tell our story."

I gasped. "Don't make a joke."

She threw up her hands. "If I don't, I'm going to cry. Although, I'd still call the police."

"Listen, she's our family. You can't be serious."

She nodded her head yes.

"Well, I won't do it." I never knew Leah's determined side could go overboard. *She'll calm down in a minute. Surely.*

"You listen to me, Kari." Leah held her hands as though she prayed. "Before we would leave Papa's and Granny-Too's, Mom and Dad will be home." Leah pointed to her own chest. "I do not want my allowance cut. I do not want to be grounded until I'm eighteen." She rolled her eyes. "And I hate it when Mom gives us the silent treatment."

Crossing my arms, I rapped the toe of my sneaker on the concrete walk. "I won't call the police on our granny."

With her eyes, Leah pleaded. "Can't we at least call Papa? He *was* a cop."

"And get him upset?" I shook my head no. "You forget he had heart surgery last year. Mom said it was because of his stressful job. I won't involve Papa in this, Leah." I raised my nose.

"Then let's call Granny-Too." Leah placed a hand on her hip. "We could make her swear not to tell anyone. She'd talk sense into Granny's foggy, old brain."

"I'm trying to remember how long it took Papa and Granny-Too to drive to Oregon before they moved there."

Pressing my belly, I needed to ease the bubbles caused by this conversation. "I think ten hours."

She glanced at her watch. "And we've been on the road—almost five." Leah stuck out her wrist. "See? It's eight o'clock. At this rate, we'll need to get a motel and another day is shot."

"Okay, we'll call Granny-Too and have her talk to Granny." My arms slapped to my thighs.

"Why are you girls taking so long?" Up ahead, Granny waited at the driver's side of the Caddy.

I nudged Leah forward. "We can't talk about this anymore."

As we came within five feet of Granny, she pointed. "You know it's rude to whisper in front of others."

Leah drew closer. "I wondered, Granny, if we'll need to stay at a motel on the way."

"Of course." She patted her own leg. "My old bones need to lay flat. Besides, my eyes are gettin' blurry."

Blurry? Leah and I mouthed.

I nibbled on my lower lip. We could become stranded because Granny can't drive the whole way to Oregon? Relief washed over every inch of me.

Wait a doggone minute. Granny's age would end this trip.

~*~

For our lunch stop, Granny pulled into Bella's Pea Soup parking lot. She maneuvered the boat which lurched into a handicap spot, shifted into Park, and turned off the relic of an engine.

This Cadillac amazed me with its metal dash of gadgets. What would it be like to drive such a classic? Ancient. Like Granny. Less wrinkles. Granny fascinated me with her old-fashioned ideas and unfamiliar vocabulary. If we'd only gotten permission for this trip, I would actually enjoy it—and her. Except for the times she made the car wobble. "Granny, you just parked in a place for the disabled."

"Don't I know it. Get my handicap sticker in the glove box and hook it on the rearview mirror. I'm tuckered out."

Handicap? Leah and I frowned. I hung the sticker.

Granny craned her neck to stare in the mirror. Digging into her purse, she whipped out a tube of brick-red lipstick and rolled it on. She smacked. Then, she pressed her lips on a tissue. "I love their pea soup."

Right then, my stomach walked off on me at the mention of cooked peas. My gag reflex kicked into go-mode.

"Stop it, Kari." Obviously, Granny understood my reaction. "If you haven't tried it, don't knock it."

"I can't help my taste buds." I pressed two fingers on my lips. A burp puffed my cheeks, and I swallowed. "I only eat raw peas. From our organic garden."

"How do you knock on soup, Granny?" Mia leaned over the front seat and blinked.

The ever-literal Mia.

"Never mind." Granny examined herself in the mirror again. She dabbed with a tissue the lipstick stuck in a crease above her lips. "I do expect you girls to sample a spoonful."

We sisters groaned.

"So, you've tried it, Kari?" Granny studied me.

"Well, no." I bowed my head.

She chuckled. "Today's your lucky day."

"Oh, but, Granny." Mia popped up near Granny's ear. "Mama says there's no such thing as luck. *Ooonnnly* blessings."

I nodded at Mia, and Granny dismissed us with a wave.

~*~

In the restaurant, my sisters slumped at the table. We'd been raised on uncooked veggies and salads at every meal. And, our parents made homemade pastas and wood-baked pizzas in the hearth.

Now, Granny's voice gave me a headache. "This will be an experience you'll live to tell your children."

If this was her attempt to cheer us, she flopped.

"Oh, please." Leah stuck out her tongue. "Or about the time I vomited pea soup on a road trip I didn't ask to take."

Granny nudged her. "You stop your sassing."

Leah *harrump*ed. "It'll be true."

"Gracious sakes." Granny stared at the ceiling and shook her head. "Give the soup a chance."

Eyes focused on the menu, one side of Leah's mouth quivered. It hitched into a smirk.

When the waitress came, Granny ordered three milkshakes. "We'll take a bowl of pea soup for me, and one cup for the girls to share." She searched our faces. "Four burgers and fries." Granny shut the menu and exposed her slightly crooked and caffeine-stained teeth.

Mia placed her chin in her cupped hands. "Granny, tell us more about you and your sister, Dori."

26

"Doreen, Mia Babe." Granny's eyes clouded with confusion. "Was I saying something about her?"

I quickly glanced at Leah. We locked eyes.

"Well." Mia's face brightened. "You said when you and Doreen decided to go someplace, you went."

Leah pointed her finger in the air. "Like now."

Granny fixed Leah with a look. "When Doreen decided we would go somewhere, she became jumpy like ants were swarming her bare feet."

Mia gasped. "Really?"

"No, Mia Babe." Granny laughed. "It's just an expression. But, I do remember one time like it happened today. I was almost fifteen and Doreen was sixteen. She had a boyfriend named Jerry Lee, and he drove a Ford pickup truck.

"Doreen was a bea-u-ty with sea-blue eyes and a smile to win any boy's heart." Granny gazed across the room. "Daddy had to shoo the boys off." She leaned in closer. "It started when Doreen was your age, Leah."

"I have no interest in the blockheads." Leah cut her eyes toward Granny. "They're so immature."

"You do have plenty of time for boys." Granny tapped her on the arm.

"Kari's never had a boyfriend." Giggling, Mia covered her mouth with a napkin.

"Hush, blabber tongue." I hoped to have one, but who knew when this would happen.

"Both of you be quiet." Leah drummed fingers on the table. "Granny's telling her story."

Before I could let Leah have it for bossing me, the waitress zoomed to the table. "Here you go, ladies." She placed two chocolate milkshakes in front of my sisters, one strawberry shake for me, and a cup of coffee for Granny. "Food will be here soon."

"Thank you, ma'am." Granny sipped her coffee. "Doreen's Jerry Lee said he'd lend us his pickup, while he worked the night shift at the gasoline station. He left it parked down the block from our house so our parents wouldn't see Doreen behind the wheel."

"You and your sister were sneaky." Mia narrowed her eyes. "We'd never be that bad, would we, girls?"

Leah crossed her eyes and sucked her shake through a straw.

"Nope." I stirred mine with a spoon. "Mama would lecture us until our ears plugged."

"Well, it wasn't my idea, it was Doreen's." Granny massaged her throat. "She always got us into trouble."

Leah waggled her head. "This is not what the family says about you, so innocent and all." Nervy enough, Leah stared at Granny.

I winced.

Shoulders pulled back, Granny coughed on her sip of coffee. "Who's talking bad about me?"

Leah's expression melted into serene. "I'll not tell."

For the sake of peace, I needed to steer the story to Great-great Aunt Doreen. I bent closer to Granny. "So Doreen drove the pickup."

But really, Granny didn't *have* to go along with her sister's tricks.

4

Does Not Insist On Its Own Way

"Anyway." Granny patted her hair and smoothed it from her cheek. "We dressed in our church clothes. Even though the season became warm, we added coats and buttoned up."

My gut calmed as Granny told her story.

"Why?" Leah squinted.

"Doreen said we didn't want Mama to see us in our good clothes." Granny's wrinkles deepened like cracks in an over cooked custard. "It seemed odd to dress so nice for where we told Mama we were going."

"Where did you go, Granny?" Mia slurped on her milkshake.

She frowned. "I thought to the movies."

Mia swallowed. "You lied to your mama?"

"Oh, no." Granny blinked and looked away from us. "*I* didn't."

What had Papa told me once? You can tell when someone lies if they blink as they tell the lie.

Granny cleared her throat. "Doreen and I hurried to the porch. She let me wear her high heels, and the right one caught a raised nail on our stairs. I tumbled and landed face down, my legs above me on the steps." Granny chuckled. "What a sight I must have been."

I flinched. "Ouch."

"Doreen laughed so hard the tears made streams along her powdered cheeks." Granny giggled. "I dirtied the front of my coat, but I brushed it clean. As we were walking to Jerry Lee's pickup, Doreen became angrier than a rain-drenched billy goat. She noticed I tore the nylons she loaned me."

"Why was Doreen mad about the nylons?" I dabbed the strawberry from my upper lip with a napkin.

"Oh, dear girls, you probably don't know, but there were eleven of us children in our family."

We shook our heads no.

"With so little money to spare, nylons were a luxury and a pair had to last a long time." Granny took a swallow of coffee. "We were more fortunate than most large families, however. Daddy drove a Nehi soda pop truck. He made a decent wage, and we never went to bed hungry." Granny smacked her lips. "Daddy brought home sodas when other kids could only dream of such treats."

"Did you go to the movies whenever you wanted?" Leah's tongue slid along her straw, cleaning off the leftover shake.

"Only once in a blue moon." Granny winked.

Mia lurched forward. Her mouth opened probably to ask another question, but this time about a blue moon. I beat her to it. "Where were you in the sibling lineup?"

"Smack dab in the middle." Her grin filled her whole face.

Mia patted the tiny flab on Granny's arm. "When's the moon blue?"

The waitress interrupted our conversation. "Here we are ladies." She set one creamy bowl of green in front of Granny and waved the cup between us girls until I pointed to Mia.

My stomach grumped. Would a milkshake be enough of a meal? Then I remembered the burgers and fries.

"Go on, girls." Granny's fingers danced in the air. "Humor me."

Reaching for the basket of crackers, Mia chose saltines. She opened the packet, and smashed them between her hands. The crumbles fell into the little bowl. With a soup spoon, she waved it between us girls. "Who goes first?"

"You do." Leah and I grimaced.

Mia held her nose as she mixed the cracker lumps into the green puddle.

"Whatever." Leah covered her face with both hands and parted her fingers to peek.

Mia's spoon clicked on her teeth as the mass disappeared. In rapid fire, she blinked.

"You're next." I poked Leah in the ribs with my spoon.

"Why not you?" She slurped on her straw.

"It's yummy." Mia pushed the miniature bowl toward Leah. "Try it."

We older sisters jerked our heads toward Mia, who always told the truth.

"I'll get this over with." Leah dipped the edge of her spoon into the goop and steered it toward her mouth. "I hope I don't throw up." When her spoon came out clean, she tasted and swallowed. "You won't like this, Kari, but I do." She ate another bite and stuck out her crunched-cracker tongue. "Ahhhh."

"I'll show you." I snatched the spoon from her, scooped up my share, and raised it to my lips. "If you can eat this—" I took a big gulp of my milkshake. The soup slid down with the shake. Licking my mouth, I shuddered.

"Two out of three isn't bad." Granny cackled. "You're good girls to please an old lady."

Little did Granny know. We'd do so only to a point. Soon enough, she'd turn the Caddy around and head home.

Somehow.

Someway.

~*~

We left behind our empty lunch dishes and piled into the car. Soon enough, Granny's Cadillac bounced from Bella's Pea Soup parking lot. Earlier, an idea took shape as I ate my burger and nibbled on the fries. And after eating, Leah agreed to carry out the plan. She now sat on the edge of the backseat.

Granny approached the freeway overpass. Leah drew closer to her and pointed. "Turn at the second right."

Granny passed the northbound sign and slammed her velvet shoe on the brake. Tires screeched. The Caddy jerked. Underneath Granny's knuckles, the steering wheel vibrated. Leah flew forward. Her waist hinged onto the middle of front seat.

When Granny let off of the brakes, Leah disappeared into the back with a thud.

"What in thunder?"

I covered my ears. Granny's voice sounded loud.

She passed the southbound sign. "You made me miss my turn north." Granny's mouth worked in a circle. She pulled into a gas station parking space and stopped.

Ah, oh.

Silence filled the interior of the Caddy. Not a peep, nor a smart remark. Leah's face became pale, and she clasped her hands in her lap. Mia stared at Leah with pity-filled eyes and patted her on the cheek.

Granny stared ahead, while I, once again, clutched my cookbook.

"You will *not*"— Granny whacked the dashboard, and I jolted about a foot off my seat —"stop me from seeing my son. Do you understand, Leah?" She eyed the rearview mirror. "No. More. Tricks."

"But, Granny." My half-digested lunch fizzled and snapped. "This trip is not our idea." I pointed. "It's yours. Mom will be scared first and angry later." I kept my tone respectful. "She trusted you to watch us." Did I just tell a lie?

In her most daring moment yet, Leah jerked the Caddy door open. She crossed her arms and walked round the front of the car. Stopping at Granny's side, Leah tapped a nail on her window.

My stomach shifted to my knees. *Oh, dear Lord, what next?*

Rolling down the glass, Granny muttered under her breath.

"It's *always* about you." Glaring at Granny, Leah waited.

Granny faced forward and angled her right brow. "Well, I *never*—"

"You never what, Granny?" Mia shot forward from the backseat.

"I've never been so insulted in all my born days."
Granny's cheeks darkened into a blush. Her lipstick long gone,
her lips puckered.

Would this be a standoff of catastrophic proportions?

No one made a sound for an awful eternity. Until, I cleared
an egg-sized knot from my throat. "This is a problem for us,
Granny, and you're old enough to understand." Now, *I* sounded
like my mom. "What I meant—"

"Get in the car, Leah." Granny stabbed a finger in the air.
"This instant."

Making fists, Leah scurried to her open door.

Because my idea didn't work, I thought of what should
come next. Having spent time in the car with Granny as the
driver, I knew our parents would be furious. A feeble granny
driving us along the freeway—not good. Actually, it bordered
on horrid. Only Papa could put an end to this sorry trip. In a
split moment, he became my backup plan.

If after a one-night motel stay we still couldn't get Granny
headed home, we'd skip talking to Granny-Too. We'd talk to
Papa. I released my grip on what had now become my security
blanket and allowed the cookbook to lie on my trembling lap.
We may not be able to win against an old lady's super-charged
grit. But Papa had been trained to deal with difficult people.

Including, I'm sure, old ladies who may be losing a grasp
on reality.

Before I called him, I'd pray his heart had healed enough
to handle *this* situation.

"Does it mean we still have to go north?" Mia snuggled
against Leah.

Granny shifted into Drive. With what appeared to me as renewed determination, her hawk eyes narrowed. Easing the Caddy from the congested parking lot, she entered the northbound freeway going to Oregon.

As Granny sped to sixty miles an hour, a finger from the backseat poked my right shoulder. Leah. To reassure her, I stuffed a hand between the door and my seat. I wiggled my fingers. Leah grabbed hold, and we squeezed.

Miles down the road I sunk deeper into the leather seat. *Granny's trip will be over tomorrow.* I no longer worried about Papa's possible involvement. He'd want to help. He would see this as an emergency for our safety. But, another idea nagged.

The farther we traveled from home the more in trouble we'd be with our parents. This idea shredded my nerves. I needed a good night's sleep before we called Papa.

~*~

"Now that we've gotten beyond you girls' pranks, where did I leave off in my story?" Granny patted the wheel. The Caddy swerved.

My arm shot out. "Keep your hands on the wheel. Please. And don't look at me, Granny. It's not safe." *How's that for taking charge?*

To my surprise, she giggled. "I'll let you be my co-pilot, Kari Rose."

Whew. She didn't get angry.

Mia's voice carried from behind me. "You had fallen and torn your sister Doreen's nylons."

She raised a hand over the wheel, but replaced it to where

35

it belonged. "My leg ached from falling on the porch steps. No matter, we ran the block to Jerry Lee's vehicle. We stopped in front of his black pickup, panting. He even had it spit-shined."

"He spit on it and it shined?"

"No, Mia Babe." Her shoulders shook with a cackle. "It just means the paint was clean and glossy."

Leah nudged Granny's arm. "Sorry to interrupt, but the map shows it would be best to get a motel room in Willows."

"I remember that place." I twisted to face Leah. "Papa said he and Granny-Too had stayed there before." A yummy thought surfaced. "We can eat at the Brown Bear Logger. Papa said it was the best food ever."

"Okay." Granny flipped the blinker and accelerated to the fast lane. "How many miles to Willows?"

Leah ducked her head. "It looks like … it's after Sacramento." She ran a finger up the map page. "About three hours?"

"It's settled, then." Granny passed a vehicle and re-entered the slow lane. "Now. What was I sayin'?"

Mia leaned near Granny. "You were—"

"—climbing into Jerry Lee's pickup." Granny nodded. "Doreen flipped a switch, worked her feet, and the engine roared to life. She *ye-hawed*, and we clapped each other's hands and sang the nursery rhyme, 'Pease Porridge Hot'."

"Really, Granny? You both turned into babies when you're about to drive a pickup?"

Would Leah never learn?

Granny glanced in the rearview mirror. "Don't intrude on my story, Leah Sassy Bedeah."

She flopped against her seat. "You're mean."

I was pretty sure Granny didn't hear her comment, but still. Why did Leah always push the issues? My stomach pitched and whirled.

"I'll never forget what happened next." Granny's voice rose to a lighthearted note.

Being Leah, she silently mimicked Granny.

Burping a giggle, I dug into my purse. I tore off a slip of paper from my notepad and wrote: *Be nice to Granny. We'll do what you said about calling you-know-who.* I folded the note into a square and slipped it to Leah between my seat and the door.

"—changed my life forever, is what it did." Granny kept her eyes on the road. So good. "Doreen told me, 'Okay, little sis, I'm going to teach you how to dance.'"

Hopefully, I flicked the note close enough to Leah's shoe.

"But, but." Mia waved her arms. "You thought you were going to the movies?"

"Yes, Mia Babe." Granny shook her head. "With Doreen, you just never knew."

Leah mumbled. "Like someone *else.*"

I wagged my head no back and forth. Didn't she get the note?

The steering wheel swayed underneath Granny's knuckles. I leaned across the expanse of seat and steadied her hands.

"*What* did you say, Leah?" Granny's voice became stern.

"She said, it sounds like someone else." Mia faced Leah. "Who is it?"

Leah groaned, covering her head with the United States travel map.

When Leah showed her face, I pointed at her feet. She bent and resurfaced.

"Oh, bother." Granny's bottom lip protruded. "Leah, if you keep babbling."

Leah hid the note behind her knuckles. Mia pointed. "What's that?" She covered Mia's mouth with the other hand.

I needed to say something. "Granny, Leah has her opinions. They don't have to agree with the rest of us." I winked at Leah to send her a signal to go along with my next words, even though we ate over an hour ago. "Besides, she gets grumpy when she's hungry."

Leah gasped. "I. Do. Not."

I pointed to the paper and wink, winked. "Yes, you do."

She read the note and grinned. "I get terrible grouchy."

Interrupting our noisy exchange, Granny snickered. "I used to argue with Doreen. She bossed me around, I'd pull her hair, and the fight began."

"I'm sorry, Granny." Leah shoved the note into her sweater pocket. "Now will you finish your story?"

Before Granny could answer, steam rose from underneath the Cadillac hood.

I slapped my cheeks. *This old tugboat may be the answer to my prayers.*

5

All Knowledge

Granny slapped the dashboard next to Grand's photo. "James, you were supposed to guide us along on our trip." She swerved the car over to the shoulder and parked. A semi *zoomed* by, rocking the Caddy.

"This should prove to you only God can guide us anywhere."

"Leah." Granny groaned.

"Yeah," Mia blurted, "and Mama says the Bible says never, ever talk to dead people."

Granny slumped over the wheel and bawled.

My heart stirred like boiling liquid in a pot. I gripped my cookbook. Was she crying because she missed Grand or because of the car? My eyes misted. Either way, I'd never seen Granny like this. Not even at Grand's funeral.

As vehicles and semis barreled along Interstate 5 and shook our existence, Granny's sobs brought on Mia's. "Help her, Kari."

Seeking a suggestion, I stared at Leah.

"Don't look at me." Her face knotted as if with regret. "I'm the one who made her cry."

"No, sir, I did." Mia sobbed into her cupped hands.

Great.

By now, a breeze swooshed the cloud of steam over the windshield. I thought *fire* and leaned over to switch off the car's engine. "I don't see flames. But in case there are, Mia, be ready to jump from the Caddy on the shoulder side. Leah and I will help Granny."

I popped outside to investigate. Stuffing hands into my back pockets, I watched the Caddy hood from a safe distance. After most of the steam disappeared, I felt satisfied it was not on fire.

Back in the car, I petted Granny's silver, feather-soft hair. "It's okay, we'll call for help." I pointed at Leah, who carried Mom's outdated cell phone. "Call 911."

Leaning back from the steering wheel, Granny swiped at her damp face and blinked. "No, I'm okay." She coughed. "Hand me a tissue, Kari Rose." Her gnarled finger aimed at the spacious floorboard where a square box sat near my purse.

While Granny blew her nose with a loud honk, I dug through the glove compartment. "We'll call a tow truck."

"Good idea." Leah held the phone. "What's the number?"

I quoted it and returned the insurance card to its place.

"Yes," Leah said into the cell, "we need a tow. It's for my granny, Adele Whitmore." She nodded. "Um, yeah. We're on the side of the freeway with something like steam coming from the hood." Pausing to listen for long seconds, Leah now covered the phone's speaker. "Does anyone know where we are?"

The moment before I spoke, a semi roared by so close I felt plunked in the middle of the truck's engine.

"It's so scary." Mia sobbed even harder.

"Mia, cuddle with your sister." I shook my head at Leah. "Honestly, I'm not sure where we are."

Leah swung an arm around Mia. "We don't know, sir, but we left Bella's Pea Soup about an hour ago." She paused. "We're headed north on Interstate 5. Okay, here she is." Leah aimed the phone at Granny. "He needs to talk to you."

As Granny straightened her shoulders, she gripped the phone with a shaky hand. She gave the man information.

Mia wiggled her fingers at me. "Tissue, please, 'cause I cried."

"Can you get someone out here any faster?" Granny listened. "Trucks are about to blow us off the road." She scratched her chin. "No, we're on the shoulder, it's just an expression." Granny nodded. "We have no other choice but to sit tight, sir."

Handing the phone to Leah, Granny clamped on her teeth.

I cocked my head to the side. "How long will it take for the tow?"

Whoosh. Another truck past with a rumble. Mia whimpered, hugging Leah's arm. "I wanna go home, please."

"Looks like we're caught between a rock and a hard spot." Granny yawned. "The man said the driver won't be here for at least half an hour. Because—as you can see—we're out in the boondocks."

"Let's sing, Granny." I motioned for my sisters to agree. Granny's eyes brightened.

"I know, I know." Leah flapped her hands. "Let's do Grand's song. How does it go, Kari?"

I wondered if it would be upset Granny, but she smiled. "He would love this."

41

Okay, this is good. "It goes like this—"

"Sing a little song," Mia sang, "it's not very long. Tulalip, Tulalip, and now the song's gone."

Even Granny sang it with us over and over. Mia and Leah stomped their feet to the tune. Suddenly, Granny coughed and wheezed. "I need my inhaler."

My brows hiked toward my forehead. *Inhaler?* My sisters' eyes bulged. We knew what this was from our cousin Teresa. "When, ah, did you—get an inhaler?"

Granny rummaged in her suitcase-sized purse. "Here— *wheeze*—it—*wheeze*—is." She pulled it out and coughed, clearing her throat. "This is for maintenance." She shook her head. "I need the rescuer."

Rescuer? Leah mouthed, her brows hiked toward her hairline.

Why did I not see her use these puffers? An image of Granny turning purple from lack of air filled me with horror. My throat muscles tightened. Pretty soon here, I'd need a puffer.

~*~

Still Granny dug in her purse for the inhaler, when she spewed an unladylike word.

Mia gasped. "Granny, you said a naughty." She clamped her teeth on her bottom lip. "Mama won't like it."

Finally, Granny found the rescuer and gave it a shake. She breathed in at the same time she sprayed the medicine into her mouth. It smelled worse than burnt food. I pinched my nose. Holding her breath for long moments, Granny finished her treatment with a sip of water and swished it around in her mouth. She opened her car door a few inches and spit the water on the ground.

Granny was full of surprises. First it was the amount of cash she's carrying. Then it was she hadn't driven her car in who knows how long. Now this. *Just how sickly is she?*

When Granny shut the Caddy door, Mia said, "Huh, Leah? Mama doesn't like it when people swear."

"Yeah. Someone has a potty mouth." Leah rolled her eyes. "If we talked like that, Mom would wash our mouths with soap and ground us for a month."

I shook my head at Leah as in *hush.* "Um, Granny?"

"What?" She drew out the word with impatience.

Frustrated, I turned my palms upward with a question. "Why didn't you tell us about your inhalers?"

"Yeah." Leah smacked her lips. "I don't mean to say one more thing to upset you, but really. It's not fair to keep secrets." Her thin smile surprised me. "You're supposed to be in good enough health to drive on a trip." She blew air through her nostrils. "Especially with children in the car. For such a long distance. And at your age."

Granny swiveled toward Leah in an attempt to look, but it was a sideways glance at best. "My age, huh?" Now, Granny stared ahead. "Where was I in my story about Doreen and me?"

Mia crossed her arms along the top of the front seat. "You and Doreen slapped hands together, and she said she would teach you how to dance."

"Doreen drove the pickup like a pro to the next town ten miles out. There, a live band played guitars and fiddles. I discovered country music." She tapped her velvet-material tennis shoe on the floorboard. "By now, I grew nervous to learn what Doreen called western square dance. Have you ever heard of it, girls?"

"Yeah." Leah raised her voice as one truck and another past. "The Aggies at our school? Their parents just call it square dancing."

"Everyone dresses like cowboys and cowgirls, too, huh, Kari?" Mia's fists mimicked holding onto a horse's reins.

I glanced at Mia and focused on Granny and her story.

"Doreen said to me, 'Watch and learn, then we'll dance with them.' So, I did. A while later, the music stopped, and the singer announced a ten-minute break. I sat across from the band members and bit my fingernails." Granny shook her head. "That Doreen. She moved through the crowd chatting it up with folks.

"At one point, I studied the musical equipment, and settled on a young man holding a guitar. A skinny fellow. He stared at his shoes." Granny giggled like the girls did at my school. "When he raised his chin, his blue eyes shined. A well-defined Adam's apple bobbed at his throat."

"What's an Adam's apple?" Mia rested her cheek near Granny.

About then, another semi came too close and jostled the Caddy.

When Granny didn't answer, I gave Leah a nod. We'd heard from our mom how much Grand enjoyed country music. He made his twelve-string guitar sing as Mom sat at his feet when she was waist-high to Grand.

Still smiling, Granny shut her teary, wrinkled lids.

Did Granny picture in her mind the bashful boy who played the guitar where she first learned to square dance? If I missed Grand so much it made me cry, how much more did Granny miss the love of her life?

I couldn't stop myself. I closed my eyes and remembered him.

6

A Tingling Cymbal

I yelped. "Look." A tow truck slowly passed, and we cheered as it pulled onto the shoulder of the freeway. Backing to within a few yards of the Caddy, the tow truck sounded a shrill *beep, beep, beep* with caution lights flashing.

"About time." Granny swiped her nose with a tissue, blinking the moisture from her lashes.

"Thank You, Lord." Leah clapped.

Mia sang, "Amen."

In gratitude, I bowed my head for a private prayer.

When the truck stopped, a tall man with an Irish flag monogrammed on his baseball cap ran toward us. He came to my side of the Caddy. I rolled down the window.

Taking us in with one sweep of a glance, he placed his hands on the door and leaned in. "You ladies are in a bind out in the middle of nowhere."

"You think so?" Granny hissed.

Leah giggled in the backseat. "Don't remind our granny, or you'll get an earful." She slapped a hand over her mouth and muttered. "Sorry, Granny."

Well, someone was being nice.

Granny pointed at the truck. "Is there enough room for everyone in your cab?"

"Yes." He opened my door and Leah's. "Right now, I need you ladies to exit the car. Stand close to the ditch. It's safer."

As my two sisters left the Caddy, Granny blinked. "How in Sam Hill am I supposed to exit anywhere? I've sat here too long, and my legs don't work."

He tipped his cap off his forehead. "I'll help you, ma'am."

His friendliness put me at ease. "We have to get Silver from the trunk, first."

"Silver?" A puzzled expression drove away his grin.

"She means Granny's walker with a seat." Leah beamed at him. "I'll get it, Kari."

Mia nodded. "Granny's eighty—" Granny flicked her fingers at Mia as in hush.

The driver stuck out his gloved hand. "I'm Paul."

I shook it. "I'm Kari. These are my sisters Leah and Mia. This is our granny, Adele."

He shook everyone's hands. "Nice to meet you, damsels in distress."

"We wish we didn't have to become acquainted, but we're glad you're finally here." Granny sniffed.

From the passenger's side, Paul kneeled on the seat. "Come on, Adele." He lifted Granny a few inches off the leather and from behind the steering wheel, holding her in his arms. Paul set Granny on Silver. "There you go." He pushed her to a safe distance from the vehicle and set the brakes.

"Thank you, Paul." She laughed. "You made it look easy."

I couldn't have agreed more.

"Look, a hairy dog." Mia pointed at the rear window of Paul's tow truck. A small, long-haired, brown-and-white dog, with ears pointed like a bat's, barked at us. Although, we couldn't hear him for the traffic noise.

"This is Hero." Paul stood at the bumper of the Caddy. "He's my co-pilot." Hero's tail wagged in time to his bark.

Chuckling, Granny stared at the dog. "I had a Pomeranian once."

Mia smoothed hair from her face. "We don't have small dogs, only big ones."

"Does he bite?" Leah pointed at Hero. "I'm not riding in there with a mean dog."

Bent over, Paul straightened. "I wouldn't carry him if he bit people."

Granny retrieved something from her purse. "I had a dog like your Hero years ago." She handed a photo to Paul, and we sisters gathered around. I gasped.

"Oh, whoa." Paul glanced up. "What was his name?"

"Understand, I'm not a liar." Granny mashed her lips into a thin line.

He grinned. "Okay."

"Hero." Her eyes narrowed.

Paul stared at Granny's Hero and whistled. "What are the odds of that?"

"All I have left is a ceramic statue of him and this photo."

"Pomeranians are fine dogs." He nodded at Granny. "Now come on. I gotta get you ladies out of here."

Paul lifted Granny and carried her to the truck. Hero jumped to the dash and stared ahead like a navigator, wagging his silky tail. The rest of us piled in. We waited, while Paul stuffed Silver in the Caddy trunk and hoisted the tugboat of a car onto the tow bed.

All set to go, Paul maneuvered the truck onto the freeway. I secretly prayed Granny wouldn't cry when she discovered the trip had ended. Relaxed in the seat, I released hours of stress with a deep, single sigh.

~*~   .

I pointed. "Look at the humongous metal tank." We zipped right by it, so I didn't catch the name stamped across the front.

Paul braked to a stop in congested traffic. "Do you need a motel, Adele?"

"I think so."

"Okay. I'll show you one a block from the repair shop." At a complete stop within the lines of vehicles, Paul flashed Granny a grin. "I'll make sure you ladies are taken care of."

"Look at the clown vehicle, girls." Granny motioned to a van painted with balloons, confetti, streamers, and a clown.

In my opinion, this type of party would cost a whole lot.

"I want a birthday with clowns." Mia gawked at the van.

Granny patted Paul's shoulder. "What you said about helping us find a motel? This is service like I remember when I was younger." She shifted in her seat. "Thank you, Paul."

It was an hour drive from where we broke down to where Paul unloaded the Caddy. We went inside to the service department and finished the paperwork. Afterward, Paul drove us to a mid-range motel. Not fancy, nor a dump.

At the sight of a pool, situated across from the motel office, Mia squealed. "I wanna swim."

Everyone unbuckled. I stretched my arms over my head, while Mia patted Hero. Leah swiveled her waist back and forth like she always did to loosen the kinks. "We didn't bring our bathing suits."

When Paul got Granny onto Silver, Granny blew him a kiss. "Thank you, Sir Paul."

He waved. "It was my pleasure, Madam Adele."

We three sisters exchanged looks. Leah covered her mouth and snorted.

Granny's chin wobbled. "What?"

Leah shrugged. "You say the funniest things sometimes."

With a wave goodbye to Paul, I pushed Granny to the front doors of Divine Sleep Motel. "I hope they have a room for four people."

"They do." Leah pointed at the vacancy sign. "See? I noticed before Paul dropped us off."

Granny patted at Leah's arm as we moved along. "You're very observant, Leah Bedeah, even if you have a smart mouth and sassy eyes."

A gurgled hum rose from Leah's throat.

I halted Silver and leaned over Granny. "What did she do wrong?"

"Not a thing at the moment." Granny sniggered. "It's the smart aleck darts she's hit me with the whole trip." She winked. "This time, I'm ahead of her."

Leah glared at Granny as she passed and opened the office door. Twisting on her heels, Leah's lips puckered. Her cheeks caved in like an impression on a thumb-print cookie.

Oh, brother. At least she kept her remarks to herself. This time. We had a long afternoon ahead of us.

~*~

I maneuvered Granny and Silver through the door Leah held open for us and nodded. "Thank you, Leah."

Her complexion flushed. She mouthed, "I've had it."

My lips moved without a sound, also. "Almost over."

As I entered the office, our family squabbles melted like butter left in a too-hot sun. The cutest guy ever with the sweetest grin stood behind the counter.

His nameplate read *Harold*. He had white teeth with two crooked ones at the top. "Good day, ladies." Harold's grin snuggled within his manicured beard.

My knees jiggled like cold mush on a plate. I stumbled. Leah caught me before I toppled. I sighed. Was it his clipped beard? His smile? Both?

Leah chuckled.

My face heated to 350 degrees as I realized my mistake. I had sighed out loud.

A burp rose toward my throat, while everyone watched me. "Um, we, uh, need a room for a night." I gulped and covered my mouth to avoid further shame. *He's staring. At me.*

"What my granddaughter means is we need two connecting rooms."

"Ah-ha." Harold checked the computer, and his grin softened.

Harold asked a question.

"What?" My bare toes curled inside my sneakers and squeaked.

"So it'll be for one night, miss?" His dark, turquoise-blue eyes sashayed.

I became dizzy. Tongue-tied. *Oh, dear Lord, help.*

"Yes." Granny pointed over her shoulder. "My car's in the shop. I hope to be on our way tomorrow."

While Harold tapped on a keyboard, his mouth relaxed over his teeth. He maintained a pleasant expression. As I gathered my thoughts to what we were doing, they scattered. His thick, black hair shined glossy, and he reminded me of the old-time singer, Elvis—.

Harold spoke. "I don't have to ask if you need a downstairs because the answer is obvious, sooo…." He focused on the computer screen. "You're in luck."

Mia sucked in a breath. "Mama says—"

I slapped a hand over her lips.

"We have two adjoining rooms downstairs by the pool right across from us." Harold nodded to the window. "Handicap equipped." He stood straighter and studied me.

"You know, young man, you remind me of—"

Don't say Elvis Presley. I slapped the counter way too hard. Everyone jumped. "We'll take it." Harold blinked and his jaw went slack.

Eyes focused on the screen, Harold told us the price, plus tax.

Granny dug into her wallet and produced cash. "Here, Harold."

Leaning over to retrieve the wadded bills, he took them.

His aftershave scent wafted like spices from a warm pie. *Oh, dear, Lord. Please get me out of here.* I waved a hand as if swatting at flies.

A giggle mingled with a gush of air escaped from Leah.
She tickled my ribs. She spoke from the side of her mouth,
"You're beet-red, sister."

My heart thumped faster.

"You can call me Harry." He handed Granny her change.

I peeked at him, and we made deep eye contact. My heart
swooshed, swooshed in my ears. Dropping my gaze, I studied
Granny's velvet tennis shoes.

She received our key card, and we moved toward the
lobby door. I led the way while Leah pushed Silver. Harry
edged next to me and opened the door.

He's in my space.

He towered above me, my eyes level with the third shirt
button from Harry's collar. A crazy desire overwhelmed all
common sense. What would his heart beat sound like? I found
myself leaning closer. To the button.

Leah shoved Granny through the doorway, which jolted
me to reality. Harry stared down at me. His brows quivered,
with an expression on his face saved for cute puppies and
drooling babies.

What, what? Once again, my leg muscles weakened.

Leah hooked an elbow through mine. "Thank you for your
help, Harry." She tugged and unglued my feet from the carpet.

Outside, a cold wind surged through my curls, startling me
from my bewilderment.

7

Love Is Patient

Leah surfed through the TV channels.

"I wanna watch cartoons."

Brushing off Mia's hand from the buttons, Leah grumbled. "We need to see what the weather is like tomorrow."

"See!" Mia flapped her arms like a frantic chicken. "You past the cartoons."

"Stop." Leah flipped her golden hair off a shoulder. "Did no one notice Harry said a storm headed our way?"

Rolling on the bed, I moved closer to Leah. "I didn't hear him."

"You didn't hear much of nothing, lovesick puppy." She giggle-snorted. "You were a complete idiot."

"No, sir." I buried my face in my crossed arms. *Yes, I was.* I'd never felt such emotions. Boys were, well, just boys. Harry stood out from the crowd of males as a guy. This couldn't happen with a complete stranger and hours from home. Could it? I groaned.

"You'll get over him." Leah kept thumbing, still not finding a weather report. "Once we're gone."

For some odd reason, I doubted this very much. I rested my cheek on a wrist. "I'm doomed." Like a fallen and half-baked cake.

Mia stuck her nose into my space. "What's doomed mean?"

Leah laughed. "It means hopeless, ruined, lost, and done for."

"Because of nice Harry?" Mia's breath tickled my ear.

"Please don't." I pushed at her face.

"I've got the weather." Leah raised the volume. "Oops. It just went to a commercial. And Mia, leave Kari alone. She's busy sulking."

"Am not." Truth be told, I wrinkled my brows for so long, the skin between them hurt like a leg cramp.

"Go check on Granny, Mia." Leah jerked, causing the bed to bounce. "Make sure she didn't fall through a hole in the floor."

Giggling, I rolled onto my back. The elastic tie in Leah's ponytail had come loose halfway down her spine. "You always make me laugh when you're not sassing. Sometimes especially then."

Before Leah could answer, Granny's voice came from the direction of her room. "Would one of you brush my hair? My arm gave out."

Mia came in and stood before me. "She won't let me do it."

"Granny," I hollered so she could hear, "please let Mia brush your hair. She's good at it." Mia left and didn't return.

During the commercial break, Leah lay on her side next to me. She spoke in a quiet voice. "I'm praying the car is beyond repair, and we have to take a plane home." She waggled her blonde brows. "And if this doesn't happen, we'll call Papa like your note said."

"Sure will." Elbow on the bed, I cupped my chin in my palm. "This vehicle problem is just what we needed." I yawned and slumped with exhaustion. "Can you imagine the hysteria this would cause if even one parent or grandparent knew where we were?"

My yawn was contagious, and Leah ended hers with a sigh. "Yeah." She pulled out her hair band. "Disastrous."

"Now for our local Stockton area weather," the announcer said.

Leah sat on the bed, legs crossed, and stared at the screen. I lay there and rubbed my tired, itchy eyes. I didn't know how people managed, driving for hours. All I did was watch the road.

The weather forecaster continued. "If you travel north tomorrow, beware of…"

I jerked upright and skidded on the silken coverlet toward the edge of the bed. My mouth gaped wide enough to accept a bite full of Granny-Too's ganache-frosted cupcakes. "Mercy, me."

This was our answered prayer. Even if the Caddy repair became successful, this would stop Granny once and for all.

Leah's lashes flickered. "This news will change Granny's mind for sure." I nodded. She pointed her chin in the direction of Granny's room. "Let's tell her." As she moved, I grabbed her. We both slid off and ran.

In Granny's room, we lowered ourselves onto the bed next to where her suitcase lay open. Still on Silver, Granny held up a blouse. "I'm freshening up before supper."

"Granny." *Lord, help us with the words.* I cleared my throat and put on a serious expression, complete with sad eyes and furrowed brows. "We have disturbing news."

Her lips parted, and her eyes searched mine. "Oh?"

Leah clasped her hands in a prim pose on her lap. "As I'm sure you're aware, we're headed for the mountains, Granny. You can't trust the weather as it changes this time of year. It can be warm or it can turn cold." She paused. "With a storm. Like in snow."

I was in awe of my sister. How did she think so quickly and seem so convincing?

"Snow?" Granny's faded-blue eyes narrowed. "In April? Don't give me the lowdown on the seasons, Leah."

My stomach clenched. *This isn't going well.* "The weather station said snow north of here." I blinked and waited.

Granny worked her mouth in a circle. "I used to live in Oklahoma." She leaned close enough to Leah for their noses to touch. "With tornados."

My confidence sank to my toenails.

No doubt. If the Caddy gets fixed, we'd have to call a cop—Papa the cop.

~*~

"It won't work, girls." Granny gave the blouse she held to her chest a few shakes. "Once the car is repaired, we continue north." She glared at us. "And this is my final word as final can get."

I sighed, my lips flapping.

Leah blew a huffy breath. "I don't believe this."

I don't either. A headache grew at my temples.

Leah spread her hands before her. "We're done with this trip, Granny." Her eyes snapped like an ignited flame. "My sisters and I are going home. One way or another." Leah sprung from the bed and stomped from the room.

Granny watched Leah's retreat. "You're not in charge, Leah Bedeah."

"Neither are you." Leah stuck her head near the door jamb. "I'll get plane tickets."

Mia crunched against me and nibbled at a fingernail. "We're leaving Granny behind?"

"How can you even think about going north into snow?" I stood, pulled Mia to me, and my voice became shrill. "Our mother will be worried sick when she finds us gone."

"No. She won't." Granny wrinkled her face into what appeared as shame.

"Why not?" I placed fists on my hips and stared at her like she regressed into a child. When she didn't answer, I raised my arms. "Well?"

Granny grabbed a hanky from her sweater pocket and wiped her nose. She spoke through the fabric. "I left a note."

By this time, Leah returned with the cell phone. "A note?" She crossed her skinny arms. "You left a *note*?" She wagged a finger at Granny. "What you've managed is to take us on a dangerous road trip. Our mom will never, ever trust you again."

Eyes streamlining into mere slits, Granny dropped the blouse. "Leah Bedeah, *this* trip is not dangerous. You should be glad to see your papa." She whipped her finger in the air like a mixer on low speed. "You should *thank* me."

Raising her eyes to the ceiling, Leah, well—she let loose a garbled scream. It jolted the rest of us. "Okay, you know what, Granny?" She bent at the waist, hands on hips. "I should have told you no. No, no, no!" She sliced her hand through the air. "I'm done going on some stupid trip without asking my parents."

"I admit it." I pushed my way between Leah and Granny. "I'd love to see Papa and Granny-Too. But, not like this. It's wrong."

Leah squeezed her face into her signature sassy look. "The truth is, Granny, you are *so, so, so* in trouble."

A stare down took place between them.

Granny readjusted herself on Silver. Doubt clouded her faded blue eyes.

I elbowed Leah to move back. "We understand better how much you miss Grand. But you took someone's children without parental permission."

"Oh, no!" Mia's mouth trembled. "You'll get arrested for kidnapping."

Her face paled. "James is gone. I need to see my son." Granny quivered.

I patted her shoulder. "I'm sorry, but my parents will be angry when they find out what you've done." I pointed at my chest. "What I've allowed."

On our own bed now, I cupped my hand around Leah's ear. "Did you get us tickets home?"

"No." Her eyelids lowered. "We don't have a credit card."

"Oh, yeah." I waggled my brows to lighten the mood. "No worries." I hugged her. "We'll call Papa and be home by tomorrow night."

~*~

We were in the motel restaurant. No one spoke.

Granny and Leah ate steaks, fish for me, and a burger for Mia. Across from me as Leah sat next to Granny, I compared the two. Their petite noses were shaped the same. On the other hand, I came to this earth with a nose like Papa's. Strong and defined, is what he told me. When I looked in a mirror, it most certainly didn't appear feminine.

Clink, splat.

Mia slurped her shake as it pooled on the table.

"For heaven's sake, Mia Babe, stop." Granny snapped her fingers for a waitress. "We'll get you another."

It dripped on the floor. I placed my napkin on the edge of the table and stopped the flow.

"Gross." Leah lifted Mia's metal shake container with a thumb and index finger. "Next time let someone else pour it into your glass."

The waitress hurried over with a damp hand towel. "We're certainly messy." She smiled.

Granny's glare should have shattered the window. "Excuse me?"

Our waitress shrugged. "I'll get a mop."

"Who does she think she is?" Granny's lips snarled. "Mia's a little girl prone to spill accidents."

I couldn't help but love Granny a bit more for defending Mia Babe—even though the lady didn't mean any harm.

"Only you're allowed to talk this way, right Granny?" Leah's laugh tingled like glass chimes.

"I'm family." Granny wrinkled her nose and swiped it with a hanky. "And, in your mother's place for now."

Leah rolled her eyes and stabbed a piece of steak with a fork. "Right."

With mop in hand, the waitress cleaned the floor beneath Mia's feet. Granny tapped the woman on the shoulder. "Do you have a gift shop?"

"Yes, we do." She straightened. "Pass the register and go right." The waitress finished her job and left.

Granny hunched over her plate. "I want to go over there and see what they have." She stuck another cube of steak in her mouth and chewed.

What was the *click, suck, click* noise coming from Granny's mouth? I stared at her teeth, forgetting until this moment they were false. I blinked at the thought of being so old. "Do you think shopping is such a good idea, Granny?" I chewed a mouthful of fish and swallowed. "We don't know how much the Caddy will cost."

Arching a brow, Granny lowered her fork. "Are you in charge of my money, Kari Rose?"

"Yeah, she is."

Granny jerked her head toward Leah. "I didn't ask you."

When Granny glanced away, Leah wiggled her shoulders. A tiny squeal in her throat erupted.

Poor Leah. I shook my head while I dipped my fish into a sauce. She had zero tolerance for Granny. "You told us to

61

guard your money." I savored the taste. "Do you even have a credit card?"

"Credit is for those who can't pay their bills." Granny slammed her hand on the table as if it were a judge's hammer. "This generation today is all about spending what they don't have."

Leah gasped. "That's what Mom says all the time."

With our meal finished, Granny left a twenty-dollar tip. My eyes widened. Granny stared at me. "What? This should make up for Mia's mess." She grinned.

With Granny saddled up on Silver, I pushed her into the gift shop. I willed myself to speak my mind, even though it would do no good. "In four more days, Mom will be home and she'll call us, Granny, and tell us to stay put." I paused for emphasis. "I know Mom. She'll come get us."

"Stop here." Granny pointed at a display case. "I want to look at this clock."

I stepped away from Granny and leaned close to Leah. "You need to leave a message on our home phone. I'll keep Granny preoccupied. Tell Mom where we are and why. Reassure her you'll call Papa next. He'll come to get us here in Stockton, while we wait for the car's repairs."

Straight-faced, Leah readjusted her purse's shoulder strap. "I've got to use the bathroom." She said it loud enough for Granny to hear. I hoped.

"Kari, come here."

"Coming, Granny." Leah and I went in opposite directions, and my shoulders grew lighter. Nothing could wipe the smile off my face. *Home sweet home, here we come.*

"This is a good price." Granny touched the glass cabinet where the clock sat on a shelf.

I leaned over to get a better view. "Are you sure you want to spend your money on a trinket?"

"*Trinket?*" Granny scowled, her wrinkles deepened like the cracks on a less than perfect cake. "This, my dear, is not a *trinket.*"

"What is it, Granny?" Mia rested her elbow on Silver's handlebar.

"It's a cuckoo clock." With her feet, she moved Silver closer to the display. "See the double doors? They pop open and a bird appears and says, 'Cuckoo.' At the same time, the clock chimes however many times for the current hour." She patted my hand. "Get the cashier to unlock this cabinet, will you, Kari?"

I did as Granny instructed and, fifteen minutes later, she held the newly wrapped and boxed clock in her lap. "I'm ready for a nap, Kari. James and I always rested at this time of day."

Beside me, Mia pointed toward the bathroom. Her shoes danced on the floor. "I need to go."

Mia took a step to leave, and I grabbed her arm. "Wait." I couldn't allow Mia to overhear Leah's phone call. She might let our plan slip. Besides. "Leah needs to go with you, and she's not here right now."

Soon enough, Leah returned. She nodded once and then looked away. I itched to know what Papa said, and I couldn't wait to get Leah aside and ask.

At the motel, Granny pushed Silver to her room to take a much needed nap. Now, what do I do with Mia?

8

Hopes All Things

In our motel bathroom, Leah and I huddled on the side of the tub. Mia watched cartoons in the other part of our room.

"Well?" I grabbed Leah's hand. "What did Papa say?"

"I didn't actually talk to him." She blew strands of hair from her eye.

"You had to leave a message?" I slumped.

"Noooo. I spoke to Granny-Too."

"What did you say?" I bit on my fingernails and spit them on the floor. "What did she say?"

"I told her how Granny insisted she drive to see Papa. That we felt we couldn't let her go on her own, and we tried several times to get Granny to turn the car around." Leah's face paled. "Granny-Too is upset, Kari. She understands how dangerous this trip is with Granny driving a long distance at her age." Leah squinted. "She's so angry, she—she cried."

"Ah, no. This is bad." I stared at my short, ragged nails. "Why didn't I think to call Granny-Too this morning and have her talk some sense into Granny?"

Leah took off the wrapper of a tiny bar of soap. She laid it back on the tub. "Granny-Too said she'd tell Papa as soon as he came home, so he could head our way."

"Where is he?"

She bowed her head. "On a turkey hunt miles in the woods."

I clicked my tongue. "When's he coming back?"

Leah crushed the soap wrapper in her fist. "Not until late tonight. He was to meet our cousin Thomas. They would be hunting all day."

"*Grrr.*" I stomped my bare foot. "Now we have to hope the Caddy needs a part they don't have, or it'll be 'snowstorm here we come.'" I grew so frustrated, tears stung like a million bees.

"Kari?" Mia called. "Someone's knocking on our door."

I sprung from the edge of the tub and let Mia in. "Who is it?" I grabbed a tissue and wiped my eyes.

She glowered as if I'd eaten the last warm chocolate-chip cookie. "I don't open to strangers."

"Good girl." I patted her head and looked through the peephole on the door. I sucked in so much air, I choked.

Leah nudged me over. "Let me see." She whirled to face me. "It's your crush."

I wanted to say, "I know," but my breath caught in my throat.

Leah unlatched the chain to greet Harry.

"Hi, ya." He did a half-circle wave. "I thought I'd check to see if you ladies have everything you need before I go off shift."

He grinned. My heart whipped into top speed. Running a hand over the side of his shiny hair, Harry's eyes glided across my face.

My cheeks grew warm in a blush. "We're good."

"Okay. I'll be at the counter at six in the morning." He cleared his throat. "I'll see you before you leave?"

I shuffled my feet. A *yes* blurted across my lips, followed by a smile. I almost giggled, but it would have been lame. "We have to wait around until we find out about the Caddy."

Leah stuck her head into our space. "They probably don't open until eight or nine."

He sort of winked. At me. "Of course." On a backward step, his eyes sparkled like moonbeams on the West Coast Ocean. "See you in the morning." He rounded the corner and disappeared.

"Bye." I released a sigh, shut the door, and leaned into it. "He's sooo handsome." Now I squealed.

"Yeah." Leah cocked her head to one side. "A real doll." Mia giggled.

With my brows scrunched, I shot Mia my most perfect scowl. "Why are you laughing?"

She poked my chest. "You love him." Craning her neck, she laughed and laughed.

"You can't love someone you don't know." I tweaked her nose between two knuckles. "Don't you have cartoons to watch, squirt?" I nudged her but she stayed rooted to the floor.

She crossed her skinny arms. "I'm not a squirt."

The cell phone rang on the desk table. I grabbed for it, but Leah beat me and jerked it up. "I don't recognize the number." She flicked open the phone. "Hello?" Leah puckered her lips. "Okay, I'll tell her. What's the cost?" She tapped her toe. "That much?" She ended the call and snapped the phone closed.

"Well?" I nibbled on my thumb nail.

Leah blinked.

"Don't tell me…" I shook my head and groaned.

~*~

Leah shook her head. "It seems the mechanic had the part. The guy knew we were travelers and stayed late to fix the problem." She plunked herself on the bed. "Can you believe they had what they needed for an antique car?"

Pacing within the small room, I wrung my hands. "Can this get any worse?" Mia blissfully watched another round of cartoons. I glared. I'd switch places with my littlest sister in a lightning bolt second. Glad to be the youngest and not forced to make decisions on this crazy … . I pressed fingers to my temples. "Oh, dear Lord, what should we do?"

"I'll tell you what, Kari." Leah cupped her hands at her waist. "I'm out of ideas."

"I never dreamed a tiny, old woman could cause this much trouble." I worked my tongue along the inside of my bottom lip. "Mom's always called Granny a spitfire."

Leah made an explosion noise in her high-pitched voice. She fell backward on the bed with arms spread. "More like a bomb who needs her Cadillac taken from her."

This description of Granny gave me a giggle fit.

"What's so funny?" Her face puckered.

Tears streamed along my cheeks. I lost control fast.

"It's nerves." Leah pressed the heels of her palms over her eyes. "Poor thing. Go ahead. Get it out of your system."

The funny-bone tears would not stop. I wept like the weeping meringue on my lemon pies.

Leah lowered her arms. "It's not like I told a joke."

Scrunching my knees to my chest, stomach muscles ached.

"Bless your heart. It's an honest to goodness meltdown." She patted my shoulder. "I'll stay right beside you until you're finished."

Mia stood next to the bed. "What's so funny, Kari?"

Leah leaned toward the nightstand, and nudged our little sister at the same moment. "Go watch TV, Mia."

I blinked hard. Was this nervous laughter?

Leah handed me a wad of tissue the size of a tennis ball. "Clean yourself up."

The bubbles of laughter threatened all over again. "Oh, oh, oh." I needed to gain control for Leah's sake, and also so I wouldn't wake Granny. I wiped my face and sat upright. "I need a wet washcloth." Propelling to my feet, I heaved a sigh.

Leah walked behind me. "Feel better?"

"I do." The damp cloth eased the rest of my tension. "As Granny would say, we have something to tell our children years from now."

"Well, I'd say it won't be many years if you and Harry become an item." Leah winked. "You're in love, Kari."

"He lives here. We don't." I peered at her from behind a dry towel. "Not going to happen."

"What's not?" Granny appeared in the doorway, holding onto Silver's handlebars.

Whoops. I woke her.

Leah explained to Granny about the car. Granny nodded. "Okay." She pushed Silver to the desk chair. "The part sure cost a bundle."

I eased out a long breath. My emotions were securely tucked, like Granny-Too does her kneaded dough into a loaf pan. "Yeah, several hundred dollars is high." After I brushed my hair, I pulled it into a tight ponytail, and fluffed my bangs.

Granny waved a hand. "Cadillac parts are pricey."

For the rest of the evening, Granny read a magazine in her room. On our bed, we girls watched a classic movie starring Jimmy Stewart.

At a commercial break, I yawned. "You'll have to call Granny-Too in the morning, Leah."

Before the movie continued, I fell asleep. I dreamed of snow deep enough to bury the Caddy tires.

~*~

We had finished our free breakfast the motel provided. I don't know why they call it *free*, because rooms are way more expensive than I could have imagined. I gave a mental shrug. Oh, well. It was, after all, Granny's money. Her spending became the least of my worries with us headed into a snowstorm.

With Granny, Mia, and our luggage in the cab, Leah and I searched the rooms a last time. We checked every corner, and even the bedding. Mia's socks were tangled within her sheets.

"The pressure of everything weighs on me." After I folded the dirty socks into a knot, I tossed it in the air like a ball. "Now, we're headed into a storm." I bounced into a sitting position on the bed. "Call Granny-Too right now. Let her know the car is ready."

Leah straightened her shoulders and punched in the number. "Hi, Granny-Too. We're okay, but I've got bad news." She paused for a moment and then explained about the

69

Cadillac. "I'll call you at the next stop and let you know where we are." Leah nodded her head as she listened. "I'll tell Kari. I love you, Granny-Too. Bye."

It appeared the depth of her eyes became dull with regret. "Papa got stuck in some mud hole in the woods, but Granny-Too got a hold of him. He'll be home in a few hours to change and be on his way to meet us somewhere along Interstate 5."

"Good." I gripped Leah's fingers and led us out of the room. "We better go before Granny asks why we took so long." I jiggled Leah's hand. "Everything will work out. You wait and see, sis."

At the office, Harry greeted us. "Hi ladies." He reached to take the keycards from me. "Did you sleep well?"

"Yes." I stared at his slicked black hair.

He printed the paid bill. "Here you go, Kari." His fingertips brushed mine, and my heart flipped. "Thank you for staying at Divine Sleep. I hope you'll come again." He then slid a folded paper across the counter and under my palm.

I made a fist and stashed it in the inside pocket of my jacket.

We waved and said our good-byes to Harry. Settled into the backseat of our chauffeur-driven car, I opened the note.

Hi Kari,

I think you're nice. Please write me at harryjr553@morehouse.com, if you're no one's girlfriend. I'm free.

Sincerely,

Harold Morehouse Jr.

I stuffed Harry's note in the fudge brownie page of the cookbook. The car pulled forward. "Stop!" I reached for the door handle. "Wait for me." When the vehicle halted, I rushed into the office. Stumbling over my own feet on the way to the counter, I called out. "Harry?" I stretched my neck and bounced on toes.

He walked through an open entryway, his turquoise-blue eyes all crinkly. "Yes, Kari?"

I leaned my arms on the counter. "Me, too. I'm free. I'll email you when I get home," I shrugged, a little embarrassed. "We don't have an updated phone." Right on cue, a bubble churned inside my stomach. It managed to stay put. I relaxed.

His eyes lit like candles on a frosted cake. "I'll look for it."

Stepping away from Harry and his beautiful face, I waved goodbye and headed out the door. Under the gray clouds, I squealed under my breath. I might have even tapped dance a step or two. Even though I'm clumsy.

Once I was inside the car, the chauffeur drove away from the curb.

If only our phone had text. We had Mom's only cell phone, and it was a dinosaur with zero options. The disappointment smarted. I made a mental note to convince Mom it was time to upgrade. She might even let Leah and me have our own phones.

Never before had I cared so much about the modern world of technology. My brain usually focused more on dice, cook, and bake. I even had a secret dream to attend chef school. Would I have time for both creativity in the kitchen and love? My heart double-thumped. Move over fine dining and hello Harry.

Leah snuggled my shoulder. "Well?" She blinked her curled lashes in a "pretty please" poise.

"Harry gave me his email address and told me he's unattached," I whispered. "I told him I'm free, also." I wiggled and continued casually, so I wouldn't squeal. "We touched fingers."

"Ahhh. Sweet." Her blinks came soft and slow. "I really like him, Kari." She nodded. "He seems—" Leah tapped her chin. "Old-fashioned like Papa."

I inhaled a huge breath and let it go between parted lips.

When the repair shop came into view, I cupped my hand and leaned into Leah's ear. "We need to refuse to get into the Caddy. Unless. Granny takes us back to the motel where we'll wait for Papa."

She gave the thumbs up.

Mia leaned across Leah's lap. "Why are you doing the thumbs up?"

I tapped on my mouth. "Shhh, Mia. I'll tell you about our new plan in a minute." Her eyes glistened.

The more important question? How will I know the right moment to tell Granny the news?

I hoped and prayed I could do this. *Not lose my nerve.*

9

Does Not Rejoice in Wrong Doing

I had lost my nerve faster than icing on a hot cake.

Our little group strolled from the repair shop to the Caddy. Leah pushed Granny on Silver. The repair guy had parked the car in a lot near the sidewalk. Traffic zipped and zoomed. The noise caused in me the worst jitters. A gurgle rose from my stomach and entered my throat. I swallowed.

Leah and I glanced at each other every few steps.

I'm sure Leah intended the eye-holdings to keep me calm. She gave me what I lacked. *Courage.*

As always, I wanted what Leah had, ever since her toddler brain decided she needed to become mobile. Determination. Strength. She learned in one day. As she fell and braced herself and stood to take her first steps. Leah walked into Mom's outstretched arms. I'll never forget Mom's comment, even though I was only three years old. "My brave baby, Leah Bedeah."

From then on, Leah grew like the fresh yeast in Granny-Too's artisan breads. She soared to any occasion. No matter the problem we found ourselves in—whether to tattle or handle it—who made the last snack mess in the kitchen and, the biggie, whose turn to wash dishes.

Our previous squabbles were silly compared to this trip.

I often thought how my life would be different. If only God had given me some of my sister's nerves of solid rock. Though, Leah's snarky attitude rated quite high on the Richter scale.

Snarky and smart. My lips lifted at the corners.

But, as we approached the Caddy, fear froze my brain. Leah would be better at telling Granny our decision. Right then, my eldest position in the sibling line made me ashamed. *I will do it.* I grabbed Mia's hand, and we stopped. As Leah continued with a glance over her shoulder, I patted Mia. "I'm about to upset Granny." She blinked hard. "I need you to trust me. Go along with my plan."

Mia's eyes grew as round as chocolate peppermint candies. "Okay, Kari."

Leah halted Silver at Granny's car door and tipped her chin upward.

Within two blinks, I stood next to Leah. "You know, Granny… " I hugged my chest to protect myself from more than a cold wind. "We're headed for a snowstorm. By the looks of the map, we'll be into it three hours before we get to Papa's."

Shaking her sliver-gray curls, Granny stared me. She drilled an invisible hole.

Trembling, I squatted to her eye-level. "None-none of us are going in the Caddy, unless-unless it's back to the motel." At my bold but soft words, my knees shuddered along with my tongue.

Granny cocked her head. "Who made you boss, Kari Rose Holt?"

"Now, listen." Leah touched Granny.

She jerked back as though Leah's hand scorched. "Don't you *now listen* me. This is my trip, my time, not yours."

Covering her top lip with the bottom, Leah worked them until she released a puffy sigh. "You're wrong. Flat wrong." She appeared ages older than thirteen. "When you do something like this, it involves our whole entire family." Now she sounded like our parents. She bent at the waist, a hummingbird's breath from Granny. "This. Trip. Is. Over." Leah snapped upright. Her shoulders flounced. "What do you say to this?"

I gripped one of Silver's handles. Granny's eyes searched mine. Was there a flicker of doubt? Should I push the issue to get ourselves headed back to the motel?

Our granny's chest heaved. Her shoulders quivered. She vibrated like a miniature earthquake, the skin on her neck flushed deep red.

I opened my mouth. *Coward.* Clamped it shut.

When the blubbering sobs erupted from Granny's throat, it shook me to the core.

As her cries grew, my sisters took backward steps. Their expressions wavered between alarm and disbelief. My conviction to change Granny's mind sank through the bottoms of my feet.

This is so not good.

A movement caught my eye. A middle-aged woman with a huge purse hurried toward us on the sidewalk. Her trimmed brows furrowed. "May I help?" Her anxious expression of concern settled on Granny.

Oh-oh-oh, no! Tongue-twisted, even my thoughts stuttered.

Of course, Leah didn't hesitate. "We've got it under control. It's just our granny's prone to hysterics." She petted Granny's bowed head like she consoled a baby. "Nothing to worry over." Leah flashed her teeth at the lady. More like a snarl than a grin.

I could only imagine Leah's thoughts, "Get lost, you nosy busy body."

Right then, Granny pointed at me and Leah. "They—my–not—" Her fresh sobs jiggled Silver. She covered her face with crooked fingers.

The lady shifted her purse to the other shoulder. Would she scream elder abuse? She pulled out her phone. "Your grandmother is working herself into a heart attack. I should call 911."

"No need." Leah dove at the stranger. "You see, Granny's sensitive." She patted the lady's hand which held the phone. "We're headed north, and we're trying to figure out if we should get snow cables for the car. Also, Granny's distressed over the car needing repairs." Leah slipped an arm around her. "Right, Granny?"

Granny dug into her own purse which perched on her lap and produced a lace hanky. "Yes." She dabbed at her face. "I-I'm okay." The gush of tears shut off.

Amazing.

A twitch at the corner of Leah's mouth grew crooked.

"Well, if you say so." The stranger nodded. "And, yes, this weather is a concern." She touched Granny's arm. "Generations of my family have lived in this valley. My folks

told me stories of the snow blizzard in April of 1880." She
scrunched her face. "I fear this storm will be a repeat. If you're
going farther than Redding, you'll need snow cables." She
waved good-bye with a gloved hand. "God bless you on your
travels." The woman glanced back with a worried frown.

As the lady hurried on, Leah's face flushed pink.
"Granny." She stooped before her. "We're all in such big
trouble. I want you to know—"

Enclosing Leah's fingers with my palm, I gave her a gentle
squeeze. "Leah."

Seeming unfazed by Leah's statement, Granny's tear-
softened expression didn't scrunch in a fit of temper. "Help me
into the car, girls, and then purchase the snow cables."

From the backseat, Mia nibbled on her nails like a starved
kid eats corn on the cob.

After Leah placed Silver in the trunk, she stepped away
from the Caddy. "I'll see if they have them."

"Wait," I hollered. "We need the cash first." Granny
handed me the money, and I ran to where Leah waited at the
double doors. "You said the right thing to the lady about
cables. I think Granny would have had a heart attack right here
in the parking lot. Besides, we'll not get far. Papa will meet
us."

Once inside the auto shop, Leah stomped along the tiled
floor. "A fit from an old lady always works." She stopped. "I'll
remember this until I'm old and dying, Kari." Leah slapped the
air. "I'll never again stay at her house."

Her statement dulled my senses. I went with habit. I
hooked my elbow into Leah's. The familiarity and security of

our arms together calmed me—two sisters against what seemed like the world. Granny's world.

The man who worked at the computer lifted his gaze. "Did you forget something?"

"Do you have snow cables for the Cadillac?"

10

Not Irritable or Resentful

Twenty minutes later, we rolled along on the northbound lane. Snow cables sat in a gray box in the trunk next to Silver. At ten in the morning, I was as worn-out as a stale piece of chewing gum. I rubbed the cover of my cookbook and longed to read the recipes where I left off on page fifteen.

But, I had to focus on the road while Granny drove. "What?" I missed what Granny said.

She *tap, tapped* on the wheel. "Who's going to attach our cables if we need them?"

Her belt buckle clicked open, and Leah leaned her arms on the front seat. "Not if, Granny, but when."

I sighed. The white lines on the pavement disappeared beneath the Caddy. "We'll figure it out." Disillusioned because we couldn't stop Granny from traveling north, I shrugged. "Leah, get back into your seatbelt."

"Okay." She hooked a finger around a strand of my hair. "Don't they have pullover spots to put on cables, Kari?"

I visualized this very thing. "They should, and highway workers will surely help us." My own words challenged me. The few times we'd traveled in winter, I never noticed. Did highway workers with their orange vests help vehicle owners or no?

It was as if Leah heard my next thoughts. "We can read the directions and put them on ourselves."

I crossed my arms. "You can put them on. I'll read. I'm such a ninny when it comes to anything mechanical." I thought of a convincing comment in case no one believed me. "Granny-Too says I took after her."

Leah moved away from me and buckled. "It can't be hard."

Mia said, "Did the cables cost a lot?"

"Ah, piddle, Mia Babe." Granny waved a hand. "It was a needed expense."

Leah rustled pages of the map. "California's so long, I have to turn the page." Several moments past, and Leah cleared her throat. "If we don't get bogged in the snow or break down, we should be in Yreka by dinner."

"How many hours?" Mia leaned across the seat next to Leah.

"About ... six from now and includes stopping for lunch." But Leah glanced at me with a wink.

Papa will meet us before then.

Mia yawned. "I'm sorta, kinda, hungry."

"Me, too, Mia Babe." Granny pushed the blinker and passed a moving van. "We'll stop at your papa's favorite restaurant."

"Yea." Mia clapped.

Leah traced a finger along the map. "In about two hours we'll be at the Brown Bear Logger."

"We'll be eating the best cuisine ever." My stomach growled.

Harry's face came to mind. I grew lighthearted but then anxious. Would he really email me back? I furrowed my brows. Leah always got the attention when we were together in public. Cute and thin, she had hair the color of shiny straw. *Did he ever stare at her?* What if Harry really liked Leah and went through me first?

Chop, chop, toss, toss as though I created an emotional green salad. With no oil and too much vinegar.

~*~

I woke to Leah's high pitched voice. "There's the Brown Bear Logger sign."

"I'm so hungry, I could eat a bear." Granny flipped on her blinker and moved to the fast lane.

Shaken by what I'd done, I'd dozed at the wheel. So to speak. "I didn't mean to fall asleep on you, Granny."

"You were bushed, besides I'm driving just fine. Right Leah?"

"Actually, yes. I took over for you, Kari."

It would have been useless, though, if Granny needed my closer, quick response to steady the wheel. "The exit is coming up." I watched for the sign to tell us where to turn off. Soon enough, I pointed. Granny gave her right turn signal.

With the car stopped, I opened the Caddy door. An extreme temperature drop reached its icy fingers and clawed my bare neck. "Wow. Where's my coat?"

"We're closer to the storm." Leah zipped Mia into her jacket.

At the idea, my belly recoiled. I found my coat and fumbled to put it on. The wind reached through to my bones as though I wore nothing.

Leah and I positioned ourselves, ready to lift Granny onto Silver. "I'm stuck in the seat." She had one hand on the Caddy door and the other on the wheel. "It's my spine, stiffer than an iron rod."

"Let me have your left hand." Leah motioned to Granny. "Kari, grab the other."

"My legs are all tingles." Together we tugged and got her to stand. "I don't think I can walk, girls." We rotated her like a chicken on a rotisserie, only in the vertical.

Mia stood behind Silver. "Should I push this closer?"

"Yes." I waved the walker chair toward me. "Ready, set, go."

Granny plopped onto Silver. "We did it." And she laughed.

My nerves on edge, it brought me a bit of calm with Granny acting happy. But would Leah blow it with her sassy mouth? She appeared serene. Was she relieved Papa would come to our rescue tonight? I had to concentrate on him. Not allow what happened earlier at the auto service parking lot to chip at me like a pick on ice.

As I pushed Silver, Mia held open the glass door to let us through. Inside, Leah inhaled, and a smirk replaced her thoughtful expression. "So, Granny, did you starve?"

"I guess I didn't." She shook her head. "Sometimes, I do sound awful."

Leah and I exchanged glances and nodded our agreement.

We settled into our booth while the first snow fell from the clouds. At the sight of it, my fingers twisted a napkin into a knot. Would we meet Papa in time somewhere along the freeway?

~*~

Across from me, Leah gazed over the top of her menu. "Here we go, Granny. The snow you doubted would come." She parted her lips, her teeth set against each other in a fake smile.

Blinking, Granny raised her nose and stared through the window.

Mia pointed. "Uh, oh, they're huge flakes."

After the waitress took our orders, I poked Granny's shoulder from where I sat next to her. "Finish your story about how you met Grand." Even if no one else needed a distraction, I sure did.

She cleared her throat. "When I spotted your grand, I fell head over heels."

Mia gasped. "You rolled on the floor in front of him?"

Leah and I sniggered.

The waitress brought coffee for Granny and for us girls hot cocoa with mounds of whipped cream *and* chocolate sprinkles.

"No, Mia Babe." Granny sipped her drink. "It means I fell completely in love at first sight with your grand."

Whipped cream clung to Leah's upper lip. She sliced it off with her tongue. "What happened next?"

"I decided to say hello."

"Did you, Granny?" Leah sat down her mug. "Did you say hi, right then and there?"

"No, to my disappointment, I became unable to speak. After Doreen and I danced together through a few songs, I told her my feelings. She said to me, 'Adele Lou, just go right up to him. Say you'll marry him one day.' Doreen grabbed my hand. 'No, on second thought, get him to talk. If his voice makes you swoon, you'll know he's the one.'" Granny tsked her tongue. "That was Doreen May—born with a restless spirit." She slurped on her coffee.

Mia leaned closer to Granny. "What happened next?"

"At the break, I smoothed my skirt with my palms, took a deep breath, and waited for the other guys to leave the stage. I hoped James would stay." Granny chuckled. "I understand now he hid behind his guitar. He was too bashful to move from his stool."

I placed an elbow on the table, chin in the pad of my hand. "Can't imagine our grand so shy."

"Over the years, I worked out of him this trait." Granny nodded. "Where was I? Oh, yes. I had only ten minutes to make his acquaintance."

Mia raised her hand. "What does *quaintance* mean?"

Granny arched her brow. "It's acquaintance, not *quaintance*. It means to introduce myself to him, Mia Babe. When I stood at the bottom of the stage, I didn't think James noticed me. But then, his neck and face became several shades of crimson. I became giddy over his embarrassment."

"Did you talk to him?" Mia filled her spoon with whipped cream.

"I'll get to that part."

"How old were you guys?" Leah cupped her hands around her mug.

"I was fifteen and James sixteen."

"Wow." Leah shook her head. "You guys were so young."

This made me think of Harry. Goose bumps slid over my skin.

What did he see in me? After all, anyone could look at me and know I enjoyed taste testing the foods I made. A roll here and a bump there on my waist and hips. I crossed my arms. My fingers touched the excess on my sides. I jerked my hands away and huffed out a breath in annoyance.

High time to eat a bit less.

~*~

We drove north. Leah, our capable map reader, spoke from the backseat. "If the lady at the car repair shop is right, I think we'll be in the actual storm within an hour."

Snow made the shoulder of the road white, and I cranked the heater to high. "We should have put on the cables in the Brown Bear Logger's parking lot."

Leah rattled a piece of paper. "No. The cable directions say to wait until needed. This part of the freeway is still pretty clean from the tires of the traffic."

Granny slowed as a semi-truck splashed us with a wall of road-kill snow. It cascaded on the Caddy, making our car appear like a slushy on wheels.

I cradled the cookbook to my chest. "Umm, I think snow is deeper than you think."

"How will we know when to put them on?" Mia's voice rose until it squeaked. "Will we slip and slide first?"

"No, silly." Leah slapped the paper. "I overheard someone talking about the storm at the diner. Right before Redding, the Highway Patrol is stopping people. They're checking to make sure drivers going farther north have cables."

The snowflakes became as large as pats of butter. No longer sheets of wet snow.

"Yeah, but, Leah." Mia sighed, as though she had great patience. "Mom says it's not nice to eavesdrop."

"*I* did not eavesdrop." Leah's tone scolded. "She means private, personal conversations, Mia. Besides, the guy was a truck driver giving information about the weather."

Aiming her nose in the air, Granny snuffled. "In my day, we'd call children like Leah 'little pictures with big ears.'"

"What does it mean?" Mia scooted from the backseat near Granny's shoulder.

Granny flipped the windshield wipers to fast. "You listen in on people's conversations."

I pushed Mia's arm. "Stay buckled."

"See, Leah, you have big ears." Mia snapped on her belt.

With Mia secured in her seat, I concentrated on the road. "Well, you guys, Leah is right. This is considered valuable information. Nothing personal." The cold seeped into the Caddy. I shivered. Up ahead, vehicles dotted the shoulder of the freeway. As we passed one car, a man grabbed a gray box from his trunk. I pointed. "He's putting on his cables."

Traffic slowed. Granny let off the gas as our wipers slapped the windshield. I leaned toward the radio. "The guy we bought the cables from said to listen to the road conditions channel." I switched on the radio. Turning the knob to low, a lady sang about a coal miner's daughter.

Slowing the car further, Granny exited to a rest stop. "I won't ask if anyone needs to use the facilities. No doubt you do."

"Yep." Leah unclipped her seatbelt and placed her chin nearer to me. "I think this storm would surprise even the truck driver at the diner."

"Yeah. I'll check the road channel after this stop."

We shivered into our jackets and placed Granny onto Silver. My shoes sank. Silver's wheels bogged into the wet snow on an unused path. By the time we reached the women's restroom, my muscles ached. My feet stung from the cold and damp. A sharp tingle raced along my spine. I not only feared this trip but hated it.

After washing her hands at the sink, Granny insisted she could walk to the car with our help instead of riding on Silver. "I need to stretch my legs." Leah and I guided Granny along with careful steps, but she slipped. "Oh, my soul!" Her knees hit the ground. Her knitted hat flew in the air. We caught Granny before she landed face-first.

Mia hovered. "Granny!"

"Let's lift her on the count of three." I readjusted my hold under Granny's shoulders. "One, two, three." Mia and Leah grabbed her around the waist, and we settled Granny onto Sliver's seat.

"My foot gave out." Granny winced and blinked, hunching her back.

Was I the only one who noticed Granny's wheeze? Leah's eyes flickered, growing as large as walnuts.

Granny pointed at the Cadillac. "Kari, do you know how to drive?"

My heart slammed on its brakes. I shrieked.

11

In The Tongues of Angels

"What?" My hand fluttered to my cheek.

A wind gust blew snow sideways. Granny readjusted her knitted cap and stuck her bare hands in her pockets. "Do you, or don't you, know how to drive?"

"You're kiddin' me."

Leah nudged my side. "She does."

"You guys—" I gasped and choked on a snowflake.

"Remember the times Papa let you drive his white pickup in our field?" Leah drew an arm around my shoulders, halting our steps. "He said you did good."

Granny motioned toward the car. "Hurry."

We pushed Granny, aiming Silver toward the driver's side of the Caddy. With a sudden jerk, Leah moved a hard left.

In frustration, I filled the side of my mouth with air and blew. "What're you doing?"

"Putting Granny in the passenger's seat." She pushed faster. I lost the grip.

My arms dangled. "Wait." *Has everyone gone crazy?*

She faced me. "What?" Leah left Granny near the front bumper of the Caddy. "Kari, I know you think this is a bad

89

idea." She flapped her arms. "Who else is going to drive this boat?"

My fingers trembled at my throat. "It can't be me." I gulped.

"What in tarnation are you two doing? It's freezing."

"You heard Granny." Leah's breath puffed like foggy mist. "Let's at least get her in the car."

Following her, I wondered if I were being coaxed into doing something I couldn't possibly—. "You can forget it, Leah." Crossing my arms, I huffed.

At the passenger's side of the Caddy, Leah and Granny yelled for me. Grumbling all the way, I stood next to the two conspirators.

Against my better judgment, we heaved Granny up and onto the seat. As soon as she was settled, Leah and I straightened. "Kari, I'll put Silver away if you'll start the car and turn the heater to full blast."

Sneaky schemer.

Traitor.

I glared at her oh-so-sure-of-herself skinny back.

While Leah opened the trunk to place Silver inside, cold wind shoved me forward. I hurried to the driver's side, mumbling. "I'm not going to do this. I'm not." I slid behind the wheel, which appeared humongous compared to Papa's pickup steering, and started the engine. Flipping the heater to high, I prayed silently. *Father, help. Please. Make it possible for Papa to reach us here—*

"Let's get this car on the freeway." Granny's finger swiveled, motioning to the instruments which made the Caddy start, shift, and move.

"Huh?" Frowning, I slapped my cheeks. *She's serious.* "Mia, stay with Granny." I stepped from the Caddy and met Leah at the open trunk. "Leah." I buried my hands into my jacket pockets.

She slammed the trunk lid shut.

My nerves grew jittery, but I kept my voice even. "Go in the restroom. Call Granny-Too and tell her where we are." I jabbed my index finger toward the ground. "Papa is to meet us at this rest stop."

"I don't blame you for not wanting to drive." Leah's complexion had paled. Lines creased along her forehead. "But, we can't get stuck here."

I touched her arm. "Tell Granny-Too we are a few miles north of Willows." I nudged her. "Go."

Leah's face flushed. "Oh, all right." She retrieved her purse from the car and trotted toward the bathroom.

For a few moments, I rubbed my jacketed arms. When I was ready to face my pushy, stubborn granny, I slid into the driver's seat and shut the door.

"What's going on?" Granny returned my former glare. "Leah already has to use the bathroom? Is she sick?"

Giving myself a moment to decide whether I wanted to risk a Granny-sized fit, I didn't. "I'm going to check on her." Granny said something about *silly girls.* I shut the door to her complaining. In frustration, I rolled my eyes to the sky. A snowflake smacked my eyeball. I squealed, blinking from the freeze.

Everyone's against me. Even the snow.

Rubbing the warmth back to my lid, I continued a wobbly trek to the ladies room with blurry vision. Leah got one thing right. Who's babysitting who for sure? What were our parents thinking to leave us with such an unreliable person as Granny?

But, Mom probably never considered such chaos, when she left me with her parting words about Granny.

In the bathroom and with the phone to her ear, Leah paced. "Uh huh." Picking at the skin on her dry lips, she nodded. "But, Kari won't agree." She shook her head yes as though Granny-Too could see her. "Okay." Another pause. "Thank you. We will." Her brows rose to meet her cowlick. "What?" She angled her head, listening. "Oh, I hadn't thought of this. Bye."

Shivering in my light-weight jacket, I rubbed my palms together. "You hadn't thought of what? And what won't I agree with?"

Blinking, Leah wiped at the moisture gathering beneath her eyes. "Kari, I-I forgot the phone charger."

My heart dipped to my navel. "Fiddlesticks. We could have borrowed a charger from Harry." Becoming impatient, I made fists at my sides. "We're not thinking." I shook my head no. "We haven't thought smart since she dragged us from bed in the middle of the doggone night."

"But worse than no charger?" Tears streamed along her cheeks. "Papa can't—come. The freeway shut down an hour ago."

I inhaled a huge, disappointing breath. *No, no, no.*

Leah coughed on a sob. "There's no way for him to get past Dunsmuir, Kari."

"Where's this?" I grabbed her shoulders. "Did you ask Granny-Too?"

"I'd have to look on the map." She shrugged. "Granny-Too said it's a tiny community off the freeway and can get snowed in during a regular winter."

At this comment, I placed my hands on the wall and leaned my forehead on the cold concrete. Thinking, thinking, I faced my sister. "She didn't tell us what we should do?"

"Well." Leah scratched near her nose. "Yes."

I searched for Granny-Too's wisdom within Leah's hazel eyes.

Shivering now, she wrapped her arms across her chest. "Call—" She cleared her throat and swallowed. "The police."

"No!" I shook my head so hard my ponytail swished across my shoulders. "What if she does have a heart attack and dies?" I stabbed at my chest. "Then it would be *my* fault. *I'm* the oldest." *I gave my word.*

Leah sniffled. I pulled a napkin from my pocket. "Here. Dry your eyes. I'll figure out something."

And my mind went blank.

~*~

Inside the Caddy, my brain not only became void for a plan of action. It froze with fear. I drummed on the steering wheel. *I'm trapped.* Granny said something, but I couldn't bother with her at the moment.

The snow fell like a raging waterfall, intensifying my dilemma. How I wanted to reverse time. Back to when Granny woke me at three in the morning and told me she was leaving. With or without us. I didn't make a conscious decision then. It was more like a pang of loyalty.

This time, I had to weigh the good and the bad of what Granny wanted.

"Well, Kari Rose, what are you waiting for?" Grouchy, unreasonable Granny broke into my regrets.

What was it Granny called it when you wanted to chew someone out? Oh, yes. I'd enjoy giving her a *tongue lashing*. Right about now. But, I hung my head. I shouldn't disrespect Granny, even though she hadn't considered us when she decided on this trip.

On the verge of hyperventilating, I prayed about the best way to answer Granny. Aren't old people supposed to be wise? I prayed for a miracle to make her change her mind. If I drove farther north, we'd be taking an awful chance. No. We *were* caught in a snowstorm from the way Granny-Too told it.

Wait a minute. What if we found a motel not far from here? We'd be safe. Granny would accept a storm halted her trip.

Should I drive in this weather?

The truth? I couldn't call the police on Granny. And Leah was correct. We couldn't stay in the Caddy at a rest stop, for who knew how long, either.

Maybe my very last hope came down to—begging.

"Please, Granny." Biting my lip, I closed my eyes from the burn building behind them. "Hear what I have to say. *Please.*" I refocused my attention on my great-grandmother. "You want to see Papa. I understand."

At her lips forming a word, I raised a hand. "Granny. Listen. We're dealing with dangerous weather. Not our mild central coast temperatures. Mountain weather, with unpredictable storms." To appear calmer than I felt, I hooked my wrist on the steering wheel. "What if, Granny, the lady at the repair shop parking lot is right? This could be a blizzard, a repeat-of-history blizzard. What will we do then?"

"Your point?" Granny's face shriveled. Her eyes pierced me with a scowl darker than the clouds overhead.

Leveling my gaze on her, the air left my lungs as though gut punched. *What else to say?*

In the backseat, Leah slapped her hands on her jean-clad thighs. "Oh. My. Word."

Narrowing my eyes aimed at Leah in the rearview mirror, I pointed. "Stop." I sounded too harsh. At least I didn't scream. She lowered her chin, her eyes as sad as a scolded puppy's. I raised my voice a notch. "Thank you. Now let me handle this."

Leah stared out the window, her right eyelashes plump with moisture.

"Don't you act like I'm the kid and you're the adult." Granny wagged her finger. "Get this car down the road."

"No, no, no." As if blood drained from my body, I became dizzy. "This is beyond unreasonable, Granny. This is delusional, because you can't fight a storm."

"I'm tired." Granny yawned and stretched, relaxing her head to the side as though ready for a nap. "Let's go, Kari." In a few seconds, Granny snored.

My jaw went slack. *Seriously?*

I jumped at a knock on the driver's window, and I rolled it down a few inches.

A wrinkle-faced, hump-shouldered woman peered at me from beneath shaggy brows. Snow speckled her silver-brown hair. It gave the appearance of a lacey veil. She moved in closer, her breath rising in the frigid air. "You girls in a pickle?" Her lips curved upward, eyes sinking into the creases of her face like raisins in a cinnamon-sprinkled bun.

My brain flickered. *How did she know?* With the windows covered in snow, you couldn't see in or out if there wasn't a guy in the car

Mia whispered to Leah. I caught the word "scary," but my whole being disagreed. The lady's face glowed.

I nodded. "Yes, ma'am. We're trying to make a decision." To my right, Granny slept, with drool teetering on the edge of her mouth.

I blinked at Granny. She truly was asleep. Who in their right mind would fake drool?

"Don't you worry none." The old lady tapped a nail on the window. "Whatever it is, Jesus wants you to work it out." She winked. "Together." Her stare grew intense.

In slow motion, the stranger moved from the Caddy and vanished within a whirlwind of snow. Leah and I huffed. As if both of us were surprised.

Without thinking, I opened the door and rushed into the cold. I stopped. There were no vehicles nearby, except ours. In the direction the lady walked, snow sat undisturbed. No human footsteps or otherwise.

My legs wobbled.

Leah came behind me with a touch to my shoulder blade. "Where did she go?" She said above a whisper.

"Just. Gone."

~*~

96

Surrounded by blowing snow, my heart still warmed from the love in the old woman's eyes. Leah startled me with a tug on my arm and a pull into the backseat of the Caddy. The three of us huddled together with Mia kneeled on the floorboard. Our heads touched.

Leah said in a hushed voice, "That was weird, Kari."

I nodded, still unable to form a sentence.

Mia peered at me, her face scrunched with worry creases. "Did she scare you, too?"

"What?" I shook my head no. "I—"

"A spooky lady, right Kari?" Leah wrapped her arms around us. She shivered.

"I believe … she was an angel." My vision blurred. "I actually spoke to an angel."

Mia breathed the word. "*Really?*"

Tears sprinkled my cheek bones.

"If you say so." Leah leaned against the seat. "I looked at the map, and Red Bluff is about seventy miles. Hopefully, we could get that far and find a motel. Or even one before Red Bluff?"

As Mia played with the button on my jacket sleeve, she looked wide-eyed from me to Leah.

In awe of what the old woman said, about Jesus wanting us to work it out, I agreed with Leah. Or maybe go all the way to Papa's if the freeway is open?

I submitted to Granny's decision for me to drive. "We'll at least get closer to Papa's which will satisfy Granny." I knuckle rubbed my tired eyes. "She can get only so far in this weather. If the road signs state the freeway is still closed farther north—" I shrugged a shoulder.

"Exactly." The corners of Leah's mouth lifted toward her cheeks. "First let's fix you up to make you look older." She reached for her handbag. "Don't know why you were the sister who inherited Mom's curls." She let out my ponytail, and the brush raked along my back. "Would you grab the green scrunchy, Kari? It'll match your brown eyes."

Thinking about what I wanted to say to Leah, I dug for it. "Leah, do you think the old woman was an angel?"

"Don't know." Leah took the velvety elastic band and twirled it around my hair. The feel of a fresh ponytail took shape.

Mia's eyes brightened. "I do. I do."

After a time of silence, I made small talk. "What do you carry in your extra bag, your whole world?"

Leah chuckled. "A girl's gotta be prepared." She wound my hair around the scrunchy band. "Kari, would you get four bobby pins?"

I found the pins and handed them to her.

Pressing on the knot of hair, Leah fastened the twist. "I'm glad we've decided no more traveling once we get to Red Bluff. I'm exhausted."

I wasn't going to contradict her, because I wanted to end this trip something fierce. If I could drive all the way, we'd sleep in one of Granny-Too's beds tonight.

Leah patted at my hair. "Let me see." She tilted my chin. "Oh, wait." Placing her fingers deep into her bag, she then pulled out a tube of lipstick. Her brows waggled.

I raised my hand as a shield. "No way."

"Think about it, Kari. You have to look old enough to have a driver's license, in case we get pulled over by a police officer."

I rolled my eyes. "Now I've got to worry about them?"

Nibbling on her lip, Leah handed me the tube. She snapped her fingers. "We'll get you something to sit on to make you look taller."

Ready to apply color to my upper lip, my hand stilled in mid-air. "This is insane, Leah. I haven't taken driver's training."

"Yeah." Mia stuck her face into our space. "Kari's too scared to drive."

Try terrified.

Cocking her head to one side, Leah placed hands on her knees. "Calm down, Kari. I've considered every detail. This will work." She swiped a knuckle under her nose. "Look. I would drive, but I'd get busted."

"Well, yeah." I snorted. "You're so short and tiny you'd pass for eleven."

"Right." She nodded her head. "Point well taken." Leah unscrewed the lid of a long tube. "Look at me. I'll add mascara to your lashes."

Leah swung the wand. I clutched her wrist. "You're not stabbing my eye with this thing. Besides, you know Mom doesn't allow us to wear it. Not yet."

She creased her lip into a pout. "I'm ready for whenever."

I whispered, "Give me the phone, Leah." I speed dialed Granny-Too and hunkered down so as not to wake Granny.

In seconds Granny-Too said, "Hello, Leah?"

"It's me. Kari. I know we're supposed to call only in an emergency."

A rush of air came over the invisible lines of cell phones. "How are you, sweetheart? We've been so worried. The storm. Mom driving." *Is she sobbing?* "Sorry, honey. I don't mean to get emotional." Granny-Too cleared her throat. "Your papa has been held up as Leah must have told you. He checks the road conditions every half hour, hoping the freeway will be drivable."

"Thank you, Granny-Too." My eyes blurred. "Thank Papa for me."

She sighed. "Of course, baby."

"Granny-Too?"

"What, honey?" Her voice rose in a hopeful note.

"We're really okay." Tears spilt through my brave front, but I swallowed. I thought of the old hunch-shouldered angel. "Granny's exhausted. And, I'm going to—"

Leah sliced her hands through the air and mouthed; *Don't tell her you're driving.*

"I mean." I blinked. "It's snowing here, but not too badly."

"Where are you, Kari?"

"We're still at the rest stop past Willows."

"Stay put, sweetheart." Granny-Too's tone became firm.

"But, it's cold here, and we have to keep the heater running." Deep down, I hoped Granny-Too's reasoning would win over what I had decided. "Won't we run out of gas?"

"Maybe not." She paused. "The Cadillac has a big tank."

Okay, *maybe not*, didn't reassure me one tiny bit. Quickly, I thought of what I should say without giving away I would drive. "We've decided to go farther north to the next motel. As soon as we get there, we'll call you."

"If you're sure this is a good idea, Kari." Granny-Too took another shaky breath.

I nodded at the phone. "Granny's eager to get comfortable. We love you."

"I love you and be safe." She gave what I could always count on for good-bye. A *mmwaa* kiss sounded in my ear. I caught the kiss on my cheek in my imagination.

We disconnected our conversation. A longing for her made me sad. I wanted nothing more than for Granny-Too and Papa to rescue us.

Leah aimed a cotton ball toward my nose. "At least let me finish making you look legal age." She dabbed foundation on my skin. My tears streamed into her efforts.

A sob caught in Leah's throat. "Mia, get me a tissue."

Leah dabbed the wet from my cheeks. I rolled my shoulders in determination, preparing myself for what I intended.

12

Childish Ways

Snow crept down. My determination flew south.

I squirmed on the booster seat Leah made for me. It consisted of my cookbook sandwiched between the car's leather and three of our coats folded on top. Settled just right, my eyes grazed the top of the steering wheel.

If I stretched my neck.

Granny rested in the passenger's seat, her mouth gapped as wide as the center of an angel food cake. I resisted the urge to touch her chest. To see if her heart still beat, she'd been so quiet. As if the Lord wanted to reassure me, Granny snuffled an old lady snort.

Taking in a deep, deep breath, I studied the dash and floorboard. I recalled Granny's hand and feet movements to get the Caddy ready to drive. I started the engine.

"I'll help you see, Kari.

I glanced in the rearview mirror.

Leah knelt facing the rear window. "If you're about to smash into something, I'll holler." Leah gave me the thumbs up.

I wasn't sure if this was reassuring.

Shifting into Reverse, I changed my mind and put the Caddy back into Park. The side mirror wasn't adjusted. Rolling down the window, I clicked on my tongue for my neglect. Fixing the mirror, I was set to go, and eased from the parking space as slow as a cake rises in the oven.

"May wonders never cease." Granny jerked upright. "We're moving."

Under my breath, I muttered. "Gee. Thanks."

Driving in reverse went well. When I hit the brakes they screeched and the Caddy jolted. With a squeal, Leah hit the back side of the driver's seat.

This reminded me of another 'first time' I did something on my own when using mechanical equipment without wise adult supervision. I added cold butter to my mom's free-standing mixer and turned it on high speed. Big mistake. The butter rattled around the wire paddle, jumped into the air, and punched me in the nose.

Think softened butter and slowly mix. My foot eased from the Caddy brake. I applied even pressure as the gas pedal melted beneath my sneakers. Then, I remembered what Papa taught me when he gave me my driver's lessons. I tested the brakes as I entered the entrance lane to the freeway. Tap, tap, let off, tap, tap. The brakes worked. I was ready.

Leah rustled around on the floorboard and popped up near my ear. "Don't forget the turn signal, Kari."

This rattled me. "Oh." Finding it, I flipped the lever and accelerated onto the freeway. *I'm sorry for making you fall,* was on my tongue, until Leah tapped me.

"Kari." She pointed. "Pick up your speed, or we'll get run over." Snow whirled all around the Caddy, making it seem way more hazardous. Leah's palm curled on my shoulder. "You can do this, sis."

I nodded, so she would believe I remained calm and could do what was needed. My intestines, though, were creating bubbles the size of snowballs.

The tires slid a bit to the right, edging too close to the slow lane's shoulder. I stiffened, let off the gas, and gained control of the wheel. *Too close.*

Trucks and cars whizzed by, and one trucker honked his fog horn. I jumped clear off my padded seat. My speedometer read thirty, but to go faster in this storm would be lame. Was this an example of road rage? Other drivers should slow down—not for me to speed.

"Orange cones. Flags." Leah sliced her finger past my temple, making the stray hairs near my face *swoosh.* "I'll bet we have to put on our cables."

"Good." My heart slowed its race. "Did you feel it when we skidded?"

But Leah didn't answer, as we drew closer to the emergency area where vehicles moved to the road's shoulder. My foot eased off the gas pedal. The Caddy became less scary to drive once I became used to the mechanics. Push the brake now. Release. Brake. Brake. I stopped behind another car and shifted into Park.

A squeal of tires and crunched metal jarred my last nerve. "Glory be." In my rearview mirror, Mia's face creased with concern.

Stirring next to me, Granny patted at the side of her hair where it had been flattened by the seat. "What's going on, Kari?"

A line of cars formed behind the Caddy. Mia unbuckled and twisted to focus on the rear window. "A wreck for sure."

I turned off the ignition as drivers everywhere opened doors.

"The guy in front of us took a gray box from his trunk." Leah opened her door. "It's cable time."

"Wait, Leah." I scooted off the jackets beneath me. "You need your coat."

Granny waved her knuckles. "Keep the engine running, heater on full blast." She closed her eyes as though she wasn't done with her nap.

Doing as Granny instructed, I then joined Leah behind the Caddy, while hugging our jackets.

Bent over the deep expanse of the trunk, Leah grabbed a wide-brimmed beach hat from one of her duffle bags. "It's freezing." She shoved the hat on her head.

After I gave Leah her coat, I shrugged into mine. "You're always prepared, Leah Bedeah." Our arms touched. "I'll never fuss at you like Mom does for carrying your world in a handbag."

She snatched a pair of gloves from the same bag. "At least someone understands."

"But." I frowned. "Why did you bring garden gloves?"

"I planned to work in Grand's flower beds." Leah smirked. "Didn't you notice his weed-infested yard?"

Leah and I worked open the box of cables. "No." My hands burned from the cold, and I blew on them.

"Here." Pulling off a glove, she flipped it. "At least one of our hands each will stay cozy."

I slipped on the leather and flexed my fingers. "Nice."

She dug in her pocket and pulled out a folded paper. "Read these instructions out loud."

As I read, Leah laid the cable over the rear tire and tucked the cable snug to one end on the ground side of the tire. "Okay, now we're to move the car back a few feet. This way you can attach the connections."

While we warmed ourselves inside the Caddy, I reversed the car. Leah connected the cables with a snug fit, and we moved to the other tire. The snow barely drifted now. *Thank you, Lord.*

Before we finished the second tire, Leah and I warmed ourselves again in front of the Caddy heater.

Granny sat up straighter. "Does it really take so long to make this car snow-worthy?" She took in the whole landscape with eyes narrowed. "Oh, my soul, we're in a blizzard."

"Not really, Granny, it's a snowstorm." Between Granny and me, Leah rested her arms on her knees, hands extended toward the heater. "But, no worries, we've got this under control. Kari and I are almost finished with the back tires."

"Slowly but correctly, Granny." I leaned over Leah and smoothed Granny's hair from her cheek.

"You figured it out, did you?" Granny yawned. "I have brilliant great-granddaughters." Another yawn escaped from her wide-open mouth. "I need coffee."

"So sorry, Granny." Leah leaned closer to her. "We're fresh out." She chuckled.

Granny angled her jaw. "When will you be fresh out of a razor tongue?"

Shaking her head no, Leah wrinkled her nose. "This is the way God made me."

"No, sir." From the backseat, Mia touched Leah's shoulder. "Mom says you have an altitude."

"Hmm, right," Leah said with an airy tone. "Mia, the word is *attitude*."

Suddenly, a gun belt above long legs stood eye level at the driver's window.

"Oh!" I patted my chest. "He scared me."

The officer who thumped on the glass also sported a mustache.

"Can't he tell the heater's running and the warmth will escape?"

"Be reasonable, Granny." Leah waved at him. "We have to see what he wants."

I rolled down the window only a few inches to keep Granny from fussing.

"I'm Officer Kelly." He stooped to look inside the Caddy. "Is everyone okay?"

Leah poked her head next to mine. "We've almost got the other cable on, but it's so cold we took a break."

He pointed his chin at Granny. "How are you doing, ma'am?"

Granny pointed a finger at the police officer. "Just so you know, Officer Kelly, my girls know exactly what they're doing."

Of course I kept quiet. It could be another delusional idea of Granny's. We'd only know for sure if we put the cables on properly when we pulled away from the shoulder. Now, Officer Kelly squinted. He aimed the squint at me an awful, forever moment. From where I sat behind the wheel, I squirmed like jelled fruit juice on a shaky plate.

Had he figured out I'd been driving? Worse yet, would he ask to see my non-existent driver's license?

~*~

"How about I take a look at—"

I grew woozy. *He's going to ask for a license.*

"—so far with the cables?" One side of Officer Kelly's mustache wriggled.

"What did you say?" I gawked at him.

"Let me check." He walked to the rear of the Caddy and stared at our unfinished job. I let out a breath. When he returned to the driver's window, he squatted. "How about I finish for you?"

There was no way he knew I was driving. I had torn down my booster because we needed the jackets. The cookbook lay on the seat between Granny and me.

Leah and I joined Officer Kelly behind the Caddy. The three of us finished the cable job. Before we could return to the car, though, a gust of wind slammed into us. A shriek with gale force tossed Leah and me into a snowbank.

After what felt like hours, Officer Kelly grabbed hold of us. He nestled us on the freeway side where the Caddy became our shield from the wind.

Leah whimpered. I snuggled her, cheek to cheek. Though words literally froze on my lips, my heart desired to shush her fear. *I'm here. You're safe.*

With a lull to the storm, Officer Kelly helped Leah and me into the rear seat of the Caddy. He slammed the door and hurried toward his SUV.

Granny hollered, but I only caught the last of it. "…blew you away."

My teeth shivered, making my jaw ache.

Yelling above the now ramped-up storm, Granny patted the top of her seat. "You girls come on. The heater will thaw you."

Silently, Leah and I slid over the seat like seals off a rock. I never appreciated warmth more, even though our bodies shuddered.

"Can … home now?" Mia's voice was no match for the intermittent scream of the wind. "…too scary."

As I sat in my soaked jeans for over an hour, the wind finally calmed to sporadic gusts.

Granny pointed. "Kari, take the keys and get dry clothes for the both of you. Be careful."

Gathering my courage, I moved from Leah's side. As I shoved my shoulder into the door, it became a tug-of-war against a flurry. With sudden energy, the door opened. Thrown off balance, I stumbled from the Caddy.

I retrieved our two duffle bags from the trunk and climbed into the backseat next to Mia. Shivering, I handed Leah the keys, and she started the Caddy. Moments later, she tossed her wet slacks over the seat. They slapped into a pile on the rear floorboard.

Mia gasped. "People might see you."

"Here." I handed Leah a pair of jeans and fuzzy socks for her continual cold feet.

"My fingers are-are stiff." Leah trembled while she dressed. Granny wrestled out of her coat and draped it over Leah. "Th-thanks. Ohhh. I'll ne-ever be-be-be warm."

Reaching for her, Granny grabbed a hold. "Honey, let's get you closer." She pressed Leah's hands between her own and moved them near the heater vent.

After we were in dry clothes, Leah sighed. "For once you're right, Granny." She nudged Granny playfully. "I'm warmer."

"I'll let this one pass, Leah Bedeah." Sniffling, Granny puckered her mouth.

Drinking from our last, newly opened water bottle, I then offered some to Leah. She gulped down the rest.

Granny tapped the dashboard. "Now what do we do?"

The wind had blown my once tidy bun to a damp mess around my jaws. As I brushed my curls, the tangles caught within the wooden bristles. "We need to hear the weather report."

Leah snapped on the radio and searched for the station.

My heart tripped. Would it be good news or bad?

An announcer said, "—is lessening south of the Siskiyou Mountains." Leah let go of the knob. "But, people are instructed to stay in their vehicles until further notice. This storm is considered unpredictable." The man repeated the message, and Leah switched the knob to off.

"We're stuck?" Mia whined. "I need tissue, Kari."

I dug through Leah's purse and handed her one.

Seeming calm, Granny waved off Mia's concern. "Don't worry, Mia Babe, we can run this heater day and night if necessary."

I frowned. Granny had been wrong about many things on this trip. Her age showed more than ever before. Now she seemed weak, instead of just old. I couldn't count on her.

Someone rapped on the driver's window, and Leah opened it partway. Officer Kelly's eyes crinkled. "How are you ladies holding up?"

Everyone spoke at once. "Okay. Fine. I'm hungry. I need some coffee."

His eyes swept over each of us. "Are you warm enough?"

Glancing at Leah, I stuffed my fists into my pockets. "Yes, sir."

Leah tilted her head. "Thank you for helping us earlier."

I nodded.

He slid his gloved fingers across the brim of his snow-brushed hat. "My pleasure, young lady." Now his eyes grew round. "Do stay inside your car as much as possible." His brows rose, disappearing under his hat brim. "The National Guard is coming with food and beverages for stranded travelers. I'll return with enough for four? Correct?"

Mia sniffed and wiped her nose on her shirt sleeve. "What are you bringing us?"

Granny nodded. "Yes, four, and, hopefully some coffee."

Officer Kelly glanced at Mia. "I'm not sure, but it's food for the belly. Something to quench your thirst." He shook his head no at Granny. "Probably no coffee." He winked at Mia. "But there might be napkins to clean messy faces."

Mia's lips curled into a pout. "I'm too old to get food on my face."

He tapped on the top of the open window. "I would like to tell you when you can expect your meals. All I know for sure is it's on the agenda."

"Are you gonna eat, too?" Mia's eager expression matched my relief.

We will be taken care of.

"You betcha. I'm starved." He tipped his hat and left.

Moaning, Granny squirmed in her seat.

"Is something wrong?" I leaned her way.

"My legs. They're cramped from sitting." She shook her head. "And, an old lady like me needs her coffee."

A howling wind rolled over the Caddy, rocking the frame. With it, clouds released snowflakes the size of the scoop-end of a soup spoon. I shuddered. Snow weaved across the windshield, the pattern as dainty as a spider's web.

A sinking feeling hit to the bottoms of my toes.

13

I Reasoned Like a Child

Is this what it's like inside an igloo?

Except for the hum of the heater, we could have been in the middle of the Arctic.

On the side of the road, three of us held up Grand's old Army blanket. It was a perfect three-sided partition around the fourth person for our makeshift restroom.

The exposed side faced a pasture, and the cows didn't pay us any attention. We couldn't care less about their hairy hides either. Except for Mia who enjoyed talking to them. Being distracted like she was, she often dropped her corner of the wool blanket. Squeals erupted from the one who needed privacy, and I scolded Mia.

After each trek to the road's shoulder, we slid inside the Caddy and beat our hands together to bring warmth into our fingers and thumbs.

Now, it was early evening before dusk, although we had to guess because of the clouds pressed over our heads.

Leah's face drooped. "I wish Mama knew we were in this storm."

We needed to encourage one another. As I searched for the right words, Granny interrupted.

"Oh, Leah." Granny scratched at her arm, where she stretched out in the backseat next to Mia. "It's best she doesn't know so she doesn't worry."

"No." With a swift shake of her head, Leah appeared stubborn. "Then Mama could be praying for us."

Nodding, Granny smoothed the hair from Mia's face.

I pulled Leah to me. She nestled within my arms, head on my chest. "We must be on national news, since storms like this don't happen in April."

"Yeah, but…" Leah tipped her chin to look at me. "Mom and Dad are at a place with no radios or cell phones. Only the front desk has communication in case of emergencies. Remember?"

I sat upright. "Didn't Mom give us the number?"

"Yes," Granny said.

"Well?" Leah popped up from my chest. "Where is it?"

"I left it at home by the phone."

Another situation where Granny didn't use good judgment.

"Oh, brother." Leah plunked her head a bit too hard against my chest.

"I need food." Mia whimpered. "When is Officer Kelly coming?"

Squirming from our cuddle, Leah peeked above the seat. "It should be any time I'd think."

"During Christmas in 1968, your papa became stranded in an Oregon snowstorm." Granny caressed Mia's cheek with her knobby index finger. "He was on Interstate 5 in a mountain pass."

Leah's head wagged with a slight shake. "All these years later it happens to us."

My stomach growled. "We're in the freakiest storm."

What little daylight we had faded. I switched on the interior light. "Finish telling us about the night you met Grand."

Chuckling, Granny waved her fingers with a flick of her wrist. "Might as well." She cleared her throat. "Where was I?"

Leah removed herself from our heap. "Grand blushed."

"Yeah, that's where." Mia clapped.

"When he looked at me, I truly fell in love." Granny's lips puckered. "As I came closer and stepped onto the platform, I held out my hand to shake his. 'I'm Adele Lou Baines. What's yours?' He actually stuttered. 'I-I-I'm James Whitmore'. His smile about knocked me over. He reached for my hand and shook it. 'Pleased to meet you, Adele Lou Baines.'

"Afterward, we sat on the stage and talked about where he lived, where I lived. Too soon his break ended, and he settled behind his drum set." Granny shook her head. "I sure didn't know then he was a guitar player as well. Oh, this guy had music running through his veins and marrow."

Silence extended for a long while. Then Granny sighed. "But, this wasn't the end of it, as you well know. I talked it over with Doreen while we danced to James's beat and told her I was going to marry him." Granny raised a brow. "You'll never believe Doreen's response."

"What?" I grinned.

"'Tell him,' she said, like it was the most natural thing. I reared back from our dance swing, and my feet stuck fast to the planked floor. 'Doreeeeen!' I squealed. 'Shame, for shame. I can't do that.' Doreen planted hands on her hips. 'Then, I will,' and she faced the stage." Granny pressed her lips into a thin line. "Before she could take one step, I grabbed the collar of her dress. 'Don't you dare.'" Granny tittered. "I yanked too hard and ripped a part of her collar right off."

Leah settled once again into our huddle and laughed.

"Instead of getting huffy, Doreen giggled. 'Adele's a chicken liver.' She reached for me, and we danced to the rest of the song."

"Wow." Leah shivered, and I readjusted my arms around her shoulders. "Your sister was bold."

"This is the truth."

My mouth went dry. Hopefully, Officer Kelly would bring water soon. "Doreen's ways didn't rub off on you, Granny?"

Leah raised her chin at me and grinned. She liked my question.

"Hmmm, well, somewhat. She made me into a stronger person when later I had to stand with James for what we wanted."

Leah sat up. "Really? Tell us about it, Granny."

She waved at Leah with a swat. "I've got to finish this part first." Granny spoke in a quiet tone. "I'm so glad you girls like my story."

Was there a catch to her voice? "We love to hear about you and Grand."

"Let me keep telling, then. When the band stopped for the night, Doreen and I stayed while James broke down his equipment. He kept glancing up. When he had loaded his drum set into his beat-up pickup, he walked toward me. I met him halfway. I had given Doreen's suggestion serious consideration. The more James watched me earlier while he played his drums, the braver I became."

Grabbing Leah's fingers, I intertwined them with mine. "Oh, Granny, how romantic."

"Well, I don't know about *romantic*. We Baines girls were like rolling rocks gathering no moss." She pursed her lips. "At least Doreen was, and I thought her the wisest sister in all creation. Anyway, James came closer, and his blue-eyed gaze reached into my soul. Stopping before him, I blurted. 'James Whitmore, I'm going to marry you one day.'"

I gasped. Leah chuckle-snorted. Mia laughed out loud.

"Now, girls, don't go copying me. I'm just telling my story, not promoting it."

We shook our heads, and I stuffed down a giggle. "We wouldn't, Granny. What did Grand say?"

"Yeah..." Leah peeked over the front seat.

"He blushed." Granny's voice caught and sounded like she needed water, also. "For the second time."

"Of course." Leah nodded.

"Then, he stared at the floor—"

A light wobbled through the Caddy's snow-curtained windows. Someone rapped on the driver's window. "Officer Kelly here." His gloved hand swiped the snow until his grin appeared.

Mia jumped. "He's back."

I rolled down the window.

Snow dusted his golden-red mustache. "Still holding up, ladies?"

"Yes," we crowed.

Mia leaned over the front seat. "Granny's telling us about when she told Grand she'd marry him."

Officer Kelly glanced at Granny. "Really?"

117

"Yep."

"I've got news." The left side of his mustache arced. "The storm is supposed to break by morning."

"Yea!" We girls hooted.

"Here are your rations." He pushed a large grocery sack through the opening.

I waited to receive it.

"Careful." He didn't let go. "It's heavy." He released the bag into my arms. "Are you still okay, ma'am?"

Granny nodded. "Oh, sure, but I can't wait to get out of this blustery mess."

"I'm in charge of this section of the freeway. If you want, I'll scrape your window and shine a light throughout the night. Check on how you're doing."

"That'd be kind." Granny flashed a toothy smile.

Officer Kelly brought another sack through the window, tiny compared to the first. "Here, ma'am." He reached in, aiming it at Granny. "I found this for you."

"What is it?" She cupped her hands. "It's nice and warm." She blinked, and her mouth parted. "Sir, did you bring me coffee?"

The corners of his eyes crinkled.

Hers shimmered, and I thought for a moment she would cry. "Thank you, so much, Officer Kelly."

I couldn't help but be grateful.

"You're welcome, ma'am." He cleared his throat. "How's the gas gauge looking?" He shined his light on the Caddy panel. "Half full. Not bad." His brows met in the middle. "I forgot to mention the snowplow is cleaning off one lane of the freeway, coming south. The plan is to shoot the snow into the fast lane. We only need a single lane in this miserable weather, anyway." He tipped his hat. "Good night now."

We said our good-byes, and Mia blew him a kiss.

Cranking on the handle, I rolled the window closed. Leah spread the contents of the sack between us on the seat. "Look here. We have some kind of meat sandwiches." She sniffed. "Roast beef. And we have orange juice and bottles of water."

Mia rubbed her eyes. "I'm too thirsty and hungry." Leah gave her a water and sandwich before anyone else.

Scraping on the Caddy windows, Officer Kelly exposed the insides of our igloo. When finished, he waved at us, and my heart warmed.

As I ate my sandwich, I counted our blessings—starting with the lady who warned us about the coming storm. Then the food and drinks brought by the kind officer.

Best of all, we had a visit by an ancient angel.

~*~

Someone groaned and it woke me. In the distance, a rumbling drew closer along the freeway. I craned my neck. A monster-sized blade moved the snow, spraying it high and onto the fast lane of northbound Interstate 5.

As the snowplow past, Leah jerked within my arms. She appeared to me in a deep sleep. Squirming, I needed a new position. I inched myself from beneath her and slipped closer to the steering column.

Hugging the wheel, I glanced to my left. In a glow of light, Officer Kelly stood next to the driver's side door. He tipped his hat. His flashlight swung as he checked inside the Caddy. I

waved. He returned the gesture and walked to the vehicle
behind us. Leah's watch showed three a.m. Oh good, more
sleep for me. I yawned, wadded my jacket into a misshaped
ball, and stuffed it into the corner space between the door and
my seat.

With a satisfied sigh, I drifted off.

Later, the sun's rays came through the glass on Leah's
side. Its warmth bathed her sleeping figure and spread.

"Granny. Leah. Look. There's sunshine."

Rising from lying flat, Granny blinked.

Leah rubbed her eyes open. Mia whimpered. "I'm cold."

In one swoop, I stretched over the seat and covered her
with the fallen blanket. "There you go, Mia Babe."

Arms toward the roof, Granny yawned loud and long.
"We'll be free from this igloo before we know it."

She also thought of the Caddy as an igloo? As I considered
this coincidence, Officer Kelly spoke through the closed
driver's window. "Turn on the radio for road conditions. There
will be information and instructions to follow." He pointed at
the front tire. "You're going to have to scoop snow from your
tires before it's time to move." He rushed to the next vehicle.

Leah leaned forward and flipped on the radio knob. "... for
further updates." The announcer repeated his message from the
beginning. "The storm dumped three foot of snow along
Interstate 5 just south of Red Bluff and into the north over
Siskiyou Pass. Those stranded on the interstate must not move
their vehicles until you've been advised by Highway Patrol it is
safe to proceed. We estimate the ban to travel will lift around
eleven o'clock this morning."

Leah and I slapped palms in a high-five.

The announcer continued. "Plows are clearing the shoulder lanes in both directions of traffic to make travel possible."

Turning off the radio, I no longer imagined driving all the way to Papa's. Meeting him at a nearby motel would be great. "A few more hours, and we'll be headed toward Granny-Too's and Papa's." I glanced at the paper bag of food. We had leftover sandwiches. I even saved my orange juice for breakfast. No one bothered to talk as the roar of the snowplow approached once again. The blade shot snow onto the left lane of the freeway.

Leah handed out the sandwiches, and we thanked God for the food. Once we finished eating, Leah and I would clean the snow from around the tires.

A thought gave me an ice-cream brain freeze. I stopped in mid-chew on my roast beef with mustard and mayo.

Would the cables really help me with my driving? I didn't want to slide off the road and fall into a ditch. Or worse, the cliff on a mountain.

14

When I was a Child

All roads drivable!

This was the news from the road advisory channel at ten minutes to eleven. With our car full of giddy females, I raised my fist in *yes*. Finally, we could continue this trip. Get to Papa's.

Officer Kelly stopped at the Caddy. "Ladies, there is a rest stop ahead. But there are long lines of vehicles at that off-ramp, backing up traffic." He tipped his hat. "So don't expect to move your car from here for a while."

We said our good-byes and thanked him, and he disappeared from my rearview mirror. I sighed and turned on the headlights. "We'll stop at the rest stop and use the bathroom."

Granny poked my shoulder. "Get me in the front seat before we leave."

"Good idea." I left the car, and Leah followed my lead. She wheeled Sliver to the shoulder side of the freeway and waited. I pulled on Granny's arms, but it seemed she stuck to the seat.

"Wait a sec." Leah trotted to the freeway side of the road and kneeled on the rear seat. She pushed Granny while I tugged. Granny slid across the seat, but her foot caught in the space between the open door and the Caddy.

I rearranged her shoe to dangle outside and lifted her while Leah pushed. Granny held onto the door and swiveled to sit on Silver's seat. *Plop.* Her mouth gaped wide in a deep-throated chuckle. "We did it."

Both Leah and I struggled to push Granny the few feet through the snow. Now, with her in the front seat, Leah put away Silver and climbed into the backseat.

Settled behind the wheel, I studied the thin layer of hardened snow on the pavement. To avoid collisions, the road advisory instructed people to wait until the vehicle ahead pulled on the freeway.

"Looky." Mia danced on the backseat floorboard. "Cars are moving."

My heart shifted. "I did this driving thing before. I can do it again." A scripture came to me. One my mom had on a refrigerator magnet from Philippians 4:6. *Do not be anxious about anything, but in everything by prayer and supplication with thanksgiving let your requests be made known to God.*

A sense of calm mushroomed through my spine. The fizzles in my belly never erupted. Releasing the emergency brake, I put the car into Drive. I pumped the brakes to make sure they worked and maneuvered onto the freeway.

Near my shoulder, Leah whispered, "He's coming, Kari. Officer Kelly."

I pursed my lips in concentration.

Mia bounced in her seat. "I feel the cables bumping."

The pickup in front of us stopped. When it moved forward, I way over accelerated and nearly hit its bumper. I wailed. "My foot is shaky."

"Officer Kelly stopped at the third car behind us." Leah sighed in exaggeration. "So no worries. And, Mia, face forward. We don't want to draw attention."

"You girls back there, buckle up." Granny patted my shoulder. "Good job, Kari Rose."

Having let off the gas, I put distance between me and the pickup. *This is not a race.* Driving twenty miles an hour, my eyes crested the top of the steering wheel.

I'm cruisin'.

~*~

After the rest stop, we cruised through Red Bluff and grabbed lunch at a drive-through in Redding. Leah leaned over my shoulder. "We're doing this, Kari."

"Yes, we are." My grin stretched so big, my face ached.

Granny yawned. "I'm full from burger and fries…I think I'll nap. Leah, help your sister watch the road."

Leah saluted. "Yes, sir, ma'am."

Granny tilted her head. "Fun-nnny."

Leah giggle-snorted.

Grinning, I exhaled. We were headed toward Papa. With the winter weather behind us, Leah agreed with me to keep going. I thought Papa would have called by now, and tell us where to meet. I had everything under control, though. No worries. The slow lane stayed clean enough, still the only lane open. Flow of traffic moved thirty to forty miles an hour. *Piece of cake.*

I decided I loved driving, especially this old boat of a car.

An image of Mom coming home in a few days flashed through my mind. My hands gripped the steering wheel. *Focus, focus, focus.*

As I hummed a song, a van in front of us made a sudden halt. I jammed the brake pedal. Going sideways a bit, I missed it and straightened the wheel. Ahead of me, vehicles were backed up. Snow drifted from a shadow-gray sky as I put the Caddy in Park. "What happened to our sun?"

"Don't know." Leah stared ahead at the road. "I was too busy helping you drive."

"What's going on?" When the traffic still didn't move, Granny ranted. "We've been sitting here long enough." She sputtered her next words. "More snow?"

Mia interrupted my sigh of misery. "Wowee. Fat flakes." Her window squeaked when she rolled it down.

Leah made quick movements to Mia's side of the Caddy. "Mia, get your tongue back inside this car."

"It's cold." Granny slapped the top of the seat behind her. "Shut the window."

Obeying them both, Mia cranked on the handle. "Oookay."

I hunched my shoulders as the process of rolling up the window created a squeak.

Instead of her usual stinging remarks at Granny, Leah reached over the front seat and switched on the radio.

"Another storm front is moving over the Pacific Northwest and will cover the upper half of California and the state of

Oregon. Please be advised this is not the same storm from yesterday, but a blizzard. I repeat—"

Listening to the full report twice, I switched off the radio. No one spoke. No one moved. *What have we gotten ourselves into?* Papa must be stuck on the freeway north of us. *Is this why we haven't heard from him?*

I needed to tell Leah to check our cell phone battery. When to get her aside became the problem, though, so Granny wouldn't be suspicious. She couldn't know we'd been in contact with Granny-Too.

Breaking the silence after our shock at the weather report, my sisters groaned and mumbled. Granny slapped her hand on the dashboard. "What in thunder?"

My chest heaved. I spoke through clenched teeth, "Leah, how far is the next town?"

She moved from her perch near my shoulder. As she flipped the pages of the map, traffic moved. I took the Caddy out of Park and pressed on the gas. "Granny and Mia, look for signs along the freeway telling us what's ahead." I didn't dare take a glimpse for myself. There were sharp curves on the freeway now. My muscles tensed for the twists in the road terrified me. "We need the nearest motel because I will not drive in a blizzard." I clamped on my lips in determination.

Snoring came from Granny's direction. I grumbled in my throat. How could she just fall asleep? At our next stop, we'd call Granny-Too and ask about Papa ... I just hoped and prayed we had enough charge to keep a connection.

An idea formed. I'll test Granny to see if she's really asleep. If she is, I'll ask Leah to check our cell battery.

126

I glanced in the rearview mirror at Leah. "I wonder if Granny wishes she were still at home."

The snoring stopped. "Well, I don't."

Another bend on the freeway prevented my eyes from roaming. "I thought you were sleeping." *Sneaky, Granny.* I smirked.

"Just a catnap." Granny yawned. "To answer your question, the house without James drives me nutty. Too quiet. Predictable."

Patting Granny's hair, Mia cocked her head to one side.

"Okay, Kari." Leah leaned the map on top of the front seat. "Dunsmuir is the next town and is about ten miles from here."

Oh, no. Dunsmuir. The town that gets heavy snow in a normal winter.

Sucking air between my teeth, the sharpest curve yet caused me to tap the brake. Up ahead, a car sat flipped on its side on the shoulder. "Uh-oh." I jerked the wheel, slowed even further. I didn't want to join this driver's route.

"Did you see that?" Granny gave a half-winded whistle. "Poor folks."

Still intent on the road, I shook off the jitters. "It seems no one's around." Right then, a man a few yards from the wreck jogged toward a stopped pickup where a man and woman sat on the tailgate. *It seems the driver's okay.* I relaxed my grip on the wheel.

Leah spoke close to my ear. "The wrecked car didn't have on snow cables."

"No." Wanting to think on happier things, I changed the subject. "I can't wait to stand under a warm shower and to sleep in a real bed."

"Sounds wonderful for these old bones." Granny's voice appeared lighthearted. "A cup of coffee is what I really need." She smacked her mouth. "With a piece of pie."

"What kind, Granny?" Mia spoke from the backseat. "Chocolate? With whipped cream? If we were home, Kari would make the best you ever tasted. With butter dough she presses with her fingers into the pie pan. Yum."

"Doesn't matter, Mia Babe, just a sweet with my coffee. What do you want for a treat?"

"I already told you my favorite." She shrugged. "But, I'll find a *candy* machine."

Relaxing as the road straightened, I nodded at Leah. "What do you want?"

"To be at—"

The wind cut into Leah's conversation and shook the Caddy. *Yikes.* I clutched the steering wheel and slowed to the speed of a riding lawn mower. As I glimpsed in the rearview mirror, the car behind me drew too close to my bumper. I braced for a thump. The vehicle swerved. *"Whoa!"*

A long line of traffic was driving onto an off-ramp. It came too sudden for me to react and stay them. I kept on the freeway.

Three vehicles were ahead of us with a snowplow in the lead. Its wide blade to the pavement, it shot snow to the side. The plow looked like a gigantic shaved-ice machine. The driver took the next exit. Cars ahead of me kept going straight.

I jerked the steering to the right. "I'm following the snowplow."

"What?" Leah hollered. "This better be right, Kari."

The snow fell faster and faster. It swirled around us like a white sheet in the wind. My belly cramped. The lights on the plow were now dim. I squinted, scared half to death. Could there be a steep overhang? A few times, I came too close to the plow for fear of losing it and flying off a cliff.

"Wow." Mia giggled. "It's shooting snow far out."

"I can't believe how deep the snow," Granny said.

But the hill grew even steeper. The Caddy slid sideways. *I'm losing control!* Terror gripped my lungs. I let off the gas pedal.

Leah flapped her hand near my face. "Kari, speed up."

Granny hollered, "Give it more gas!"

Do not be anxious about anything.

"Go, go, go!" Leah slapped the top of the seat.

The Caddy engine revved as my foot pressed on the gas pedal—tires spinning. *Ahhh.*

Time slowed. The cables clawed the road. Moved us forward. *Thank You, oh, thank You, Lord!*

The snowplow parked at the top. Close to the side of a building. I turned the wheel to the right. When I slowed to a stop, I shifted into Park across from the plow.

My heartbeat pounded in my head.

Leah spoke near my shoulder. "Is this place vacant?"

Before anyone responded, a howling wind shook the Caddy. It was as though a monster had the car in its teeth and tossed its head about with violent jerks. I leaned against the steering. I gritted my teeth and hung on.

Mia's muffled sobs yanked on my nerves.

Do not be anxious.

Granny curled her fingers around the seatbelt at my thigh.

Help, Father! My eyes blurred.

All at once the wind stopped. The Caddy stilled. The engine sputtered, the heater purred, and the windshield wipers slapped. With less intensity, snowflakes drifted from the low-hung clouds.

I attempted to loosen my fingers from the steering. They were stuck. I relaxed all the muscles in my arms. My hands moved. Fingers unpeeled from the wheel like the rind on an orange.

Freaky.

Settling myself against the seat, I collided with a lump. Granny's face hid in the space between me and the seat.

With her body curled into a ball, I unbuckled and scooted forward. *Pow!* An object hit the top of the Caddy. The impact slammed my eyes shut. I covered my head with my arms. "Our Father, who art in heaven, hallowed be thy name."

My lids shot open with a scuff sound near my door. The outer edge of our headlights shined on the blade of the snowplow, resting against a mound of snow. *Where's the driver?*

An invisible hand from outside knocked on my window.

I gathered my nerves where they belonged. With no clue as to what the face would look like, I rolled down the glass a few inches.

"I'm the plow guy." The bearded older guy blinked. Concern in his gentle eyes eased my fears. "You okay in there?"

Tears dotted my lashes. "I think so, but something hit the roof of our car."

"You're parked under a fir tree." He peered over the top of the Caddy. "A mound of snow fell from one of its branches."

Behind him, a sign read Dunsmuir Restaurant & Lodge.

15

Love Bears All Things

"Thank you, Lord," I whispered, dabbing the wet from my cheeks with the heel of my palm. *We're safe.*

Leah grunted, shoving her shoulder into the passenger door. It wouldn't budge.

The plow guy yanked opened both Leah's door and mine. "My name's Derrick." His lips crinkled upward within his grizzled beard and made creases around his eyes.

I pointed. "This is our granny, Adele Whitmore, my sisters Leah and Mia."

Mia quit crying and sniffled.

He rubbed his gloved fingers together. "And you?"

Blushing because I had forgotten myself, I shrugged. "Kari."

"Well." His breath rose like smoke from a chimney. "I don't want to frighten you ladies." He exposed his watch from underneath his jacket. "A major blizzard will hit us in under an hour. We have to break into the building and get you inside." He moved as though he would leave.

"But…" Leah buttoned the top snap of her coat. "Wasn't that the blizzard just now?"

"Sorry. No."

"So this lodge is closed?" Leah shivered.

Derrick pulled his knitted hat off his forehead and scratched at his balding head. "And vacant."

Granny leaned forward in the seat and stared at him. "Do you have to go back to your job plowing the freeway?"

"My boss just told me to get the plow to the county yard. They're closing the freeway indefinitely." He coughed. "It's an act of mercy we have the weather warning." He waved for us to follow. "Before I leave, I need to get you ladies settled indoors."

Mia hopped out and tugged on his jacket. "But, my papa says this is breaking and entering."

Derrick bent to her level. "We're in an emergency." He glanced at the freeway below us. "I'd love to lead vehicle loads of people here. My plan was to get this lodge open and get some folks settled inside. I hope I still have time." Shaking his head, he stared at Mia. "Do you understand?" She nodded.

Leah and I exchanged glances. I scooted from the Caddy and stepped in calf-deep snow. "Would you help us with Granny, Derrick? She can't walk very well."

In response, he rounded the front of the Cadillac and opened Granny's door. He scooped her into his arms. Leah, Mia, and I waded through the snow, stepping inside his boot prints. Under the porch-like overhang of the lodge, he faced us, waiting.

Once we met them at the glass double doors, Derrick lowered Granny to her feet. "Okay, Adele, the girls will help you stand." As though handling a newborn, he held Granny under the arms until we wrapped ourselves around her.

He dug into his pocket and removed a folded knife. "I've never picked a lock before. I'll try this." He stuck the blade in the keyhole and squinted, making deeper lines at the edges of his eyes. Derrick twisted while he gripped the handle and shook and shook.

"Maybe we could break the glass with a rock."

Everyone stared at Mia. Not a rock in sight, but probably buried under the snow.

"I don't have much time." He waggled the door handle once more. "Wait. You gave me an idea, Mia. Everyone stay put." Retracing his steps, Derrick headed in the direction of his plow.

Circling Granny, we shivered.

On his return, he carried a long metal bar. He ushered us away. "Keep your backs to the doors." As I squeezed my eyes, he hit the glass and it shattered. "I've made a mess, but we can get inside."

Through the ragged hole, Derrick reached in. He opened the lock with his gloved hand. With the side of his boot, he swept most of the snow and glass off the cement. Swinging wide the left side of the door, he motioned. "Come here, Mia, and hold this." He swung Granny into his arms.

She patted him. "Be careful with me."

Chuckling, he carried Granny with ease into a spacious room.

I swayed as a rush of wind came from behind and pushed me through the doorway. "Hope there's electricity."

"Me-me, too." Leah pointed. "Look. A huge pile of wood next to a fireplace."

Tears smudged my vision. *Thanks, Lord, we'll be warm.*

Leah sighed. "We've had a rough two days." Next to me inside the entryway, she looped an arm through mine. "I could sleep for a week next to a raging fire."

Derrick settled Granny on a metal chair near the fireplace. "I'm going to find something to cover the hole I made." He hollered over his shoulder. "Will you girls find paper to make a fire?" He disappeared into another room beyond the left side of the fireplace.

Mia followed me, but I waved her toward Granny. "Sit in Granny's lap to keep you both warm."

She rushed into Granny's waiting arms. I nodded. We're getting organized before the blizzard hits.

Leah walked toward a staircase on the right side of the fireplace. "I hope to find some blankets up there."

Derrick called out. "I found the paper."

Hurrying into what I now knew was the kitchen, I skidded to a stop. "Where are you?"

"Here." He poked his head from a doorway to the right deeper into the room.

I stepped into a huge pantry lined with mostly empty shelves. Derrick's finger waved to a barrel full of newspapers. "I also found something to block the snow and cold from coming inside through the hole." He readjusted his knitted hat. "But I need your help."

He stopped beside a tall, paint-chipped cupboard on rollers. "Let's empty this thing." We removed dishes, outdated foodstuffs, and cook pots. I knelt before the lowest shelf. I pulled empty and rusted canisters with lids marked salt, garlic granules, and baking soda. Standing, I grew jittery.

I didn't want this stranger to leave. In the few minutes we'd been at the lodge, he brought order and made me feel safe.

With the last Mason jar cleared out, he grabbed hold of the hutch. "Take the other end. Guide it while I push."

I flexed my miniature muscles, wondering if I could. We rolled the solid-wood furniture along the linoleum, Derrick taking backward steps.

Once it was through the two doorways, we entered the fireplace room and stopped for a rest. A figure on the stairs caught my attention. Leah dragged quilts behind her. Lips curved in obvious pleasure.

Good. We won't be too cold.

"Ready to finish, Kari?" Derrick's words returned me to our task.

Guiding the cupboard along, I caught site of the double-glass doors.

Before we reached the entryway, Leah spoke. "These will help us stay cozy." I imagined her draping Granny and Mia with a quilt. "Isn't this better?"

Settling the cupboard to within inches from the entrance, Derrick grinned. "There. Protection."

I blinked hard. "Thank you for staying to help us."

Behind me, Granny said, "Thank you, Leah."

I faced my sisters and Granny as Mia tugged her quilt closer to her chin. "I'll be warm before I know it."

"You'll feel shut in," Derrick said, "but you girls could easily move this cupboard."

"Before you leave, we need to bring in Granny's walker and our luggage."

As though in warning, the wind whistled through the space between the hole and the door.

Hurry, rush, rush.

16

As For Knowledge

After another scurry of wind escaped through the hole, Derrick rolled the cupboard from the doorway. "Okay, Kari. I'll need you and Leah to help. I've got to beat this blizzard."

I shivered from more than a chill. We'd soon be left alone. "Leah." I waved her over. "Let's get our stuff from the Caddy before Derrick leaves." I adjusted the collar on my jacket to stay snug high at my neck. Leah zipped and snapped her coat.

Derrick led the way on the path he'd made earlier. The air grew cold enough to freeze my nose and ears. He retrieved Silver and one duffle bag and went round us on his way to the lodge.

Inside the Caddy, I grabbed my cookbook, purse, and a duffle. Leah searched for her phone. "When I find it, I'll call Papa and tell him where we are. Go on ahead, Kari."

"Good, but I hope the battery's not dead."

Halfway on my return to the lodge, the wind screamed through the trees. Snow blew in a whirlwind of white. Stung my eyes shut.

Leah.

Heading back in the direction of my sister, I hugged tighter to my belongings. *Get Leah.* But the wind grew vicious. It blew me off the path and ripped the duffle from my hand. I stumbled and fell face down into a snowdrift. My arms were pinned beneath me as I hugged my purse and cookbook. *Leah.*

Every time I struggled to sit, the wind knocked me into the same spot in the snow. I grew more and more tired. Strong arms lifted me. Derrick hollered, "Where's your sister?"

I pointed but my arm flopped in the frenzy of another gust.

Scooping me into his arms, Derrick waded through the snow. He steadied me inside the lodge entryway.

Crying now, I blubbered. "Leah's in the car." I shivered at the open door. "Hurry." Derrick pivoted on his boot heels and re-entered the storm.

A small palm brushed the snow off my back. "You okay, Kari?"

"Hush, Mia Babe." Granny stood next to me. "She's frozen. Let's finish our fire. I'm going to assume Leah's safe." Granny handed me a blanket. "Come away from the door, honey." She pushed Silver with one hand and pulled me across the room with the other.

Who held up whom while we leaned shoulder to shoulder?

Mia nudged me toward a metal chair. "We'll start a fire for you and Leah." She wadded newspapers and tossed them inside a fireplace big enough to fit three men. "It'll be a *huge* fire."

I shook so hard, I struggled to keep the blanket over my shoulders. My back ached and I uttered. "Uhhh."

Granny sat beside me on her Silver chair and held a long match. "We've only this one as far as I can tell."

Continuing her chatter, Mia piled a few sticks of starter wood on the paper. "And, we found kindling. Oh, and some newspaper on the other side of this wood pile." She pointed to the left of the hearth. "We prayed for Derrick and you and Leah. Now you're here. Derrick and Leah are coming." Mia nodded at the wood. She placed a larger piece on the sticks.

An icy quiver raced along my spine. "So-so cold."

Mia's dainty brows drew inward. "You okay, Rosy?"

The way she used my middle name made my lips twitch. "I'll hurry." Mia hefted one log with a grunt.

Bring Leah, please, God, bring her.

"Who wants to strike this?" Granny still held the match in the air.

I reached for it. Raking the fire end of the match over the rock hearth, the tip glowed to life. I handed it to Mia. "He-here. You light it."

Her almond-shaped eyes widened. Pursing her lips, Mia took the match and placed the flame on the paper. It caught like a tiny forest fire. Dry sticks crackled on my next blink.

"Ahhh, it's gonna work." Mia rubbed her hands near its warmth.

"You did a good job, Mia Babe." Granny reached for the heat.

Teeth chattering, I shuddered. Even the skin over the roots of my hair had goose bumps.

Granny waved me over. I scooted my chair between her and Mia, and Granny grabbed our hands. "I need you to pray, Mia, for Leah and Derrick."

Pulling in a breath, Mia bowed her head. "Dear God." She paused. "Please keep Leah safe, and help Derrick get her in here right now. In Jesus' name. Amen."

"I-I…" Tears stung, and warm streams ran along my frozen cheeks. "Le-left her."

Granny jerked her head and stared. "In the car, I hope."

Nodding, I swiped at my damp face.

"Well, Leah's not dumb. She'll stay put." Granny's eyes scanned our pile of belongings Derrick brought inside. "She's got James' wool blanket?"

"Yes." I kneeled before Granny, and rested, ear down, on her growling stomach.

She patted me. "You'll become toasty, Kari Rose." Her hand lifted from my arm as though she pointed. "Mia, you add more logs to the fire, and don't try to lift bigger ones. You're not so strong, you know." The pressure of her hand now massaged between my shoulder bones.

Mia's footsteps scurried near the hearth. A chunk of wood clunked. Two more pieces hit the pile. The crackles and pops filled the silence, and I grew sleepy.

My little sister's prayer stayed with me, while in the background Granny and Mia carried on a conversation.

"Where did you learn to make a fire, Mia Babe?"

"I've seen Daddy do it before he bakes our pizza in the wood-oven hearth."

"Good, good." Granny patted me as though burping a baby. "You paid attention."

Moving from Granny's lap, I sat on the floor to heat the front of me. Mia squatted and peered into my eyes. "Are you feeling better, sweetie?"

"Yes, warmer." But a shiver made it seem like a lie.

A high-shrill wind *swooshed* around the outside parameters of the lodge. It rattled windows. It jiggled doors.

Trying to think of anything other than Leah in the cold, I craned my neck. A deer antler chandelier hung from the high-beam ceiling. "Look up, Granny."

"Oh, that's pretty." She reached closer to the fire. "This room would make a great place to square dance."

Twirling, Mia extended her arms. "Yea, let's."

I stared at her, not sure I could do anything carefree.

Her feet stilled, and Mia intertwined her fingers. "I forgot why we're here." Her expression sagged. "I'm too scared."

"Let's see if there's canned food in the kitchen." I tugged on her elbow. "Aren't you hungry?"

Lifting her pointing finger, Granny wagged it over her shoulder toward the double doors. "There's a noise."

Mia lunged for my chest, and I held her.

I stood. "It's okay, Mia Babe. Come on, we'll check for something to eat." My heart wasn't into this anymore than to dance. Our sister was in the freezing storm, but I needed to distract Mia. Truth be told, I had to engross myself in something else. Or, I would break down and cry.

An object hit the side of the building, and the wind screeched through the hole in the door. Mia wrapped her arms around my waist.

Shadows of dusk moved over the plate-glass window near the double doors. Would Leah and Derrick make it before dark?

17

Believes All Things

At the hearth, I reached inside Granny's super-sized purse. "You say it's in here somewhere?"

"Yes." Granny bent forward from where she sat on Silver. "There, I think." She touched a pocket.

Lifting a tiny flashlight, I pressed my finger on the switch. "I'm glad you have this. I'm afraid there's no electricity." I gave Mia the flashlight. "You take charge of the light."

"Okay." Mia giggled. "I'm the boss of seeing." She gripped my coat. "Older people carry a lot of stuff, huh?"

"Well, of course." Granny zipped the pocket closed.

We moved from the light of the fireplace and into the gloom with our tiny beam. "Leah brings half her room with her everywhere she goes." I patted Mia's head. "She's not old." Inside the kitchen entryway, I flipped the light switch. The room stayed dark.

Mia shinned the flashlight around in the kitchen. I became more aware of the objects than when I helped Derrick move the cupboard. Stainless steel and cast-iron pots and pans hung above a large chopping block. A few feet from one wall sat a huge black-and-white wood-fire cook stove. Its stovepipe rose into the ceiling.

Mia ran to it and passed her hand over the surface. "Looky, Kari. This metal thing is named Grand, like our grand."

My gaze settled on the big letters, and my lips parted. "Well, sure enough." I touched the shiny white porcelain on the doors. "Mom and I saw one similar to this at an antique shop in the village."

I opened the biggest door on the right front. "This is an oven."

She peered inside. "It's rusty."

"Look, Mia." I reached above the stove. "These are doors to the warming shelves which keeps the food hot." On the stove's surface to the left of the oven sat round cast iron covers. With a metal handle, I hooked into each cover and set them aside. The third part, a middle brace, held the covers in place. A few charcoaled sticks lay at the bottom. "Down here is a grate." I pointed. "You make a fire on the grate to heat the cook top and the oven."

"It's so tiny for a fire." She yanked on my coat, eyes wide. "Why is Derrick taking so long, Kari?"

Moisture pressed within the bridge of my nose. My idea to keep Mia occupied while our sister was in the blizzard wasn't working. Nor for me. "I don't know, honey." I knelt before her. "We have to trust in God." I nodded my head up and down for her to agree. "Now more than ever, Mia. No matter what happens."

The lids over her chocolate-brown eyes closed for longer than a blink. "Yeah, but."

I cupped my hands around her face.

Her eyes grew round. "What if he needs help?"

Yeah, what if?

I jerked upright and grabbed her hand. We stopped a few feet from where Granny stood, where she held onto the handle bars of Silver. "My old knees couldn't sit another—"

A gust of wind forced its way through the gaping hole in the front door. The cupboard shot across the room like a skateboard. Our dreaded blizzard reached inside. It knocked Granny to the floor. "Oh, my hip."

More snow blew and spread across the floor. I helped Granny to Silver's seat. With her settled, I shoved the hutch with all my might. The wind had greater strength. It blew me backward where I sat hard on the wood floor.

18

Rejoices With The Truth

Getting up off my backside, I hurried to the fireplace. "I need your long coat, Granny."

Frowning, she readjusted herself on Silver. "Why?"

"To stay warm outside."

"What?" Granny screeched. "Just where do you think you're—?"

"You can't stop me." I wiggled my fingers for her jacket. "Derrick needs help."

"You're going?" Mia pressed her teeth on her bottom lip.

"He's trained, and you're not, Kari Rose." Granny's eyes went soft.

I wrinkled my face into a fierce pucker. "I'm getting my sister."

"Don't get lost." Mia begged, folding her hands as if praying.

Granny slowly stood. "Take my coat, then."

I took off my jacket and slipped on Granny's smaller one. The fit gripped way too snug, but I got it on even though the front couldn't zip. Having added my coat, I was bundled and ready. Though, my movements were stiff.

Granny hugged me roughly. "Take our flashlight."

At the door, I glanced back at my family sitting in the fire's light. I stepped into the storm thick as clam chowder.

~*~

Pinpricks of snow pelted my cheeks. *Leah.*

Keeping my head bowed, I followed Derrick's path. It curved to the right. Before I could count to twenty, I bumped into a mountain of metal. Staggering in the deep snow, my wrist jammed while I broke my fall. "Oh, ow, ow." I braced myself against the blade and pushed to a standing position.

By now, my feet were blocks of ice. I clomped to the plow door. "Derrick!" I moved away as it opened.

Thud, thud. A pair of boots clumped on the hard-packed snow at the trail's end. "Kari, what're you doing?" He scooped me under my arms. He raised me high in the air and placed me on the front seat.

"Leah's in the Cadillac?"

"Yes." He nodded. "Wrapped in a blanket. I couldn't get inside because snow's piled against the car. Besides, the doors froze shut. Right now, I'm grabbing the snow shovel. I tried the radio, again, but no one answers." The lines in his face deepened. "I'm sorry to say." He huffed a sigh. "I can't find my cell phone, either."

My teeth chattered from cold and now fear.

Derrick's smile didn't reach his eyes. "You stay here. I'll get Leah. You won't see me without her."

I offered my flashlight.

"Keep it." He tapped a headlamp secured on top of his knitted hat. "I have mine." Derrick reached in and started the engine and turned the heater to full draft. "You'll be warm soon. If it's too hot, turn this knob like so." He fiddled with the adjustment. "See?"

Cupping my hand over my injured wrist, it still throbbed. "Okay."

Outside the plow, Derrick reached for his shovel and shut the door behind him. The windows were thick with snow. I could only keep track of him by the headlamp's glow.

Soon, Derrick stopped near the Caddy. His movements were those of shoveling away the snow. I moved to the other side of the cab and waited for him to bring my sister. Fidgeting, I stared at the radio mike.

"Need to do something…" The mike felt solid in my palm. I pressed what I figured should be the talk button. "Hello?" Letting off the knob, a scratchy static echoed. "Too loud." I lowered the volume. "If you can hear me, please bring help." Shuddering, I didn't like the idea no one to hear me at the other end.

"My sister is trapped in our car. I'm in Derrick's snowplow. He's digging the snow from the car so he can get to her. We're at the vacant Dunsmuir lodge off the freeway." My finger grew weak. I released the button. "So tired—" I rested my head on the back of the seat.

"Kari." I jerked awake. "Open up."

I fiddled with the handle and pushed with my shoulder. The door wouldn't budge.

"Kick with your feet, Kari."

Turning in my seat, I bent my knees and shoved hard. The door flew open. I scrambled to the passenger seat to make room. Derrick held a Leah-sized bundle, and a whimper of relief churned in my chest.

~*~

I lunged for my sister. "Leah!"

Derrick readjusted her from his shoulder to his arms. "She's cold."

I lifted the wool blanket, "Leah?" and pressed my fingers to her face. "You're freezing, poor baby." Her teeth clicked. Her whole body shook.

"Sit back, Kari." Derrick placed her in my lap. "Snuggle with her to give her body heat. I couldn't shut the Cadillac door, so I'll be right back."

When he left, I placed my jacket over the front of Leah for added warmth. I hugged her close and rocked. "He saved you." Pressing my cheek to her cold one, she groaned. What could I do to make her feel better? I remembered part of a song Mom used to sing. It soothed me now. *This will help Leah.* In a shaky voice, I sang, "Mama's little baby loves short'nin', short'nin', Mama's little baby loves short'nin' bread." I tucked a strand of hair behind her ice-cold ear.

A shiver convulsed Leah. It lasted forever, making me cringed at its violence. I held her tight, afraid she would fall off my lap. I cared little if I had bruises on my face from her wild hands. Finally, the shudders quieted. She trembled in a softer rhythm.

I relaxed my sore muscles. "Granny will have to finish her story of when she met Grand." Reaching under the blanket, I massaged Leah's jacketed arms in a downward motion to her fingers.

Her head at an angle, Leah's lids hooded over her eyes.

"Mia and Granny are safe inside the lodge."

She ran her tongue along her upper lip. "Thirsty."

"I'll see if Derrick has water." After scooting from underneath her, I searched the cab. Soon, I found a small ice chest. When I opened it, my eyes bulged. "Food and drinks, Leah. There's grape and apple juice. Which do you want?"

Eyes still closed, she appeared asleep. "I'll pick one for you." I opened the cap on the grape. Lifting Leah upright, I brought the bottle to her mouth. "This has natural sugar and will give you energy."

She allowed the juice to slide between her lips. "Mmmm." Never opening her eyes, Leah curled into a knot.

Taking my own gulp, it tasted delicious. Though, I needed to save the rest for my sister. I set the bottle in Derrick's container holder. "I found a pudding cup. You need to eat so you won't get grumpy. You know, like you do when you're hungry."

Leah struggled to sit but collapsed. "Tired."

Her shivers would not stop. I rubbed her limbs. Then, I gripped her under the arms and heaved her upper body on my lap. "You're still shaking, sis." By now, sweat formed on my brows from the heater's warmth. I reached for the pudding cup on the dash and dipped in the spoon. "Leah, you've got to—"

Derrick opened the door. Wind-blown snow rushed through the cab. "How is she?" His bulk, frosted with snow, shook.

I clutched Leah closer. "She talked once and drank a few sips of your juice."

He took her from me. "I'll return for you soon." Derrick covered Leah's head, and they disappeared in a frenzy of plump flakes. I grabbed the door and pulled it with all my strength.

Turning down the heater, I rapped my foot on the floorboard to the tune of "Short'nin' Bread." In the world outside the cab, wind shrieked and howled. The scary stories my uncle Josiah told of the abominable snowman came to mind. Could that be Big Foot with his fur cloaked in snow? And wasn't it so the mountain monster was taller than this plow? *Hurry, Derrick.*

My leg muscles ached now from the tapping of my foot, so I quit. "Any minute he'll come." Growing hungry, the snow-covered windshield reminded me of thick cream. If I had sugar and vanilla, I could make ice-cream with the snow.

What if Derrick can't come?

"I'm okay. I can be stuck in a snowplow in the middle of a blizzard. Really." How did we get from a promised dull week with Granny to this? The most exciting thing I had planned was to try recipes from my new cookbook. I swallowed. The knot in my throat would not budge. "I have heat and food and juice. It would take a tornado to knock over this plow."

Or Big Foot.

Or a blizzard.

Terror struck my heart as huge as any monster. But, Jesus taught for us to count our blessings. *Leah is safe.*

Needing to do something, I grabbed the mike. "Is anyone there? My name's Kari Holt from Pismo Beach, California.

We're stuck here in Dunsmuir. My sister may need emergency help."

No one heard me.

No one knew we were here.

No one can care.

I threw the mike to the floor. "Stupid. Stupid. Stupid. It should work. It—" I leaned my head against the frozen driver's window. The world outside the plow moaned and screamed.

I jerked to a kneeling position on the seat and tucked my chin to my chest and folded my hands to pray.

19

I Thought Like A Child

I jolted awake from a nightmare. *I'm cold. Need to go home.* Blinking, cold air blasted on my face. The plow no longer made its normal engine noise. "What happened?" I turned the ignition switch to off. Flicked it back on. Nothing. Pressing my forehead to the steering wheel, I wailed.

The interior light still glowed, and I glanced at the fuel gauge. "Empty." Would I become an icicle?

I buried my hands into my pockets and touched a soft lump. Digging through the layers, I found a knitted cap inside Granny's coat. Now the hat sat snug over my head and ears. I needed one more thing.

On the roomy floorboard, I walked my fingers along a solid wall below the seats. No space underneath there. What's behind the driver's seat? I felt around and found a large compartment. Shining my flashlight on it, I discovered tools: flares, chainsaw with oil, and other small equipment.

I studied the front of the dashboard and slapped my forehead. Opening a little compartment, a candy bar perched on top of leather gloves. "Oh, yea. Thank you, thank you, Derrick." My teeth ripped off the wrapper of the bar. I munched into nutty, gooey delight. Flavors burst on my tongue. I closed my eyes. *Mmmm.*

After the last bite and swallow, I licked my fingers clean and pulled on the gloves. My hands were way too small. Surely, they'd be warm soon.

I touched my throat. *Water.* I drank the leftover grape juice and also the apple.

A nut chunk loosened from between my teeth, and I coughed. Mom said I ate too fast, not chewing my food well. 'Digestion starts in the mouth,' she claimed. As I nibbled on the nut, I figured Mom had a point.

Don't think about angry parents! But what else could I do trapped in this plow? Sleep sounded good.

If I slept, this night would go faster. So I curled my arms around my knees and snuggled. I prayed, thanking God for Leah's safety. "And if you don't mind, please stop the blizzard?" Yet, I lay there wide awake unable to doze. All the sugar I ate and drank.

A glow lit the driver's window, and I bolted upright.

The door opened with a yank. "Kari?"

I leaped at Derrick's chest. He staggered under my weight, and I heaved to control my sobs.

His voice soothed. "You're okay. So is Leah."

Once inside the lodge, Mia ran to meet us. "Kari, Kari, Kari!"

Derrick set me in a chair near the hearth next to Leah. She circled her arms around me in a sideways hug, her cheek on my shoulder.

Now, I could no longer stuff my jumbled emotions, and I cried.

Granny touched my hand. "I'm glad you're safe, Kari Rose."

"I thought you would die. You, too, Leah." Mia sniffled. "But me and Granny, we prayed real hard. Now, see, you're both here."

"You girls have been through a lot." Derrick placed another blanket over our shoulders.

"Please, Derrick, move my chair closer to the fire." Granny groaned. "I need to talk with my great-granddaughters."

"Yes, ma'am." He rose from one of the chairs within our half circle and pushed Granny closer.

I peered at Derrick. "Your plow ran out of fuel." He nodded a yes. "You're stuck here." He kept nodding. Derrick's eyes shimmered with what looked like regret. I felt safe for the first time since we left Granny's.

~*~

Granny settled next to me and my sisters. "I need to—" She bowed her head but lifted her lashes beneath crumpled brows. "I'm sorry, girls." I waited for her to finish. "I was only thinking of myself." Granny pulled her hanky from inside her sweater sleeve and wiped her nose.

Leah, Mia, and I exchanged glances, and my sisters' round eyes mirrored my own.

Granny lifted her chin. "I've done a lot of thinking while you girls were in that blizzard." She raised a hand and let it fall to her lap. "This trip shouldn't have happened."

When Leah gasped, I reached for Granny's hand. "I've been upset with you."

Her eyes became slits. "And you were correct to have been. I'm so sorry. After what I've put you through, and then you nearly froze tonight ..." She muttered under her breath. "Sometimes I'm a stubborn, old hag. You're still so cold, Kari Rose." She cupped my hands between both of hers. "Let me warm them." Granny massaged the circulation into my fingers. In the quiet, the fire crackled.

With a sleepy sigh, I nodded. At least she apologized. My eyes darted open at the sound of a strange noise.

On the floor Derrick snored. Lying on his side with one arm under his head, the other crossed over his chest. I pointed. "Mia, cover Derrick with a couple of blankets."

A breath escaped from between Leah's lips. "I'm ready to sleep on the bed I made for us, Kari." She moved to a small pile of quilts at the edge of the fireplace and stretched out. "He saved us, didn't he?"

I settled next to her. Touching Leah's golden hair, I let the strands escape through my fingers. "Yes. He did."

"I'm sleepy, too." Mia yawned.

"Mia, let's go over there." Granny pointed to the left side of the hearth. "Our bed is ready for us, too."

I stood and helped Granny to her floor bed.

Once I snuggled next to Leah, the room grew silent. Even the storm hushed. The fire's snap and crackles relaxed me to the point I drifted almost to sleep.

Leah swung an arm over my shoulder. "Feels perfect now that I'm warm."

My lids lost the tug-of-war long ago to stay open. "I know, huh?" Wondering how Leah had felt being alone in the Caddy, I squeezed her hand. "Did you think you would die?"

She shuddered. "Completely."

"I was so scared, until Derrick brought you to me."

"We'll be okay. Even though I'm shaky from missing dinner." Leah drew closer, making soft settling-down-to-rest noises.

A pang of guilt stabbed. It might as well have hauled off and slapped me. I ate a candy bar. The pudding. I didn't need it like Leah did.

"Mia told me you two started to look for food."

"I meant to. You were more important. I couldn't sit around waiting for Derrick to bring you into the lodge."

We sighed at the same moment. I fell into a fitful dream where snowmen chased me around the snowplow.

20

Endures All Things

A screech woke me. I bolted upright ready to punch a snowman in his corncob piped mouth.

Mia was jumping in place near the large plate-glass window next to the entryway double doors. "Raccoons! Three of them. Come see, girls."

Leah snuggled her head deeper into the pillow. I blinked to fully awake.

Rubbing the sleep from my lashes, I glanced around. "Mia, where's Granny and Derrick?"

Mia waved. "Hi, raccoons." She kissed at them, making smacking noises. "C'mon, now. I won't hurt ya."

I hugged the blanket to my shoulders. "Mia Babe."

"Please don't holler." Leah rolled onto her side.

"Ahhh." Mia stomped a foot. "The raccoons are running away. Granny's in the bathroom. Derrick is gonna see if the radio works."

Covering a yawn with my palm, my brows raised toward my curly bangs. "It stopped snowing, didn't it, Mia?"

"Yep."

As I buried deeper under the covers to keep warm, Mia screamed. Leah and I jumped. Our baby sister ran toward us. "Ba-ba, ba-ba, ba-ba."

The terror on her face scared me all the way to standing. I grabbed her shoulders and shook her. "Make sense."

Her mouth rounded like a donut hole. She heaved a breath. "*Bear!*"

I reached the window before Leah. "Where?" My eyes focused—a huge mass of cinnamon-brown. Wagging its head, the creature lumbered through the snow. It sniffed the ground at the bottom of the mountain just yards from the lodge. Suddenly it stopped. *Big as a couch.* "I've got to tell Derrick before he meets up with it." I grabbed my coat and moved between the cupboard and the glass door. "Mia and Leah, watch for the bear. If it comes any closer, I want you to scream as loud as you can."

Mia pressed hands on her pale cheeks. "Do I have to?"

"Wow." Leah swayed near my shoulder. "It's *huge.*"

Peeking from the doorway, I got a good view of the plow. Covered with snow, it looked like a white monster. I stepped outside. Waving my hands in front of my waist in Derrick's direction, I didn't want to attract the attention of the enormous fur ball.

Behind me, Leah spoke a tad above a whisper. "It's digging in the snow now with its back to us. It's not moving."

I drew in a deep breath and stepped on Derrick's path. My tennis shoes made burping sounds in the snow. Cringing, I tip-toed. Partway, I twisted to check. *No bear.* I kept on toward the plow. By the count of twenty, I stood at the driver's side.

"*Psst.* Derrick. *Psst.*" A movement at my side view caught my attention, and I startled. The bear?

Leah waved her hands for me to come back. Now, she flailed her arms in wild, frantic motions to stay put.

Oh, dear Lord.

Leah stomped her feet. "Bear."

I froze. *No, not the bear.* The cry in my chest rose and lodged near my tonsils.

~*~

My sister disappeared into the building. *Don't leave me.* For what seemed like forever, I waited for Leah. Kept my eye out for a lumbering fur ball. Toward me. With a sudden clash of metal, Leah stepped outside banging a pan and lid like a dinner bell. She hollered. Walked closer in the direction of the bear. "Get! Shoo!" Jumping up and down, Leah added to her performance with rapid barks.

Leah's barking at the bear?

The plow door slammed into my shoulder. What happened? Buried. Can't breathe. I imagined I clawed at the snow. *Arms. Legs. Useless.* My heart raced faster, pounding in my ears. My brain dulled. I was pulled into a dark, black as night.

~*~

Rough hands jerked me by my shoulders.

As I met fresh air, the icy cold burned my lungs.

Gloves scraped the snow from my closed eyes. Now, a face wrinkled with worry came into focus. Derrick's lips moved. He held onto me as my legs failed. No stronger than cooked noodles. "You okay?" His eyes widened.

I coughed, stretching my chest for more air.

Leah stood next to us, panting. "What happened?"

"Kari, I'm sorry. I didn't know you were there." Derrick's breath gushed in a sigh. "I opened the door and hit her. She fell into the snow and got buried."

Leah reached for me. "Oh, no."

I still worked to catch a normal breath, sagging against him.

Leah swished the snow off my pant legs. "I scared the bear."

Derrick swiveled his broad shoulders. "What bear?"

"It's gone." Leah brushed snow from my hair.

"I wondered why you were making such a racket." His cupped hand swept the snow off my back.

"It was headed this way. I had to do something." She hugged me too tight. I wiggled away to catch another solid breath.

As I breathed a bit easier, my eyes focused on a shape in the snow. Where I had landed. My body created a messy impression of a snow angel.

~*~

An hour later having shaken off the shivers, I waved for my sisters to lead the way into the kitchen. "Let's see if we can find food."

We left Granny by the fire, scowling. Not happy with this. Not happy with that. She wanted coffee.

Never mind the fact I didn't want to take this dumb trip. *All Granny's fault.* I gritted my teeth, feeling light-headed from being buried. And so cold. *I shouldn't complain.* At least earlier she said she was sorry.

"I sure wish the radio would work." Behind me in the fireplace room, Derrick spoke. "I'm going to look around on the second floor, Adele."

"Go ahead. Everybody just leave me here."

Even though Granny couldn't see, I waved at her as though I swatted at a fly. *Her fault.* I didn't know who I spoke to in my head. Myself or God. Both?

Leah passed through the entryway of the kitchen and stopped before the wood cook stove. "Mom always wanted one of these." She stroked the white enamel doors on the front and opened the largest one. "This oven would hold a lot of cookie pans."

"Get us a fire going." Mia clapped her palms on the stovetop.

Bending to eye level, Leah tapped Mia's nose. "Let's."

To put wood inside the fire grate easily, I lifted off the three cast-iron sectional parts. Mia and I twisted newspapers. We added them to the grate. "Would someone get the smallest pieces of wood you can find?"

"I will." Leah reappeared in moments, with an armload of kindling. "Are these small enough?"

"It looks like it." I placed the wood she brought on the paper.

As I wondered about matches, Leah pulled one from her pocket. "I found a few of these in a box next to the fireplace woodpile."

Cocking one brow in surprise, I reached for it. "I like these bigger matches." I raked the flint end across the rough surface of the stove. It scratched to life. "Here we go, girls." Sticking the flame to the paper, it ignited. Smoke rose from the opening. "Hurry." I grabbed the center piece of cast iron and dropped it into place. Snatching the handle attached to one circle-shaped lid, I let it clang onto the hole.

Leah plopped the other lid down. Mia waved off the smoke and coughed. "Good job, girls."

"Thank you, thank you, everyone." Leah curtsied.

"What's all the ruckus?"

Jolted by the deep voice behind me, I placed a hand over my throat. "You scared me."

Derrick, resting a shoulder on the kitchen doorway, grinned.

Mia tugged at the hem of his coat. "We built a fire so we can cook."

"I'm starved." Coming closer, Derrick rustled his palms above the almost warm stove. "I guess for now, I've got to give up the idea the radio should work." He moved to the kitchen cupboards. "Maybe I'll find something to drink in here." Derrick dug around on a shelf. "Ah, ha. What's this?" He held in his hand a can of cocoa. He popped open the lid. "Let's make hot cocoa." He turned the faucet to on. "Now, why did I expect water to come pouring out? You've got to have electricity to make the pump draw water from the well."

With my grumpy thoughts, my shoulders slumped because of Derrick's broken radio and lost cell phone. "What if you gathered snow, and we heated it on the stove?" At least this was something we could fix.

"Good idea." He searched the cupboards down below. "I'll fill the largest cook pots." Once he found two large kettles, he went outside.

After Derrick left, I walked into the pantry. Thick, large cardboard barrels with lids lined along one wall.

Mia came behind me and counted. "Seven of them."

"Yep, you're right, but how am I supposed to open them?" On closer inspection, though, the tops on the barrels were clasped on with silver bands and latches. I flipped the latch open and lifted the lid. *Pinto beans.* About two gallons was my guess.

Mia skipped in a circle. "Beans, beans, a musical fruit—"

Biting down on a chuckle, I sighed. "Stop, you."

She relaxed her neck, eyes to the ceiling, and giggled.

I popped open another barrel lid. It was full of what looked like whole-wheat flour. It smelled stale. Another had a fine layer of cornmeal on the bottom. The other barrels sat empty. A much smaller tub on a shelf was half filled with white powder. I dabbed in my index finger and licked. "This is a little bitter like baking powder."

"Let me try." Mia buried her finger, tasted, and scowled. "Gross."

"If we find powdered milk, we can make a yummy batch of cornmeal pancakes."

"Oh, I like those." Mia's tongue rolled along her lips. "I could eat three."

"I'll wash and soak beans in case we're here tomorrow." How I hoped and prayed the blizzard had stopped. At least there was no wind, and the snow had let up.

"Do you have the recipe in your book for the pancakes, Kari?" Mia ran her thumb along one of the empty shelves, making squiggly lines in the dust.

"I'll look, but if not," I shrugged, "I'll figure it out." I tapped a finger on my chin. "In a pinch, we could use plain water instead of powdered milk."

Back in the kitchen, I rummaged through the lower cupboards. A large metal bowl sat to the rear out of easy reach. It was about the size of Granny-Too's bread-making bowl. I stuck the front half of my body into the shelf. When I grabbed it, boots scuffed along the floor. I backed on out and straightened.

Derrick settled the kettles of snow on the cook stove. "I'm going to get more in case we're here for awhile."

He left again with more pots. I reached for a small-sized pan, dipped it into the kettle of snow, and placed it on the hottest spot of the stove for cocoa water."

On his return, I had the pinto beans rinsed with melted snow water. I filled a cooking pot with the pintos and water. "What's upstairs, Derrick?"

"There are eight rooms and half of the beds are stripped of blankets." He carried the pot of beans and set them on the stove.

Leah waved an arm. "I did that."

"There's also a bathroom upstairs we can use." Derrick stood over the chopping block. He placed down five mugs and

165

the tin of cocoa. "We'll have to add water to the upstairs and downstairs toilet tanks if we want to flush, though."

"How weird." Leah wrinkled her nose. "We'll be carrying a whole lot of snow water to the toilets."

"No baths for us." With potholder in hand, Mia opened the fire grate door. "It needs more wood, Kari."

"Be careful there, Mia." I gathered the few pieces left on the floor next to the stove. "We'll need to stack a pile of wood here to keep this fire going."

"It burns fast, doesn't it?" Leah peered over my shoulder. "It's a tiny fire compared to the fireplace."

"Yep." I shut and latched the stove's grate door. Peeking at the beans, I pointed. "Would someone hand me the salt and pepper over by the sink? And, Leah, check the cupboards for cumin. That'll add a wonderful flavor to the beans."

"Did you girls see the snow changed to rain?" Derrick dumped spoonfuls of cocoa into the mugs. "It started before I came back inside just now."

Leah and I shook our heads, and we stared at him.

With a snap, he sealed the lid on the cocoa. "We'll be able to leave sooner than later once the rain melts the snow." He chuckled. "In my unprofessional opinion, the blizzard is over."

Giving Derrick my best grin, I high-fived Leah with a smack. This was what I wanted to hear.

Mia unzipped her jacket. "Will you drive us outta here in your snowplow?"

Placing hands on his knees, Derrick winked. "Sure can. First though, I'd need someone to bring us some diesel. It's out of fuel."

"Yea!" She spun in a circle, waving. "I'll tell my class at school I rode in a snowplow."

Standing, he scowled. "Besides, I ruined your granny's car when I smashed the window."

Mia stopped spinning. "Why did you do that?"

"You shouldn't have told Mia. She might tell Granny." I didn't know this was how Derrick rescued Leah.

He scratched the thatch of hair on his balding head. "Yeah, well, I had to. The door was frozen shut."

Leah stared at the floor. "Thank you, Derrick, for saving me."

"You're welcome." Leaving the room, Derrick called over his shoulder. "Mia, come help me gather smaller wood for the cook stove." She hopped and skipped from the kitchen, humming a tune.

After a late breakfast—more like brunch—we cleaned the kitchen of our cornmeal pancakes mess. With beans simmering on the stove, I joined the others near the fireplace. Everyone reclined on their blankets. Some of us in conversation. Granny napped, her snores whirring like a blender on low speed.

Between the heat from the fire and the downpour of rain on the roof, my eyelids swelled with a need for sleep.

~*~

"Hurry for the stairs!"

Derrick's yelling? The floor moved beneath me. I stumbled within a tangle of blankets.

Derrick roared. "Follow me!"

I tugged on Mia's hand. Leah and I intertwined our fingers. We hit the first stair behind Derrick as he carried Granny. *Thunder?*

Behind me at the double doors, the roar deafened all other sounds. Icy fingers scratched along my spine. Derrick topped the stair landing and disappeared.

Boom! Whoosh!

21

Tongues, They Will Cease

Glass shattered. My heart slammed in my chest.

Horror escalated me forward.

Derrick shouted, "Mud slide!"

Waves of gooey, thick, wet rained on my sisters and me when we reached the middle of the staircase. The force shot us closer toward the landing. A tangle of feet and legs and arms. My head slammed into someone's skull.

Crawling, crawling, crawling on the stairs. We stumbled and slid.

I lost my clutch on Mia. My hands fumbled for any part of her. A glob of hair connected with my fingers. I made a fist, tightened, and yanked. Mia hollered in pain. *I won't let her go.*

Leah hung onto my leg at the same time hair covered my face. I spit and spat. My efforts useless.

Strong arms scooped Mia and me off the step.

Slipping, Leah clawed at my ankle.

I arched my body, but couldn't reach her.

Leah gripped even tighter causing my foot to pop. *Oh, dear God, help.* Winching, I lunged for my sister. Derrick lost his hold on me.

He hollered for Leah, grabbed me around my waist, and pulled Leah by her shoulder. He tucked her under his other arm and carried us like footballs.

When Derrick let go, we fell into a heap at Granny's feet.

~*~

The lodge shifted. I gulped more than once to keep my pancakes where they belonged.

We huddled with Granny as the building settled.

Derrick motioned for us to move farther from the stairs. I helped Granny, while my sisters scooted on their backsides. Someone whimpered.

Below us, there was a drip, drip, dripping, as though the entire downstairs became soggy. I raised my hand and waved it to get Derrick's attention. "Shouldn't we see how high the mud is?"

"In case we need to climb higher?" Derrick glanced toward where we came from. "Yeah, while there's yet time."

Tasting mud, I stuck out my tongue and wiped it on the hem of my jacket sleeve. Leah hugged Mia while they shivered.

"Come on, Adele." Bending at the knees, Derrick gathered Granny into his arms. "Let's get you ladies even farther back."

Derrick situated us in a corner at the end of the hall. He retraced his steps to the top of the stairs. Crossing his arms, his shoulders slouched.

My heart sank to the toes of my filthy sneakers. *What does he see?*

"Has the rocking stopped?" Granny's teeth clattered.

"Yes." I rubbed her arm.

Derrick disappeared into one of the bedrooms. Long seconds later, he returned with his arms loaded with blankets and pillows.

I hurried to take two of the patchwork quilts from him. "What's it like down there?"

He shook his head.

Granny coughed. "My-my bones ache."

"I feel sickish." Mia's voice. As soft as a kitten's meow.

I covered my sisters with quilts. When I kissed Mia on the head, some of her mud came off on my lips. *She could have died.*

After Derrick draped a blanket over Granny, he handed out three pillows. "Mia and Leah, would you share one?" He pursed his mouth. "I can tell you this, Kari, we're lucky."

Little Mia jerked upright. "No, we're not. Mama says there's no such thing as luck. Only blessings." She lay on her side and tucked her chin near her chest.

"We're getting deeper into trouble." Granny gathered the blanket around her tighter.

"You think?" Leah snapped.

Granny leaned against the wall, staring at her. "I've told you I'm sorry, and yet—" She bowed her head. "I can't take another smart aleck word."

Leah pulled her quilt to her eyes and mumbled. "Not another immature, negative remark from you, either."

"What?" Granny's eyes grew sharp. "Speak up."

Bolting upright, the cover fell off Leah. "I thought once you apologized things would be different." She slouched back down on the floor. "Just call me dumb."

"Ladies, ladies." Derrick's expression sagged. "This doesn't help us." He scratched at the graying brown of his beard.

"True." I tucked Mia's cover around her. "Let's at least be quiet for a while and rest."

Reaching for Leah, I snuggled down next to her. Granny lay on the other side of Mia. Derrick stretched a few feet away, closer to one of the lodge's rooms.

As I gazed at the ceiling, my feelings a jumble, Leah rolled over. Her wobbly smile made my vision blur. We touched foreheads. "I'm sorry, Kari," she whispered. "I can't seem to quit sassing."

"You're saying how we all feel, Leah." I wiped a thick smudge of mud from her cheek. Although, it made little difference she being covered in it. All of us girls were. I made a mental note to find towels and clean us up later.

"Right when we think she'll act nicer." She tsked her tongue. "But, I make things worse. I know I do. I never realized until now it's true what Mom's been saying."

"Yes, but a sassy mouth is not the worst thing." Tears I'd held onto escaped from my lashes. *I could have lost my sisters.*

She sniffed. "I love you, sis."

"Me, too, I love you." I closed my lids.

In my half-awake, half-asleep state, Leah touched my face. "Are we going to die?"

My eyes shot open. "Don't think like that." I squeezed her hand. "I'm praying for God to send help."

Leah blinked. "Good."

We intertwined our fingers. *Father, which art in heaven . .*
.

~*~

The warmth on my face woke me. The sun gazed through the small hexagon window above us at the end of the hall. Before I left Granny's home four days ago, I lived in safety. The air an even temperature on my skin.

So much for that.

At this point, I'd take Mom yelling at us every morning before school. 'Hurry, hurry, hurry, you'll miss the bus', over our current mess. Which got messier.

Unsettled questions poked me like an accidental prick from a paring knife.

How long would we be stuck? Is anyone trying to find us? Would the food run out? *I want to be at Granny-Too's home.*

Choking back a sob, my noises woke Leah. She sat up and looked around. "Kari, I'm sore from the floor." Her tone of voice, deeper than normal, carried proof of having slept.

Blinking away fresh sniffles, I pointed at the window. "We've got the sun."

"No snow?" She crossed her legs under the covers. "No rain?"

"Nope." I tweaked her nose with my thumb and forefinger. "We're going to survive this." I winced. Did I tell a bold-face lie? Deep inside my middle, a huge doubt churned.

Bobbing her head like a chicken when it walked, Leah sang, "We're cool, yeah, we're cool."

"Who's cool?" Granny squirmed in her spot on the hardwood surface.

Sucking in a breath, I waited for Granny's first complaint.

173

With Leah's back to Granny, she mouthed, *My bones ache.* I covered my lips and giggled. This fed Leah's tart mouth. *This place isn't fit for humans. When is help coming?*

Laughing out loud, I hiccupped.

Granny propped herself against the wall and glared at no one in particular.

What happened next for my part could only be explained as hysteria. Laughing even harder, tears drenched my cheeks. I'd lost control for the second time on this trip.

I'm certain I woke Mia as her head bobbled. "Where am I?"

"You're still at the lodge." Derrick yawned and stretched his arms. "You okay, Kari?"

I embarrassed myself long enough. Gulping air, I nodded.

"Good. Let's put away our bedding and take a look at the downstairs."

Near me, Mia whimpered. "I want to go home."

Leah moved to Mia's side and finger combed her tangled hair. "We all do, don't we?"

Bursting into tears, Mia bawled. "I-I-I mi-i-iss my ma-ma."

Her sobs were like a slap to the face. I forgot about my giggles. Leah and I petted her and calmed her. Afterward we gathered our blankets off the floor. Mia sniffled, but I was certain she'd be okay. She followed us to one of the bedrooms. When she threw the pillows on the bed, her tiny shoulders shook. She shattered like fine china, blubbering into her hands.

Leah and I knelt on either side of our baby sister. We wrapped her in our hugs. Both of us spoke. "Shush, now. We'll see Mom soon. Honest, sweetie, it's okay. Are you hungry?"

Mia quieted. We led her along the hall, while Derrick carried Granny ahead of us to the stairs.

At his first step below the landing, Granny screeched. "We're done for."

Peeking round their shoulders, I wheezed. "Ah, no."

22

Not Arrogant Or Rude

Leah, Mia, and I gathered in a cluster next to Derrick.

Tree branches and rocks within the mud oozed through the lodge's blown-out double doors. In the vacant room to the right of the stairs, mud had piled below a row of broken windows. A trail of mud filled the room at least a foot deep.

I shivered. "How did this happen?" Now the place was more like a cave, wet, stinky, and even colder.

"It had to have come off the closest mountain." Derrick readjusted Granny in his arms. "Look at how high the mud is outside."

Leah broke the short silence which followed. "This means we're doubly trapped."

"Mud's got to be at least one foot deep in here." Derrick took a step down. "Be careful not to slip. This is one disaster waiting to break a bone."

Following Derrick, we held onto the rail. Goo squished under my tennis shoes. I settled on the second from the bottom step. Do I tiptoe on the miry floor—which probably wouldn't save my shoes—or let the sludge overflow and work its way between my toes?

What? Wait. I'd be walking in mud almost to my knees.

Leah whimpered. "I hate dirty."

Mia tugged on my hand. "Please, Kari, let's go back upstairs."

I agreed. "Mia can't walk in this, Derrick."

On the first floor, he stood in the clay which covered over the tops of his boots. "Unbelievable." He raised one knee, and the suction made a glug sound. Twisting to face the second floor, he placed his boot on the bottom stair. "I really don't know where to put you, Adele."

"I don't want to be down here. If that's what you're getting at." Granny's lips shriveled. "Take me to one of the beds upstairs where it's clean and dry."

"You and Mia both." I blinked at the mess.

"Kari, would you get Mia and Granny settled?" As we returned to the second story, Derrick glanced my way. "Then come downstairs where Leah and I will be. I'll inspect the damages. We'll rekindle both fires. Maybe you girls can cook us some food?"

I nodded.

Granny muttered. "If you don't forget about me."

"Well, now, Adele." Derrick led us along the second story hall. "If we're able to clean an area for you, and after we build up the fires, I'll bring you down." He chuckled. "You can get those tiny feet of yours toasty."

Granny scowled. "They're so cold now, I can't feel them."

Derrick set Granny on the bed, and he and Leah left.

"Help me take off my shoes, Kari Rose." Kneeling, I unlaced her clean suede sneakers. "It's a good thing I'm still clean. My suitcase is in the Cadillac."

"It sure is, Granny." I settled her in with fluffy pillows. Stepping away, I dug through Mia's bag and found clean clothes for her to change into. With Granny and Mia settled in bed, I waved from the doorway. "I'll bring you two some hot cocoa."

"Oh, how I crave my coffee."

Angling my head, I remembered something. "You know, I saw a rusty coffee can. I'm not sure if it's really coffee or something else. I'll go check."

"What?" Crossing her arms over her chest, Granny huffed. "All this time, and you didn't check to see if it's coffee?"

Leaning against the door jamb, I pressed on my achy, empty belly. "It's been a bit hectic. Don't you think, Granny?"

She raised her chin. "I suppose." She fluttered her lashes. "Please, bring me just one cup?"

"If it's really coffee, I will." I loved Granny more for asking nice. I blew her a kiss. "Give me time, though. We have to add wood to the fires and get them going." With that, I spun on my mud-clogged heels.

I came into view of the downstairs. Derrick scratched his neck and stared at the fireplace. "Look at this."

"No, way." Mud filled the fireplace.

"'Fraid so." He faced me. "They'll be no more fires here."

"What'll we do?" The dismal sight caused me to shudder.

Derrick looked around. "This fireplace is beyond my ability to clean without the proper tools. Maybe we can make a path to the kitchen. The mud didn't reach in there."

Passing him, I tip-toe slogged through the mire and stopped at the kitchen entryway. "Thank goodness." After wading through the mud, it squished between my toes. I poked out my tongue. "Nasty." I jiggled off first one shoe, and then the other. My stocking feet left mud splats on the linoleum.

A mound of twisted newspapers lay in the stove grate. Leah added sticks of kindling.

I squeezed her shoulder and headed to the cupboards. "Pigs would love to wallow in the mire on the other floor."

Leah laid a piece of wood on the kindling. "Thank the Lord it missed the kitchen."

Sighing my own prayer of thanks, I searched for the coffee. Where had I seen it? "I hope to make Granny happy." Opening another cubby door, I stuck my head inside.

"How?" Leah clattered the metal lids over the grate.

"Here it is." I shook the contents. "Sounds like coffee." I opened it. "It smells and looks like coffee. There's enough to keep her satisfied for a while."

"Ah, I see." Leah lit a match, and touched the newspaper through the front of the fire grate's little doorway. "By making Granny coffee." Shutting it, she slapped the debris from her hands. "Did you see what I did?"

"Yeah and smart going." I filled a small pan with snow water.

"Placing the lids on the stove top after adding wood and lighting the fire from the front makes more sense." Leah fanned her fingers. "Tada! No smoke in our faces."

I wanted to praise her with a smile, but acting grumpy fit more my misery. By now, I could barely feel my toes in my dirty, squishy socks.

Derrick entered the kitchen and looked around. He strode to a smaller door to the far left of the wood cook stove and opened it. "A closest." He thumped around inside. "Well, look here." He pulled out a wide push broom with a long handle, two large metal dustpans, the stub of a kitchen broom, and an industrial cotton mop. Derrick held up the push broom. "This can be used on its wood side to push the mud to make our path." He scratched his beard. "What I really need is my snow shovel."

Leah waved an arm at Derrick. "We have halfway decent tools to get rid of some of the mud, then."

"Yeah." I pointed. "The dustpans will make good scoopers."

"Clever." Leah nodded her head in agreement.

Derrick began pushing mud to make a path from the kitchen entry, through the fireplace room, and beyond the stairs.

As I watched him, my bones ached from the cold. *Can feet freeze in this chill?* Would I know before it's too late?

Turning, I placed the pan of water over the hottest part of the stove. In my mind, I changed the subject. "Granny's going to have to settle for cowboy coffee."

"Ahh, this water is so warm." At the sink, Leah washed her hands in our large bowl of dishwater. "For sure, Granny will complain about the grounds in her mug."

Shrugging, I set a cover on the pan for the water to boil quicker. "It depends on how desperate she is for coffee."

Leah faced me and pressed a finger to her chin. "I bet she grumbles."

While she hunted through the cupboards for something else to eat, I stirred the half-way done pintos. I imagined Granny's pleased expression when she got her coffee.

Leah wagged a small container. "Popcorn!"

~*~

Later, upstairs in Granny and Mia's room, Derrick bowed his head. "Lord, bless this food we're about to eat, and thank You for keeping us safe so far. In Jesus' holy name."

And everyone said, "Amen." Derrick brought a little bit of home by saying the blessing. So right and good, the prayer made me even more homesick.

It was mid-afternoon, and we shoved popcorn down our throats. The very act of chomping took some of the chill from my body. And, at her spot on the bed, Granny held her own small bowl of the crunchy and fun food. Earlier, with her first sip of coffee, she flashed me the sweetest smile. Such a victory.

Next to Granny, Mia spoke around the popcorn in her mouth. "When we see Mom—" she chewed and swallowed— "she's gonna be happy, huh, Kari?"

With a fingernail, I picked a kernel from my tooth. "Oh, yeah. Dad, also." *Then Mom will let us have it.*

Leah dotted the air with her index finger. "And Granny-Too and Papa."

Halfway to his mouth, Derrick's fistful of popcorn halted. "Who are they?"

"It's our mom's dad and mom." Mia closed her eyes. "We miss them a terrible lot."

Visualizing the one who was newly gone, I remembered Grand's chipmunk-like chuckle. "Our Grand, Granny's husband, died several months ago." Tears churned behind the bridge of my nose.

Derrick nodded. "I'm sorry, Adele."

"No need." At Granny's sharp tone, she broke into my memories and gave Derrick the hawk-eye.

"*Granny.*" I bent forward in the chair. "Why are you being rude?"

She moved the popcorn around in her bowl with a hand. "Well—he didn't know my James."

Derrick chuckled. "I'm sure he was a fine man."

"He was more than this." Shaking her head, Granny ate a single kernel of popcorn.

"Grand and Granny were like twins." At my comment, Granny's lashes creased with moisture. "Mom says they even had the same handwriting."

"Tell me about your James, Adele." Derrick shoved another fistful of popcorn past his teeth.

Mia yanked on Granny's sleeve. "Yeah, finish your story about when you met Grand."

She tapped a finger on her upper lip. "Where was I?"

"You told Grand you were going to marry him. He blushed." Leah's eyes became soft and eager. "So then what happened?"

Derrick's gaze switched from Leah to Granny.

Granny pulled a hanky from her sweater pocket and wiped her mouth. "Your grand said, 'What fer?'"

"No, way!" I huffed. "Grand said fer, instead of for?"

"Yep."

Leah stopped chewing. "Our Grand talked like a hillbilly?"

Granny's eyes glimmered. "At one time he had a strong Arkansas accent. Anyway, I said, 'What do you mean what for? Does a girl have to explain her reasons?' James took my hand, bowed his head, and kissed my knuckles. Oh, my heart burst into twittery."

"Get out, Granny." Leah slapped her knee. "That sounds like Twitter on the Internet."

"I don't know about this Twitter." Granny frowned. "I said *twittery*, like your heart giggles."

"Never heard of it, Adele." Derrick chuckled. "Although, this describes my experience. Once I got to know my girlfriend, who is now my wife of twenty-four years."

Granny dismissed us with a wave. "You young people don't know much."

"Not about twitter *whatever*." Mia fell backward on the bed and giggled.

Leah's laughter ended with a snort.

"Are you two through?" Granny nibbled on another single popcorn. "I've got a story to tell."

"Enough, Mia." I pulled her by the arm into a sitting position. "Go on, Granny, we're listening."

"Like I was saying." Granny glared at Mia and Leah. "Your grand kissed my knuckles. I said, 'Mr. Whitmore, I'd be pleased if you'd come to see me at my home.'" Granny leaned forward, her eyes pinning me to the chair. "Do you know what your grand did?"

"No." Our voices rang through the tiny room.

"He swooned." She pursed her lips in a straight line. "Yep, he told me months later after we became secretly engaged." Granny cackled. "He figured I was a little blind to want to see him again."

Secretly engaged? Hmmm.

"Blind?" Mia raised her brows. "Why?"

"Silly girl." Leah poked Mia. "Grand thought of himself as ugly. Right, Granny?"

"Yep, he sure did, and James was gawky at this age. He fleshed out and became truly handsome later on." She rested against the headboard of the bed. "Do you know what he told me?"

Everyone shook their heads no.

"James said, 'Adele, yer easy on the eyes. As a matter of fact, yer down right purdy.' With a blush deeper than before, he grinned so big, he showed off more of his crooked teeth. 'I'll come a callin', Adele. Will tomorrow be okay?' I let go of his hand and gushed. 'Yes, James, come way before five though. My daddy isn't afraid to point his shotgun at the boys who come to our house. Just ask my sister, Doreen.'"

"Shotgun?" I gulped. "Are you teasing?"

"You heard me." Granny's eyes became mere slits. "By the end of my warning, James' complexion turned as pale as the underbelly of a dove. 'I'll see ya, Adele, at five, so we can start off on the right note.' He put out his hand to shake mine."

Intertwining my fingers near my throat, I sighed. "This is so romantic, Granny."

Her left shoulder rose and fell. "Yes, my James had a gift for romance. He showered me our entire married life with roses, trinkets, and cards."

Derrick finished the last of his popcorn. "Welp, this is a great story, Adele. But what I want to know is, did your James outgrow being shy?"

Her eyes twinkled. She didn't speak for a long moment. "He had to being married to me."

Harry's face popped into my mind. My heart *twittered.*

~*~

We'd finished eating our popcorn. Granny drank her coffee without a fuss over grinds at the bottom of the cup. Smelling the beans simmering all the way up to the second floor, saliva pooled in my mouth. Cornbread would go with it. *Rats!* I clicked my tongue against my teeth.

There would be no butter between the slices.

Downstairs, we began to work while Granny napped. Because of window and door glass in the mud, our jobs stretched out until it became tedious. Derrick continued to drive the wood edge of the push broom to make a path within the mud. Leah followed him with the metal dustpan. I could now see the floor as I came behind her, using the kitchen broom to make a cleaner streak. Mia scooped mud from the stairs with the miniature fireplace shovel.

When Derrick came near where Mia worked, he turned and checked our progress. But some of the mud oozed into the path we just made. Derrick started over. He moved more mud to widen the space for us to walk through. With our shoulders and backs aching, we finished after a few hours.

While we girls entered the kitchen to make cornbread, Derrick rummaged through the same closet where he found a few carpenter tools. He tore apart another free-standing cupboard and used the wood to nail over the right side of the blown out front doors. For the left side, Derrick attached a tarp he discovered in the rear of the same closet.

The tarp wouldn't keep out the cold as well. It couldn't be helped. Our first cupboard in front of the hole in the door broke into pieces from the mud slide.

Now, the four of us sat in our metal chairs before the toasty cook stove. Derrick crossed an ankle over his knee. "I want you girls to take the other bed where Adele is staying. The cook stove pipe runs along the other side of that wall. It should give you ladies extra warmth."

I stretched the strained muscles in my arms. "You'll need extra blankets to keep warm won't you?"

"I've got plenty." He straightened in his chair. "Don't know about you ladies, but I'm tuckered." He yawned as if to express his point. "Can't wait to get some sleep." Then he sniffed the air. "That is, after Kari's beans and cornbread."

I copied him by inhaling. "It does smell yummy and should be done in a few minutes."

Leah slapped her palms on the top of her thighs. "I'm going to see if there's any tea for a hot cuppa." She rose from her chair. "Anyone else want some?"

Raising my finger as in yes, Derrick and Mia did the same. "No more stale cocoa." I rubbed my stomach. "It burns my belly."

Derrick and I talked about the possibilities of getting rescued sooner than later. Leah carried a pot of water and placed it on the hottest part of the stove. "Actually." We stared at Leah. "I found several flavors." She pulled a couple of tea bags from her coat pocket. "In a small ceramic bowl hidden behind an electric can opener."

"What kinds?" Mia peered at the selections.

Leah opened her fist. "Peppermint, cinnamon, lemon zest."

"Somebody come *help* me!"

Sighing, Leah placed one set of knuckles on her skinny hip. "Whose turn is it to help the—ah, Granny?" Her cheeks flushed.

I'd bet my cookbook, my sister was about to call Granny 'the old lady'. I shook my head. "It's yours." I flapped my hand. "But I'll go instead. Please pour me a cup of mint."

"Thanks, Kari." Leah wiggled her fingers at Mia. "Come on let's gather the mugs."

When they left the stove area, I leaned closer to Derrick. "Have you figured a way to get outside and try the radio?"

His friendly expression faded. "Sorry." Lines on his face deepened.

Granny called out. Her voice rose in what sounded like desperation. I headed for her room. Lifting my heart to God, I prayed we had enough food to last until this nightmare ended.

23

Faith, Hope, Love Abide

The next morning, I jerked awake from a dream.

I suffocated in mud.

Tromp, tromp, tromp.

A bear on the roof?

Slipping from underneath the blankets, I yawned. Tiptoeing so as not to wake my roommates, I grabbed shoes and stalked from the icicled room. The noise above me moved to the stair landing. I arched my neck toward the octagon-shaped window right below the ceiling and squinted.

Shadows plugged the glass. A face peered at me.

Yelp crawled toward my throat, but a hand waved. "Hi, Kari." Derrick. "I climbed on the roof to see if I could spot the freeway. I can, but there's no traffic." He disappeared and clomped in the direction of the girls' bedroom.

I shoved my feet into my shoes and walked down the stairs. Dried mud showered to the first floor in soft plops. The front entryway remained untouched from Derrick's handy barricade. I scratched my ear. How had he climbed on the roof?

In the kitchen where I now stood came a shuffle-thump from the pantry. Seconds later, Derrick appeared. "Hi."

I jumped, lost my balance, and grabbed the air. I fell, seat first, on the floor. "You scared the life out of me." I patted my chest. "Where did you come from? How did you get on the roof?"

"Sorry, Kari." Grinning, he offered his hand and helped me up. "Early this morning, I searched the lodge for an attic entrance. On the pantry wall behind the door there is a ladder. It led me to what I was looking for."

"Really?" I brushed a bit of moist dirt from the seat of my jeans. "I want to see." I moved to follow Derrick, and he hurried through the open pantry door.

Inside, he pointed with his bearded chin. "Look there."

Behind the door, a rough-cut ladder nailed on the wall led to a flap of wood. A tiny door on the ceiling. I pointed. "Let's climb it, so I can go on the roof."

"I don't know." His thick brows met in the middle. "The roof has a dangerous slant with lots of snow."

The toe of my shoe rested on the first board. "I'm not scared." Halfway up, I gazed over my shoulder. "Are you coming?" At the top, I pushed on the little attic door. It lifted with a scrape of wood against wood.

~*~

We stood on the solid attic floor. Derrick moved toward a large window on our right. He released a side latch and pulled. The window squeaked inward. "I'll go first." Once on the roof, he wiggled his fingers. "Come on."

I grabbed Derrick's arm, held onto the window frame, and stepped on a snow-cleared patch. A wind, cold and moist, lifted my hair. The strands tickled my cheeks. As I peered over the expanse of cloudy skies and fir trees, goose bumps crawled along my skin.

Derrick pointed at my shoes. "Don't leave this spot. Everywhere else is too slippery." He waved a hand toward a mountain range. "What a view, huh?"

I stuffed fists into my jacket pockets and jiggled the warmth into my fingers. "We can see tops of trees." A bird screeched in a high pitch. "Derrick." I pointed. "Is that a bald eagle?"

"Well, looky there." He laughed. "Sure is."

"I've seen them in pictures." Smiling, I murmured more to myself. "I don't know why they're called bald."

I focused on the eagle's flight. It soared behind a clump of trees. Snow clung to the branches: emerald green and white, and above were gray clouds with swatches of blue sky. The view made me forget for a moment. We were stranded. I blinked. If only I could fly like the eagle and escape.

At the entrance of the lodge, mud and debris had forged its way and rearranged the landscape. "Wow. Granny's poor Cadillac." Mud and snow came halfway to the doors.

He waved a hand. "We're hemmed in by the mountain on the east side, but see over there?"

Following his fingers with my gaze, it directed me to beyond where the Caddy and plow were parked. "Is that—"

"What does it look like?" He rubbed his gloved hands together.

"Part of the freeway?" Without vehicles, it appeared the world had stopped which made me feel weird. *We're so isolated, Lord.*

"Yep, Kari." He shielded his face with a hand as the sun topped the eastern mountains.

Overwhelmed by the intrusion of the mudslide and the vacant freeway, I made a joke. "I'm going to jump from this roof and get help." The lines in Derrick's face deepened. I giggled. "Just kidding."

"You had me for a second." His grin quivered. "I thought you'd lost your brains from being nearly frozen in my plow. Come on. Sit a minute on the ledge." Derrick pointed to the window. "I decided to find a way to the roof after a helicopter woke me this morning. It sounded as though it flew over the freeway." He stared at the empty four lanes. "I'd like to think they're searching for us, Kari."

His tone and words brought hope. "Do you think they noticed your plow?" I settled into a more comfy position on my perch.

Instead of answering me, he spread his arms behind his back. "I need to somehow get down there. To shovel snow off both vehicles, so the helicopters can't miss them." A snap on Derrick's quilted coat popped open during his stretching. He pressed it closed.

I blew on my hands, stuffed them deeper into my pockets, and sniffed. "My nose is leaking, and I'm too cold." I swiveled my jean-clad legs over the window opening and into the attic. *Also starved.*

Derrick followed and shut the glass and secured the latch.

I knelt near the attic door. "Do you really think help will come soon?"

"I believe so." He shrugged. "If people have serious injuries they get first attention."

"Like people stuck in their cars?" I climbed down the ladder into the pantry.

"Sure. Just because we didn't see any cars buried under the snow on the freeway doesn't mean there aren't." His steps echoed above me. "And, some people had already been stranded for a whole day and night. Many of them ran out of fuel. You know, from running their vehicles on account of their heaters. This is what my boss said at the emergency meeting." He whistled. "No one expected the first snowstorm, let alone the second."

My foot reached the last step, and I jumped the few feet to the pantry floor. I moved aside and Derrick landed. His boots pounded with a thump.

"You ladies were stuck on the freeway, also, weren't you?" His lips became a thin line.

"Yes, but Granny's Cadillac had plenty of gas, so we kept warm. I got out of there as soon as—" *Oops.* My neck flushed with heat. Although surely Derrick knew it was me who drove up the hill to the lodge. With my head bowed, I hurried toward the pantry doorway. "It was nice on the roof." I flung the words over my shoulder to change the subject.

He stood next to me at the kitchen sink. "Glad you enjoyed it." Lowering his voice, his brow rose as though he had a secret. "Do you mind if I bring up something personal?"

I gulped but shook my head no. *It's about me driving.*

"You do an excellent job to stop the tension between your granny and Leah."

A soft breath escaped from between my parted lips. This wasn't about me driving illegally. I so wanted to avoid this topic. "Leah has never been close to Granny like Mia and I have." I rinsed a dish cloth and wiped at a food smear on the kitchen counter. "She was closer to Grand."

"I wondered." Derrick rummaged through a cupboard. "Just wanted you to know I noticed. And, I think you're a mature and responsible person." He chuckled. "Unfortunately, I haven't seen this in some of my own teens at your age."

It was nice to be appreciated, even if it was for throwing water on blazing conversations. "What are you looking for?" Feeling a chill in the kitchen, I opened the little door to the fire grate in the cook stove.

"I'm tired of corn products." He grinned. "Although your beans are great, I've got to have something else." He patted his stomach. "I've lost weight."

Adding more wood to the fire, I laughed. "You've got a ways to go before you starve."

"Hey." Derrick shut one cupboard door and opened another. "That's my middle-age paunch you're poking fun at." He moved kitchen equipment this way and that. "I'd really enjoy a slice of my wife's New Orleans chocolate cake."

For a moment my mouth watered at the mention of dessert. As I closed the little door to the now flared-up fire, I thought of Papa. Surely, he would pitch enough fits so people came looking for us. Or come himself. "He'll pull strings to make the police take action."

Derrick's rearranging came to a halt. "Kari?" He rounded the wood stove and stared at me. "Who will? And to act how?"

"My grandfather, Papa, was a police detective." I slapped the wood debris from my palms. "Last year before he retired, he solved a case of a bunch of jewelry store robberies."

Derrick's grin stretched across his face. "Really?"

I raised my hands over the rising heat. "In our area, Papa became pretty famous."

His voice pitched to a higher note. "This is great news, Kari. To know you're connected to emergency personnel who are probably searching for us as we speak." He shook his head. "And it doesn't matter your papa is retired."

"That's what I'm thinking." With the fire popping, I halfway closed the stove damper. We'd have more heat coming off the stove and less going up the pipe. "I'll help you look for food." I searched a cupboard across from Derrick.

With his arm deep inside a length of shelving, he sighed. "I sure miss my three kids, and I'll bet my wife is panicked. Now, there's someone who will squawk until she finds me."

I shut the cabinet door to the mouse-infested droppings and sneezed. "Shooey." I covered my nose with a coat sleeve. "What ages are your kids?" Opening another cupboard, a bag of wild rice was torn into and spread across the shelf. *Gross.* I'd have to be starved to eat this. Even if I washed it.

The idea of being this hungry sent shivers along my backbone.

His voice echoed like he'd stuck his head in a hollow log. "Seventeen, eighteen, and twenty-one, all daughters."

"Wow, Derrick, you're out numbered." I moved to the last of the cupboards and rummaged through the lowest shelf.

"What are you doing?"

Granny's voice startled me. I hit my head on the higher shelf at the same time my fingers latched on to lumpy, soft plastic. "I found something." Pulling it out, my eyes widened. "I can't believe the mice didn't chew on these."

My sisters stood on each side of Granny. Leah tilted her head. "What is it?"

I wagged the bag. "A treat hidden and forgotten."

"Have they been opened?" Granny pushed Silver toward me.

"Nope." Mia squeezed the contents.

Leah pinched it. "They're getting hard."

"Who cares, Leah, it's a sweet treat." I hugged them.

"Now all we need is chocolate bars and graham crackers." Derrick smacked his lips.

Granny hovered over my shoulder. "Well, we don't have those." She maneuvered Silver closer to the stove.

Having recovered from my surprise at seeing Granny, I tapped her shoulder. "I can't believe you're down here and looking perky."

She stared at me. "I got lonely. Besides, I felt my ears burning and worried someone talked bad about me."

I waved her off. "Oh, Granny, honestly."

"I wish we could get to the Caddy." Leah played with the drawstring on her jacket hem.

"We didn't bring in everything?" Mia squinted.

"I happen to have a king-size chocolate bar in my little what-not bag." Leah flicked strands of hair behind her ear. "Which is in the Caddy."

Derrick buried his fingers into his beard and scratched. "I have some stashed in the plow."

"Oh, no." I wailed. "I found a candy bar in the glove box and ate it."

"Well, now, you didn't look behind the driver's seat." He winked at Mia.

I tapped my fingers on the bag. I guess I wasn't a complete hog to have eaten every single one of Derrick's snacks.

"We need to get our chocolates." Leah danced a jig. "Then we'll make almost s'mores."

Mia rubbed her hands above the cook stove. "We could open one of these lids and roast the marshmallows here."

As we were talking, Granny had moved away. She now stopped at the pantry entryway. "Would someone please get me unstuck?" Her wheel had caught on the door jamb.

"I'm coming, Adele." Derrick trotted to her.

"Listen." Leah motioned us girls into a circle. "I think we can get my candy bar. We'll take a rope and tie it around my waist and the other end to the door. I'd wade through mud for chocolate."

"Nuh, uh." I shook my head. "It's too dangerous."

A few yards from us, Granny fussed while Derrick worked to loosen the caught wheel. "How did you do this, Adele?"

"Where will we find rope?" I placed fists on my hips.

As I waited for Leah to answer, Granny mumbled something to Derrick.

"I know!" Leah's eyes lit like pure sunshine. "We'll rip sheets into wide strips and tie them together to make a rope."

"No, sir, that's destroying private property." Worry-creases lined Mia's forehead. "We could go to jail."

Slapping her thigh, Leah leaned back her head and snorted.

"Jail?" Derrick pushed Silver, with a frowning Granny on the seat. He tilted his head. "What are you girls talking about?"

"Leah's got an idea." I shifted my weight to the left foot. "But it's too risky."

"Let me help to decide, okay?" His stomach growled, and he patted it. "Hurry and tell me, so we can fix breakfast."

I hugged the bag tighter to my chest. "Okay, but you may think we're nuts."

~*~

"Uh, no, you're *not* going." Tucking his thumbs in his jean pockets, Derrick squinted.

"Why?" Leah stomped her foot. "I'm not a baby, you know."

"Well, now, did I say you were a baby?" He removed his knitted hat and raked his fingers through his oily, thinning hair. "No, I did not." His expression remained calm and his voice soft.

I wrinkled my nose. Without showers we were all getting pretty oily and scruffy. I made a silent vow *not* to look at myself in Granny's compact mirror.

Rolling her eyes, Leah groaned. "So, we're not getting my chocolate."

Derrick held out his palms in defense. "Let me think on it for a moment." He chuckled. "You're about as stubborn as my seventeen-year-old daughter Chelsea."

Leah tapped her tennis shoe several times. "Is this long enough?"

"Calm down." I bumped her hip with mine. "Are you this starved for sweets?"

Her bottom lip flipped into a pout. "You ate Derrick's candy bar." She stretched her neck. "And, yes." She hissed.

"I'm dying here for a sweet besides the decayed cocoa you've been serving." Leah stuck out her tongue. "Disgusting."

"I'm hungry." Granny pointed her knobby finger at me. "You girls need to fix breakfast. I want my coffee first. And, you won't go to the Cadillac." Granny glared at Leah. "There's a ton of mud out there even an elephant couldn't wade through." She faced Derrick. "Are you going to hang another blanket over the front door like we talked about? I'm freezing."

He slapped his forehead. "I got sidetracked overhearing these girls." He sprinted from the room.

"Wow." Leah crossed her arms. "Talk about service, Granny. You've got him wrapped around your crooked knuckle."

"Don't start." Granny shifted on Silver's seat. "Did you hear me about the idea of you getting your candy?"

"Since when are you my boss?" My sister planted hands on her hips. "You couldn't even drive us to Papa's." Her eyes shimmered with tears.

"'Cause it's too dangerous." Granny wagged a finger. "Your mother would have my head if something were to happen to you."

Staring at the floor, Leah dug the toe of her shoe at what appeared like ages-old gum. She muttered. "Mom would've had it long before now."

"I heard that." Granny puckered her lips and narrowed her eyes.

"Well—you heard Derrick. He's thinking on how we might get the candy. He might figure a way so it's safe." Leah crossed her thin arms. "So there, Granny bananny."

I gasped, and my hands flew to my mouth.

"Over chocolate?" Granny screeched. "Have you all lost your minds?"

I stood between them. "Come on, let's not fight." I touched Leah's wrist. "I'm sorry, but I agree with Granny."

Leah made fists, and she bent close enough so her breath skimmed my nose. "Fine. Just *fine*." She ran from the room and stomped on the stairs.

Derrick said, "Excuse me," and I imagined him in a side step from Leah's path.

Reaching down, I grabbed a piece of wood to add to the fire. I'd make a breakfast no one would probably like.

24

Give Away All I Have

Now at mid-morning, Mia and I made pancakes with what we had: the last of the cornmeal, water, salt, and baking powder (which had gone mostly flat ages ago). With the lack of a fresh rising agent, the pancakes cooked up heavy and wrinkled.

Derrick got busy dragging away our muddy blankets from where we had slept by the fireplace before the slide. He used these to cover the blown-out door. He also covered the three windows at the east wall.

While I cooked, Derrick's process had been easy to follow. Like a foreman, Granny sat on Silver in the kitchen entryway and barked orders. I guess being grateful for the first cup of coffee had worn thin.

Groaning, I grew exhausted with fussy people.

Mia shook the bag of marshmallows. "Let's put these on our pancakes."

"What a good idea." I hugged her, kissing the top of her sweet head. "We don't have chocolate for the almost s'mores anyway." I opened the bag with a sharp knife. Mia topped each pancake with two plump marshmallows. All the while, she hummed a tune.

Her happy attitude rubbed off on me. The weight of our situation floated away on her tune and disappeared.

Soon enough, Mia and I displayed the pancakes as though they were platters of exotic foods. "Tada!"

With everyone gathered around the cook stove, Granny reached for hers. "Well, doesn't this look scrumptious?"

From my apron pocket, I lifted forks and butter knives and passed them to waiting hands. "I'll get you and Derrick a second cup of coffee, Granny."

I hollered for Leah to come and eat. Derrick shushed me. "Shh! I checked on her and she's asleep."

"She's worn out from being stuck in the Caddy half frozen." I nibbled on my lip.

Mia stood behind me. "Yeah." She clicked her tongue on her teeth. "Poor, poor, Leah."

After I brought cups of coffee, I got myself one. Though not a coffee drinker, I wanted something for energy. To make it tasty, I tossed cut-up pieces of marshmallow into my cup. I filled it half-full of coffee and the rest of the way with hot water. I gave Mia a hot cocoa topped off with a marshmallow. Derrick led a prayer to thank God for our food. Everyone said, "In Jesus' name. Amen."

We chatted and laughed. More than grateful for this bit of peace, I started a new day in hopes of a rescue.

"Yummy, this is so good." Mia spoke with her mouth full, but I chose to ignore it. Who cared about manners with our laps for a table? "The marshmallows were my idea, huh, Kari?"

I hurried to chew the food in my mouth. "They sure were, Mia Babe." Her eager expression tugged at my heart. Loving her all the more, I brushed strands of hair from her cocoa-stained chin.

Finished with his meal, Derrick let his fork clatter to the plate. "I've been thinking about how best to get Leah her chocolate bar."

"Risk your life for chocolate?" Granny aimed the fork tines at him. "How will you get through a landslide of mud?"

He waggled his brows. "I won't have to." He looked at me. "Kari already knows this, already. You can get onto the roof through the kitchen pantry."

"Really?" Mia's eyes grew wide on her oval-shaped face.

"Yes, really." I winked. "It's so neat there." Granny raised her index finger and opened her mouth. I rushed my words to silence her unwelcomed opinion. "I went a few steps on the rooftop, just outside a window." I pursed my lips and gave Granny my most mature and confident expression.

Derrick crossed his arms. "On the roof I noticed something interesting."

"What is it?" Mia leaned toward him.

"There are three trees which stand near the roof." He twitched Mia's nose. "Guess what one of the trees is close to?"

"Don't know." Mia shrugged.

"The plow." Derrick beamed. "I'm figuring a way to reach the first tree and climb down. If I have to, I'll jump into the rear of the plow."

He could probably pull it off, he sounded so certain.

"You guys are noisy." Leah walked into the kitchen, rubbing her eyes.

I explained the plan to Leah and smiled. "So see? You had an idea, and Derrick will make it happen."

"Yeah, but, what if he breaks his neck?" Leah yawned.

"Oh, no." Mia covered her mouth.

"I used to jump from planes in flight to help put out fires in the forest." Derrick nodded.

Granny placed her empty plate on the floor. "You were a smoke jumper?"

"Correct." He curled his hand, brushed his row of fingernails on his shirt, and blew. "They called me Hot Shot."

Leah took the plate of pancakes I offered to her. "We'll never forgive ourselves if he gets hurt."

My fussy sister thought more about what could happen to Derrick instead of her craving for chocolate.

Maybe we should be worried for Derrick.

~*~

Having swept the floor and wiped clean the mess I made on the stove top, I borrowed Derrick's flashlight. I decided to see what might be in the few cupboards I hadn't searched. But, nothing, nothing, nothing.

I opened the last door. "*What?*" On the bottom shelf as pretty as a present sat a bar of chocolate. "Hurry, everyone, look."

In a scuffle of shoes and boots, my sisters and Derrick stood before me. They stared at what I held in my palm.

"I was fixing to tell you more about me and James." Sitting on Silver, Granny craned her neck. "My, my, now what have we here?"

As a group, the rest of us swiveled in Granny's direction. Everyone eyeballed her. I cocked my brow, suspicious of her tone of voice sweet as pecan pie.

Glancing at me and then Granny, Leah took the candy bar. She gave it a jiggle. "Where did you get this?"

I had to stuff the giggle rising into my throat. Sometimes, Leah sounded like a miniature version of our mom.

"Me?" Granny batted her eyelashes, and her hand fluttered to her chest. "Why, I do declare. I don't know what you mean."

Oh, brother. She was a terrible liar. "Now, Granny, you might fool Derrick and Mia. When did you put the candy bar in the cupboard?" I narrowed my eyes. "Confess."

The coloring in her cheeks became a soft pink. *"What?"*

There was the word *what* again drawn out like a train whistle.

"I betcha' she found it here in the lodge and horded it." Leah bobbed her chin. "Isn't that so, Granny?"

"Well. I didn't." Her mouth drooped to her chin. "I've had it with me in my purse. When you were planning a reckless attempt to get a silly chocolate bar—" Granny shrugged. "Now, we can forget about it."

I slumped. "We could have used some fat and more energy in our diet before now, Granny, don't you know?"

Leah returned the candy bar to me and extended her arms in exasperation. "You are the most selfish person I've *ever, ever ...* " She rolled her eyes heavenward, twisted on her toes, and left the room.

Granny pointed after Leah. "Do you want us to save you some?"

Leah shook head no, her ponytail flinging.

"I'm still going to the plow." Derrick averted his gaze as though embarrassed by Leah's outburst. "To see if the radio works yet."

"We don't need you flying off the roof." Granny glared at Derrick. "It's not like you have a parachute strapped on like when you were a young punk."

His brows met in what appeared a stubborn frown. "I can handle myself, Adele. Thanks for your concern."

Right about now, Derrick probably wishes he was stuck with a group of guys instead of a girl, two teens, and a rude, bossy old lady.

I divided the chocolate bar into five even pieces and handed them out, keeping Leah's serving in the wrapper.

Sitting on Silver, Granny pushed with her feet to get closer to Derrick. "What will happen to me and the girls if you don't return?" She squinted. "Hmm, Derrick?"

Not sure if I should interrupt, I waited for him to answer. Would he be able to jump without hurting himself?

If he didn't make it back for some reason— How would we reach him? *We're surrounded by mud.*

~*~

Early the next morning, my eyes were clogged with sleep. I forced them open.

Today Derrick would jump from the roof.

My sisters and Granny slept while I threw on my shoes and tiptoed toward his adventure. I passed the cold fireplace and headed to what my body begged for in the kitchen. Warmth.

Derrick leaned against the counter and drank a mason jar full of water.

I yawned, reaching my arms over the fire grate. "Nice fire."

"Morning, Kari." He tipped the jar and gulped down the rest.

"Good morning to you." I finger-combed my hair and made one long braid. "I need a brush for this mess, but, oh well."

"You're not going on a date." He set the glass in the sink.

"Not allowed to until I'm seventeen." Raising my brows, I added. "Mom's orders."

"That's been our rule for our daughters. Yet my youngest isn't interested in dating." Grinning, he wiped a hand over his mouth. "She's what we call our bookworm." Washing the jar, he nodded. "I think today will be freedom day."

"Really? I hope you're right." I filled a dipper with the snow water and overflowed my glass. "Oops. I shouldn't waste." Taking a sip, my eyes became teary from the chill. "So cold but tasty."

"We're lucky to have wood for our fire to keep us a bit warm, to cook by, and to melt the snow for water." Derrick turned his back to the heat.

I shook my finger and said in a sing-song voice, "What did Mia say?"

He frowned, scratching behind his ear. "About?"

Blinking, I smirked. "'Mom says there's no such thing as luck, only blessings.'"

"Ah, yes, blessed even though we're stuck. Your little sister is somethin' else." He rubbed his stomach. "I plan to jump after we eat. What's for breakfast?"

I raised my hands. "Cornmeal's gone."

"Oatmeal?"

"Some and I've been saving it." In the pantry, I checked the container. There was about two cups. After cooking the oats on the hot-enough stove, I served Derrick a large portion. I got a smaller one with enough left for Granny and the girls.

"My wife always makes meat breakfasts and oatmeal with brown sugar and cinnamon once in a while." Derrick shoveled a spoon of the hot cereal into his mouth, grimacing.

"It's dull without sugar, huh."

He nodded and gulped.

"What's your wife's name?" Oatmeal by itself tasted bland for sure. I stifled the urge to gag while it slid down my throat. I burped. "Excuse me."

"You're excused." Derrick nodded. "Terry. She's a wonderful woman. I fell in love with her garden first."

I stopped eating. "Garden?"

"Yeah, her veggie garden." Scraping the bowl clean with his spoon, he shoved in the last bite. "She sold her veggies at a stand and her tomatoes"—he pressed his finger and thumb together and kissed them—"were the best. Twenty-five years later, she still feeds me her home-grown, juicy tomatoes."

"Sounds almost romantic." I giggled.

"You know what they say." Derrick wagged his head. "The way to a man's heart is through his gut."

As we washed and rinsed our bowls, I wondered what foods would win Harry's heart. Just to make double sure he would never forget me. *Hmmm.* Were he and I headed for a relationship like my great-grandparents, Granny and Grand? I couldn't wait to email him and find out his favorite cookies. Home-baked cookies travel well through the mail.

I daydreamed about Harry until time to climb on the roof.

Derrick and I buttoned our coats and headed for the ladder. Once we got in the attic, he unlaced a boot.

"What're you doing there?"

His fingers turned white as he yanked on the strings. "My boots straps must be snug as possible. Otherwise, I will surely twist or even break an ankle."

"What a horrid thought." I covered my mouth. "Please, don't jump."

He tightened the other boot. "I thought you wanted to see if the radio works so we can get off this hillside?"

I lowered my eyes to the wood-shake roof. "How could I help you if you get hurt?"

He chuckled. "Nothing's going to happen." Now, Derrick crawled toward the roof's edge. "I know how to roll."

I scooted on my backside to follow him, becoming icky wet. "Roll?" *Did he say roll?* Then it hit me why I grew especially nervous. He seemed a bit old to fly off a two-story roof.

Derrick lay on his stomach, where earlier he'd cleared a path. "I've decided to jump near the plow in the snowbank." He pointed at the fir tree. "Sturdier branches are too far away for me to grab hold. Besides, the snow might be deep enough to cushion my fall." He stood. "Pray for me, Kari."

Covering my eyes, I whispered, "I can't look." Praying, I waited for the bones and flesh thud.

25

We Know In Part

Staring wide-eyed at where Derrick disappeared, my heart thumped in panic. A Steller's jay bird scolded from a nearby fir tree. Right before Derrick leaped, a curious need to watch him fly made me open my eyes. Had the jay's noisy call muffle the sound of his landing?

"Derrick?" I hollered.

When he didn't respond, my brain became muddled. *What do I do?* By now he should have said something, anything. I inched my way toward the attic window along the snow-cleared path. Growing dizzy halfway there, I rested my forehead on my crossed arms. Tears burned behind the bridge of my nose. *What if Derrick is hurt? Or worse?*

A muffled shout.

I jerked my chin.

The roar of a cheer rose from the ground. "I did it, Kari."

I scooted farther from the window ledge to hear Derrick better. *Thank You, God.*

"I'll try the radio. Afterward, I'll clear off the snow from the vehicles, and get Leah's candy bar." Derrick cleared his throat. "Go to the front door, but don't come out until I call."

In pure relief for him and us, I nodded even though he couldn't see. When I reached the window, I grabbed hold of the ledge and stood.

"Derrick made it?" Leah's voice jolted me. My foot slipped—landing me on my side. She reached out her hand through the opening. "Grab on, Kari." I stretched my fingers. "Gotcha!" Leah pulled me through as I pushed with my shoes. Mia jerked on my coat with a grunt.

All three of us tumbled to the attic floor. "I'm going…" My chest heaved. "…to meet…" I coughed. "Derrick."

"Thank the Lord." Leah helped us stand. "He's not hurt."

From the attic ladder we took turns jumping to the first floor and ran to the lodge's front double doors. We ripped one side of the plastic and blankets from its nails. I peeked through the doorway. How would Derrick wade through a ton mud?

"There's another problem." Leah spoke near my ear. "Granny won't get up."

"Yeah." Mia yawned. "She says it's too cold out from under the covers, and she doesn't ache in the bed."

Rubbing my palms together, I chuckled. "I wondered when she'd give in and rest."

"In her own words about others, she's 'a trial and a tribulation.'" Leah sniffled.

"You know." I nudged her elbow. "She is our great-granny. Let's give her a break."

Mia's eyes roved between Leah and me.

We left the entrance and entered the kitchen. Leah added more wood to the fire. "I never thought I'd say this, Kari." She wiped her hands on her pants. "But you're right." She grabbed a kitchen towel off the counter and settled into one of the metal chairs near the heat of the stove. "Granny's *old*."

I studied Leah, but she wasn't acting sassy. "Did it take the trip for you notice?"

"Guess so." She picked at dirt under her paint-chipped fingernails.

Sitting on the floor, Mia leaned against Leah's chair. "She can't walk like we do, either."

I lifted loose strands of my hair and tucked them behind my ear. "Grand died six months ago. People say when one old spouse dies most often the other lives for under a year."

"This means Granny could die soon." Mia gazed at the ceiling. "So, so sad, girls."

"She's too stubborn." Blowing her nose on the towel, Leah furrowed her manicured brows.

"*Eeuw*, Leah." Mia pointed. "You just blew your nose on our kitchen towel."

"Don't sweat the small stuff, Mia. We'll get another." I leaned closer Leah. "Remember, Mom says they were like twins. You know what this means."

"No." Leah's eyes grew round. "What?"

"Granny feels even more lost without him, with three strikes against her." I counted on my fingers. "She's ancient, madly in love with Grand, and he's her twin at heart."

"I never imagined old people still being so in love. What a concept." Leah crossed a leg and jiggled her foot. "I wonder if Granny will finish her love story."

An ache in my back reminded me of my tumble on the roof. I stretched. "When Derrick comes, we'll go upstairs and visit with her. Take her a bowl of oatmeal and a cup of coffee."

Leah stood. "I'll check on him."

I twisted to face her retreating form. "Be careful." But I decided to follow not wanting left out of the loop.

Moments later, Leah shouted, "Hey, Derrick!" She paused. "What? Can't hear you."

His deep voice responded, but it was muted.

"Just a minute." Leah almost ran into me as she headed for the stairs. "Derrick needs a sheet. Then he'll tell me what comes next."

When she returned with her arms full of the linen, we poked our heads out the door. He stood near the plow, his face bright as a wet lobster. In a pile in front of him sat the rest of our luggage. In the mud.

I mumbled to no one in particular. "I'll have nightmares about mud for a long while—there is so much of it everywhere."

Leah cupped her fingers around her mouth. "We've got it."

"Good." With a hand, he shielded his eyes from the sun's glare. "Take the biggest log you can carry and tie it to one end of the sheet. Whoever is stronger can toss it my way."

Being older, I should throw it. But Leah inherited the athletic genes. I nudged my sister. "Go ahead, muscle girl."

She nodded. "Sure." After marching inside, she returned with a medium-sized, round log.

Mia tapped my arm. "Should I tell Granny what's going on?"

"That'd be best." I waved Mia toward the stairs.

Leah set the piece of wood on a chair. "Until you do, Granny won't stop fussing." She wrapped one end of the sheet around the log, tied it into a double knot, and stepped outside. "We're ready, Derrick."

He pointed at the ground in front of him. "Stand across from me, Leah, but you'll have to wade out a few feet."

Her shoes disappeared into the mire. "Eeeww!" Her face wrinkled but she raised her knees high, slogging even farther from me and the front door. Stopping, she lifted the log. "One, two, three." With a grunt she sent it sailing. It landed closer to Derrick.

"Wow." I raised my thumb. "Good job."

Leah scowled down at her filthy pant legs. "How's that, Derrick?"

He moved toward her. "Great. Thanks."

Mia stood in the lodge entryway. "Granny needs to use the potty."

"I'll go." I scurried to the stairs and raced to her room.

Granny's face scrunched like a shriveled mushroom. "That's about enough of this monkey business."

Sucking in my breath, I remembered my advice to Leah. *Patience, Lord.* "I'm here now, Granny." After her bathroom run, I helped her back into bed. "I'll bring your oatmeal."

"Good. I'm half starved." She shook her finger at me. "Don't forget my coffee."

Once in the kitchen, I spooned Granny's portion of oatmeal into a bowl. As Leah and Derrick talked outside in muttered tones, I grew torn between delivering Granny's breakfast and taking a quick sneak-a-peek. I stepped outdoors.

Derrick took steps toward us, tugging the sheet-wrapped luggage through the deep mud. "Gross." *More mud to deal with.* I ducked inside, hurried upstairs, and handed Granny the oatmeal with a spoon. "Your coffee should be ready in a jiffy." I left Granny eating, her mouth too full to get a word in edgewise.

I returned with a warm washcloth, a kitchen towel, and the coffee. Granny reached for the steaming cup. "I should have stayed here all along after the mudslide. When was that, Kari?"

"Two days ago." I came at her with the wet cloth. "Let me clean your face." She lowered her cup and raised her chin. I wiped the sleep from her eyes. "Derrick's bringing your suitcase." Hopefully, he got through on his radio.

"Oh, good." She pulled the quilt to her chest. "Would you get me one more blanket, please?"

I folded Mia's side of the cover over Granny. "How's this?"

She smiled. "Better."

As I reached the open doorway, Granny spoke. "Thank you, Kari. You're such a thoughtful child."

I picked at the peeling paint on the doorjamb. "I'm fifteen, Granny, practically an adult."

"This is true, Kari Rose." Her eyes gleamed.

Thinking of Harry, I hesitated. "Granny?"

"Hmmm?" She sipped on her coffee.

"Later, will you tell us more about you and Grand?"

She set the cup on the nightstand. "I'd love to." She scooted lower under the covers and closed her eyes.

Leah would call me silly, but my eyes misted. Granny appeared fragile and tiny in the double bed. Not our normal cranky and stubborn granny. As she appeared to drift off to sleep, I missed my Grand even more. Grand. The name my mom gave him when she was a toddler. Short for Granddad.

26

The Perfect Comes

A commotion on the first floor below drew my attention from Granny's room. I perched at the stair's landing. Derrick tossed Granny's suitcase next to duffle bags at the bottom of the stairs. Task completed, he stood beside them, wet and muck-covered, gulping his breaths. He staggered from sight toward the kitchen and surely to the warmth.

I carried Granny's empty tray to where Derrick sat hunched close to the cook stove. "Thank you for the rest of our luggage." He nodded.

Derrick's expression seemed closed off. Clamping on my tongue, I moved toward the sink. I vowed not to ask him any questions about the radio. The poor guy. I swear he had more gray in his hair than before he jumped.

What's going to happen to us?

A rush of regrets stormed through me, while I washed Granny's dishes. If only we would have recharged our cell phone at the motel. If only Derrick hadn't lost his phone who knows where. Would we even have cell service out here in the middle of nowhere? If only—*Shouldn't have taken this trip in the first place.*

I nibbled on my lip, wanting to kick myself.

"Derrick, I'll get you hot cocoa with a marshmallow."
Leah placed a comforter over Derrick's shoulders.

I turned back to wash the dishes.

She raced to the counter a few feet from me. "Uh, oh,
Kari, look."

What's the problem now? Moving from the sink, I faced
Leah.

She held the cocoa can upside down. "Empty."

"We still have plenty of coffee." I peered into the small
pan of leftover grinds from Granny's cupful. "I'll add more
water to this to make it stretch."

"I'm sure you'll take anything hot, right Derrick?" Leah
tossed the can, making a three-point basket into a trash barrel.

"Yeah." He kept his head bowed.

"What's wrong, girls?" Mia sauntered into the kitchen.

Leah folded her arms. "No more cocoa."

Mia moved to the opposite side of the sink to the butcher
block. "We have lots of teas." She peeked into the blue ceramic
bowl. "The cocoa was gross."

Leah opened and closed the little door to the stove fire
box. "I need to get this hotter." She went into the other room
and returned with an armload. "Mia, help me by stacking your
wood here on top of mine." Leah squatted and let the logs roll
on the floor within easy reach of the stove.

Once the fire crackled and the coffee boiled, I served
Derrick a well-deserved hot drink.

He accepted it after slipping off his gloves and placing
them on the warming shelf of the stove. "I got too cold."
Sipping, he closed his eyes. "Nothing could taste better right
now than this watered-down coffee."

I shrugged. "I'm making it last longer." Sitting next to Derrick, I worked on grateful thoughts. We were safe in this lodge with a brave and kind man. Though, his outdoor adventure about did him in.

Long minutes later, he gulped the last drop. "That hit the spot. I'm glad you're thinking ahead by making our coffee stretch."

"Radio still doesn't work?" I slapped my mouth, having broken my own word. "I didn't mean to bug you."

"Sorry." The narrow space between Derrick's brows puckered. "No."

"Somebody come help me!"

"Whose turn is it?" Leah cupped a mug between her hands.

"It's yours, but I'll go." I stretched. "Would you take the rest of our bags upstairs, then? I'm so ready for clean clothes." I hurried to the staircase and stepped over our luggage. At least we have plenty of water. *Food's almost gone, except for stale flour.* We won't starve to death on whole-wheat flour. Right?

~*~

Within earshot outside Granny's door, it didn't take much for me to realize she started a huge pity party. "I have never in all my days been treated so badly. Left a poor old woman alone. I've called, yet no one comes." Granny heaved a sigh. "James, I just want to be with you."

Granny's crying became a moan, which stirred my emotions. And the words about Grand. I quivered with worry. What should I do? Go to her?

Let her grieve alone?

But, I couldn't do it, so I entered Granny's room on tiptoes. I sat on the bed. Hugging her to me, her back poked sharp as bird bones. She laid her head on my chest. She heaved with more sobs. I smoothed gray hairs from her cheek.

Long moments later, Granny grew calmer. I gathered a wad of tissue. "Here you go." Placed it to her nose. "Blow."

"Thank you, Kari Rose." She made the noise into the tissue one does when they've been crying. "I need to use the bathroom."

Hooking my arms under her shoulders, I lifted.

An idea came to me on how to make her feel better. "Later, why don't we make a shallow, warm bath for you in the tub?"

Her smile reached her eyes. "That would be wonderful." Long minutes later settled back in the bed, Granny rested against a pile of pillows.

"I'll get the water heated." I kissed her forehead and pulled the blankets to her chin.

I raced down the stairs, where Leah waited for me at the bottom. She hid an arm behind her back. Her smile claimed it was good news.

She thrust out her hand. "More chocolate!"

"You did bring a large bar on our trip." I yipped with my happy dance. "There's plenty to go around."

She knocked the candy bar on the handrail. "Yeah and plenty frozen."

In the kitchen, I rummaged around for food to see what was left. We had salt, flat baking powder, and I stuck my head closer to the inside of the whole-wheat flour barrel. I wrinkled my nose. Yep. No doubt it's old. *Is it buggy?* I shuddered. If so, though, wouldn't it be needed protein?

"Here's my contribution." I twirled round. Derrick stood in the entryway, waving his milk chocolate bar.

I reached for it. "I'll make pancakes and melt chocolate to add to the batter."

He let the bar go into my open palm. "We have enough flour?"

"We sure do, but it's stale. A whole barrel full." I hurried past him and opened my cookbook to the pancake recipe, ready to measure and mix the ingredients. "The milk and sugar in the chocolate should make a tastier pancake."

My sisters came to help, with Leah on my right side. "With Granny crying while you were up there, I decided not to barge in. I'll haul the bags upstairs later."

"She was pretty sad, talking to Grand like he stood right there." I stopped pouring water into the dry ingredients. "I really wonder what God thinks of people talking to those who have died." I wiggled my fingers at Mia. "Grab the wooden spoon off the dish drainer. Leah, would you melt Derrick's bar in a small pan over a warm—not hot spot on the stove? Be sure to stir it constantly, so it doesn't scorch."

"Sure." Leah moved to a cabinet.

"Don't forget, Kari." Mia handed me the spoon. "We need to warm the beans."

"Right." I snapped my fingers. "When the chocolate melts, Mia, would you add it to the batter? Then combine the dry and wet ingredients until they are mixed. I'll get the beans heated." After placing them on the hottest area, I stirred them. "Derrick, would you fill two large cooking pots with water and place them on the stove?"

He rose from his chair. "Do we still have plenty of snow water in our barrel?"

"I just checked and we do." I hummed a made-up tune and then stopped. "Granny will feel so much better after a warm sponge bath."

"You're giving Granny a bath?" Leah's jaw sagged.

"Well, yeah." I stared at her. "It was my idea, and she'll need my help."

Leah broke the milk chocolate bar into chunks. "Well, I hope we don't run out of water because of a silly bath."

Derrick set the first pot of water on the burner.

I placed a hand on my hip. "Didn't you hear me tell Derrick we have plenty?"

Placing the last piece of chocolate into a pan, Leah shrugged. "Guess I was day dreaming about the sunny coast."

After setting the second cooking pot on the stove, Derrick stood next to Leah. "If you have something else to do, I'll take over melting the chocolate."

Nodding, Leah handed him the spoon. She gathered plates, bowls, utensils, and cups for hot tea and arranged them on the kitchen counter. "We can serve ourselves cafeteria style."

With the batter ready, I griddled pancakes. I set each cooked one on a plate in the warming drawer above the stove.

When our meal was ready, I clapped. "Let's take our food upstairs and eat with Granny. Afterward we'll hear another story about Grand."

We girls carried our plates filled with several chocolaty pancakes and bowls steaming with beans. Derrick carried a tray with his food, Granny's, and our cups of hot peppermint tea. One thing I discovered while being stranded in this lodge, peppermint kept my stomach happy, happy. Even when I ate beans.

I followed everyone up the stairs. My grin stretched so wide I hoped no one noticed. They'd think I'd become too goofy. But really, we had everything we needed for the moment.

Within my glad thoughts, I imagined the *whelp, welp* of sirens.

~*~

Balancing the tray, Derrick hurried up the last of the stairs and entered Granny's room. When I came in, he had placed the tray on a round table. Peering through the window, he barked out a laugh. "Well, I'll be a monkey's uncle."

We squeezed next to him. I covered my mouth. "I really heard it." I twirled away from our cluster. "Help is here, Granny. We're saved, we're saved."

Her mouth opened as though she would laugh. Leah and Mia held hands, dancing around the room. Peeking a second time through the window, I gave Granny the details. "There's a bunch of red and blue emergency lights. Looks like a police car, and an ambulance. No. Two ambulances." I tapped the window. "A fire truck."

Derrick chuckled. "You missed what's leading them."

"Oh, Granny." I shot her a quick glance. "At the front of the line there are two snowplows side by side. They're scrapping the mud off the lodge road."

Wrinkling her nose, a silent *oh* had formed on Granny's lips.

"Let's go meet them." Leah darted for the doorway.

"Whoa, there." Derrick grabbed her arm. "I'll carry your granny down the stairs so we can go together." He nodded at Granny. "You ready, Adele?"

"Yes, if the girls will help me into my coat." Her face flushed, her trembling hands attempted to yank off the covers. "Then, I shall be, sir."

Leah and I helped Granny throw back the blankets and get into her jacket and shoes. After we swaddled her into one of the quilts, Derrick cradled her in his arms. "You're light, Adele." He winked. "A golden feather."

She kissed his cheek. "You're a strong hunk of a man, Mr. Derrick."

We giggled, and the burden of worry fell from my shoulders. *We're saved.* "Thank You, Lord."

Derrick blushed from pink to a cherry red. "Thank you, ma'am." He gestured at the door with his arms, "Let's go, ladies," and Granny floated upward in her human swing.

At the landing, I peered over Derrick's shoulder and slumped. No one stood at the blanketed doorway. As we descended the stairs, my questions whirled like ingredients in a blender. Was Papa leading our rescue? Would our parents be with them? What about Granny-Too?

We waited at the bottom of the stairs. My belly churned on a knot as big as a Granny Smith apple.

Leah poked my ribs with her elbow and said what I was thinking. "I hear the plows."

Mia jumped up and down in front of us. "Me, too. Me, too." She stumbled, heading for the bank of mud on one edge of our path. I grabbed her by the coat collar and stood her upright.

The ground rumbled louder. The plows drew close enough it seemed they would drive through the lodge walls.

"Everyone stay put where it's safe." Derrick sat on the second to the last stair, still holding Granny. "The plow drivers have to move the mud somewhere, so let's sit tight."

Leaning against the stair rails, Leah cupped her hand near my ear. "Derrick must think I'm lame. I wanted to run out and meet them." She crossed her arms and a pout trembled on her lips.

"What's wrong, Leah?" Granny's brows scrunched into squiggly lines. "I thought you'd be happy now that this nightmare is almost over."

Staring at her muddy sneakers, Leah remained silent.

The left side of Granny's mouth lifted. "Always something bothering you, Leah Bedeah."

"It's not like I chose my family genes, ya know." Leah's eyes sparked with anger. "I wonder *who* I took after, Granny."

At first Granny blinked. She nodded ever so slight. "Spoken like flesh and blood." She clicked her teeth. "You're true kin."

The ground grew silent. The plow engines shut off. It was as though we, as a group, held our breath.

Mia broke from our huddle, passing Derrick and Granny, running with arms whirling. "*Mama, mama.*"

I bolted from the stairs. "Mia!"

An axe blade slashed through fabric covering the door. Mia froze. A uniformed firefighter sidestepped into the room. He scanned the interior with a sweeping glance.

Wrapping my arms around Mia, we shuffled backward.

Behind the firefighter, another man's hooded head poked through the rip. He seemed familiar, even with the white beard on his face. I felt drawn to him with his blue, hawk-like eyes. That nose. "Is everybody okay?"

"Son!"

"Papa!" Rushing at him, I threw myself into his jacketed arms.

"Everything's going to be just fine, Rosy."

I believed it true as the Gospel. My ear pressed against Papa's chest, and his heartbeat raced.

27

The Partial Will Pass Away

A highway patrol officer, several paramedics, and a few firemen crowded inside the muddied entrance of the lodge. People talked all at once, creating a dull echo in the fireplace room. We crowded around Papa. "In just a minute, girls, we'll have you stand next to the hearth after the guys shovel away more of the mud."

With huge snow shovels, four men scooped a clean area for the additional people to fit.

"Papa." I jerked on his arm. "We've got chairs in the kitchen. Should we get those?" He nodded his response and followed me into the other room.

We brought the chairs to the cleared space, and we settled Granny on Silver next to us. In the kitchen, Derrick mingled with the other snowplow guys and spoke in low tones. The officer and the paramedics had their own discussion.

When they stopped talking, the officer cleared his throat. "I'm Officer Mcpherson. The ambulance technicians are ready to begin examinations, starting with you, ma'am." He nodded at Granny.

"Why me?" Her hawk-eyes glared. "I'm a feeble and old lady?"

His face flushed the color of a ripe strawberry. My sisters and I giggled. The paramedics drew closer. One of them opened a case and pulled from it a blood pressure cuff. I knew what it was, because Granny kept this on her dresser at home. She had used it on Grand.

Officer Mcpherson nodded at Leah and me. "I'll be asking both of you a few questions. Afterward, you'll be checked by our technicians."

I quick glanced at Papa. He winked.

Leveling a pen over his miniature notebook, Officer Mcpherson wrote. Then he leveled us with a gaze. "Young ladies, it's been reported one of you may have driven the Cadillac parked out front."

Leah's fingers found mine and gripped. I gave my own signal with an *It'll be okay* squeeze.

Officer Mcpherson bent on one knee. "Now, I want you to understand no one will be arrested."

Arrested? The hair on my neck prickled.

Mia nodded yes. "See, Kari, we shouldn't have broken into the lodge."

My hand stilled the top of her head with a grip. "Shush."

The officer's serious expression settled on me. The corner of his mustache bobbled. "I'm quite sure you ladies are not old enough to drive." He scratched his neck as though gathering his next words.

The itch must have been contagious. My nose tickled.

Before he spoke, he flicked a look at Papa. "An officer who worked the night of the first storm reported what he suspected." He leaned closer. Leah stabbed her nails into the creases of my palm. "Though under the conditions of the weather"—he slapped his notebook closed—"this officer and myself have agreed to forget this whole driving situation."

I raised my eyebrows at Leah. She at me. We sighed in unison.

"But, I'm curious." With a thumb, Officer Mcpherson readjusted his uniformed hat on his head. "Who drove the car through the storm?"

Within Leah's hand, my fingers trembled. My brain ordered me to tell.

Leah leaped off the chair. "I did."

What is she doing?

Officer Mcpherson studied her. "Really, now?"

Leah dipped her head yes, with the straightest expression ever. Chuckling, it rumbled between my ribcage where no one could hear.

A corner of his mouth curled. "You're sure you were driving, uh, I'm sorry, what is your name?"

Papa crossed his arms. His eyes twinkled.

"My name's Leah Bedeah. And yes, I drove the Caddy." Her chin rose in a challenge.

Papa moved and pressed fingers at the middle of my back. He whispered, "Kari?"

Now, my silent chuckle died. A monster bubble gurgled within my belly. It slipped to my lower extremities, popped, and released, sounding like a windshield wiper across dry glass.

All gazes lobbed over to me.

Mia giggled.

A flush spread to my cheeks and heated them to the temperature of a Ghost Pepper. "Officer Mcpherson?" There was no way to escape. Papa had spoken, and so must I. "My sister says she drove because she had the idea. I'm the one who got behind the wheel. Through the snowstorm." I gave myself a mental 'good job' pat. My lips pursed.

He stood. "I thought as much." Officer Mcpherson drew his attention to Leah. "We know your sister doesn't have her learner's permit."

How did he—? Papa. Again.

Leah nibbled on her cheek, before answering. "Granny's foot hurt. She couldn't drive."

His blond brows rose to meet the ripples on his forehead. "And where was this when you decided your sister should drive?"

Leah never took her eyes off the officer. "At one of the rest stops." She released our grip and fumbled with her fingers.

Officer Mcpherson motioned to our papa. "Why didn't you call your grandfather to come and get you?"

I stepped closer to him. "Papa wasn't able to come right away. And then, when he could, the freeway closed."

Officer Mcpherson rested his fists on his gun belt. "No more driving until you *earn* your permit."

I shifted my shoulders and swallowed a sigh. "Yes, sir."

~*~

When the paramedics had examined Granny, they started with Mia and finished with me. They gave each of us a good-health pat, all except for Granny. Her foot had swelled to twice its size. She was dehydrated.

"I don't need a hospital." Scrunching her face into a snarl, Granny growled. "Give me a warm bed in my son's house. My blood's near froze."

Although Granny fussed, it appeared to me most everyone ignored her rant—except Papa. He stood alongside her stretcher and touched the top of Granny's head. "Mom, I'd go with you in the ambulance, but then I'd have to leave my car."

"No, you wouldn't, Son," Granny wagged her hand. "Kari is a good driver." She raised herself partway up as though searching for me. "She'll drive it for you." Her eyes grew wide. "What about my Cadillac?"

Papa hollered over his shoulder before he walked through the doorway. "Mcpherson, would you get one of the extra men to drive my mother's Cadillac?"

"Sure thing, Jacob."

Derrick ran over to the officer. "You'll have to call for a tow, instead. I had to break into the car when one of the girls got trapped inside. The door's warped so bad it probably won't open or close. I broke the window when I couldn't get the door to work."

"Okay, will do, Derrick." Officer Mcpherson began the call for a tow.

Mia, standing next to me, gasped. "Breaking and entering." She yanked on my jacket sleeve and stared up. "But, he had to, right Kari?"

I tweaked her nose with a thumb and finger. "Yes, Mia Babe. Granny doesn't care, because Leah is more important than a car."

Papa caught up to Granny and hunched closer to her stretcher. "Mom, about your car—" His voice faded as they made their way to the ambulance.

Derrick rushed over and reached for my hand to shake it. "Ladies, it's been good knowing you. My boss just called. I'm to get checked at the Shasta City hospital."

His skin was rough against my palm. "We were safe with you here, Derrick."

Leah received his handshake with a nod. "Thank you, again, for saving my life."

Mia pushed her way into the middle. "You said I could ride in your snowplow."

"Can't, sweetheart." The line between his brows deepened. "My boss told me to go in the ambulance."

Mia's eyes grew round. "Are you sick?"

"No." He shook his head. "Just a check-up to make sure I'm okay. How about I carry you on my shoulder to your papa's car?"

"Yippee!" Mia's feet walked along Derrick's leg as he lifted her and settled her on his broad shoulder. "I'm flying." She waved her jacketed arms to the sky.

"I can't believe I'm such a dork." Leah stared at the lodge. "But, Kari, I'm going to miss this place."

"In a strange way so will I." We held bags and Granny's suitcase in front of us near the entryway, waiting for Papa to help carry them. "Not at all what Granny had planned, was it, Leah?"

"Oh, no!" Grabbing my arm, her eyes grew to the size of walnuts. "We still have to face Mom."

"You never know." I bumped Leah's hip. "She might be so relieved we aren't dead, she won't yell and have a fit."

Nudging me, she bowed her head. "And grounded for life?"

"Mom's not so unreasonable, Leah." *Please make this true, Lord.*

"Oh, no?" Squinting, she twisted a long strand of her golden hair around a finger. "Just wait until she's over being scared and all happy."

"I'd say." Papa stood in the doorway of the lodge. "Are you two ready?" He lifted most of the luggage, leaving us with one each.

I walked beside him. "What do you mean *I'd say?*"

"Kari, open the rear door of my car with the clicker." Papa stopped and stood sideways to me. "It's in my jacket pocket."

Oh, brother. I'd have to wait to find out what he meant. I pressed a button on the clicker, and the door rose in slow motion. Papa moved forward and tossed in our luggage. "Why don't we make sure everything is removed from Granny's car?"

Leah opened Papa's back passenger door where our sister sat. "Mia—

"I heard." She scooted across the seat. "Help clean out the Caddy."

We carried what little was left in Granny's car in one trip. I claimed the front seat with "shotgun." Papa slid in and pressed the starter button and headed downhill. We waved at Derrick. He grew smaller and smaller. Papa made the corner, and our plow hero disappeared from view.

The only sound came from the squishy, splats of tires on the lodge's winding, wet-paved road. On the freeway, Papa kept his police-trained stare on the slow lane in front of him.

Twisting in my seat, I asked the easy question first. "How did you find us?"

"Well." Papa sighed. "I did some investigating. It took a while, but I discovered a tow truck driver's last call-in mentioned a Cadillac. That it followed him to a vacant lodge on a hill." He shrugged. "The local officials agreed the place you stayed at was the only lodge it could be."

I nodded, nibbling an already short fingernail. "Is Mom furious?"

A long silence, and then he chuckled. "Let's just say, she's been calling me every hour today."

"Oh, yeah." I squirmed in my seat. "Mom and Dad would have gotten home today."

Papa passed a semitruck where it was parked on the shoulder of the freeway. "And, no, Kari, I can't say whether or not she is angry. When I told her I found you, she became emotional."

Shame seeped through the pores of my skin. I sagged. "We didn't mean to scare everyone." I clasped my hands on my lap. "It just … well … happened."

"Kari Rose, the point is you did worry us." He clutched my shoulder. "Granny made a bad decision. But we wished you would have used better judgment." He removed his hold on me, placing his hand at the wheel. "When I spotted the Cadillac, I called your parents."

I gulped, but a lump as large as an onion stuck in my throat and brought the sting of tears.

In the backseat, my sisters slept. I attempted the same. Since Mom's verdict loomed, I doubly needed my rest.

~*~

"*Ouch.* I'm not a turnip, you know. There is blood in there without digging." Granny scolded the nurse while Papa and we girls waited nearby.

The doctor checked Granny, pronounced her in okay health, but said she must stay overnight. "We don't want you to go home, Adele, until you're hydrated."

"Well, don't you think I can drink plenty of water at my son's house?"

There's that again—Granny still trying to get to Papa's.

"I'm sure you have a good point." The doctor's smile grew thin. He spoke as though she were a child. "But you've been traumatized." He angled his head. "Understand?"

"Don't have to tell *me.*" Granny waved him off and her hand dropped to the bed. "I lived it."

I exchanged a glance with Leah. She snorted.

Granny pointed a gnarled index finger. "Don't start, miss sassy pants."

Crossing arms over her chest, Leah stared at the wall. "Can't even express myself around you."

"If you can't say something nice, don't say anything at all." Mia peered into Leah's face. "That's what Mama always says."

Leah looked down her nose at Mia. "I didn't *say* anything."

"Mama says it's not nice to snort at grownups." Mia crossed *her* arms.

My gaze wandered to Papa, but he gave his attention to the doctor. When the conversation ended, the doctor patted Granny's arm and left.

"Fiddlesticks." Granny's lips puckered, reminding me of two inch worms.

Papa drew closer. "What is it, Mom?"

"My bones ache." She pushed strands of hair from her face. "This bed is hard as packed dirt."

"We'll get you to a comfy room." He swiped a thumb across Granny's cheek. "Hang in there, tough lady."

She blew air through her closed mouth, making her inch worm lips race.

I muffled a laugh with a hand. Moments later, a nurse placed graham crackers and a tiny container of orange juice on Granny's bed tray.

"About time." She pushed up as Papa rearranged her pillows. "I'm starved. We were rescued before I ate Kari's pancakes." Granny patted the nurse's arm. "Did I tell you my great-granddaughter, Kari, not only drives real well, but she cooks good too?"

The nurse shook her head no with a smile and left the room.

This warmed my heart, Granny bragging on me.

Mia tugged on my arm. "Let's go to a food machine, I'm hungry."

"Here, Kari." Papa lifted his wallet. "Get everyone something to eat. I'll take a root beer soda."

"Thank you." I stuffed the bills in my pocket. Stretching on tippy toes, I kissed his bearded cheek. I giggled. "It feels like fur, soft and ticklish."

With a grin, the corners of his eyes crinkled.

Three sets of tennis shoes padding down the hall made a lot of noise. Added to our loud feet, Mia chattered up a whirlwind. "No, maybe I don't want a soda. Hot cocoa sounds yummy." She patted her tummy. "Not the old stuff like at the lodge."

Leah stopped. "We need to ask somebody for directions, guys." I waited for her, but she didn't move.

I continued to where we were headed. A large room with bright lights was on the left. "I think this is the cafeteria."

For a second time since coming to the hospital, Leah snorted. "This'll cost too much, Kari."

Leading the way inside, I rushed to several vending machines loaded with snacks and drinks. "Ha, see?"

Mia ran to the hot cocoa dispenser. "Here's *my* favorite." She hugged the machine and made licking noises.

I laughed, but Leah growled. "Oh, stop being babyish, Mia."

Somebody's hungry.

After choosing our sandwiches, we ate a lot and spoke little. Appearing much calmer, Leah patted her lips with a napkin. "When do you think Mom and Dad will be here?"

Before I could answer, I finished chewing the whole-grain bread, tuna, mayo, pickle, and swallowed. Unexpected gas rose to my throat. I burped. Mia sniggered. "Excuse me." I covered my lips with two fingers. "Papa said tonight."

"I'll be giddy with joy when we get to Granny-Too's." Sighing, Leah munched on her corn chips. "She'll probably make our favorite dishes. Have our beds ready." She closed her eyes. "Granny-Too will spoil us as always, and I've never been so exhausted."

Shifting her shoulders, Mia sat straighter. "What's our favorites?"

"Well…" I laid down my half-eaten sandwich. "Chicken and dumplings for one thing. Granny-Too will surely make this special meal." I blinked. "She always did in the winter. Before they moved a long ways." Boy, I really missed my grandparents. Fluttering my lashes to shoo away the moisture, I took a drink of my cocoa. "With lots of dumplings swimming in the pot." *Doggone tears want to take over.*

"Hmmm." Leah grinned. "I can hardly wait."

Mia licked around her mouth. "Let's go ask Papa to take us to his house right now."

"He won't leave." I shook my tangled ponytail. "Not until Granny's settled into a room."

"I'll ask him if he'll call Granny-Too." Leah wadded her chip bag and made a basket in a trashcan. "I want to see her."

Mia copied Leah, but in the cup's flight, drips of cocoa splattered on the floor. Mia and I rushed to wipe the mess with a napkin.

Stuffing the last of my sandwich into my mouth, I spoke around my food. "Definitely."

~*~

Outside the emergency door, we waited for Papa when a pair of nurses rushed by us in the hall. They disappeared behind the double doors. Where Granny lay in a cubicle. On the dirt-hard bed.

With the hall cleared, Leah took off in the same direction. I pulled at her arm. "We shouldn't go in there."

"Why not?" Her question laced with innocence, almost pleaded.

Is Granny in trouble? I softened my voice. "Leah."

28

Does Not Envy Or Boast

Leah's eyes bulged like popover rolls. "Someone needs help?"

Mia drew closer, and we created a cluster. "Who is it, Kari?"

Grabbing both their hands, I steered them to the waiting room we'd just past. "It's probably an ambulance bringing in a patient."

I collapsed into a faded green chair. Leah frowned. "I'm not touching this one."

Staring at the chair she referred to, I understood. She once again stirred her emotions into a meltdown. "A rip doesn't matter, Leah." I sat on the torn one. "See? No big deal." Pleased with my patience, I brought a fingernail to my teeth and chipped away.

Leah scowled. "What's eating you?"

I pointed at myself. "Me?"

Leaning toward me, Mia touched my arm. "Something's eating you?"

"You're biting your nails and acting nitpicky."

"*I'm* picky?" I forgot about being patient with my sister. "You're the one who doesn't want to sit on a stinkin', tiny, stupid rip."

"Stop with the nail biting." Leah paced, arms crossed. "It grates on my nerves."

I stuffed my hands underneath my thighs and huffed a breath. Slumping in the chair, I stared at the ceiling. Curled paint would flake off any second and fall in my greasy hair.

Poking my leg, Leah grumped. "You know it's not good for your back to slouch."

"For the love of cupcakes." I slammed my feet on the floor and bolted upright.

I stared at the silent TV screen. "What if?"

"What if what?" Leah's expression softened.

The contents of my stomach curdled. "I'm worried about Granny." Raising my chin, I made fists on my thighs. "There, I said it. Are you happy now?"

My sisters faced the open doorway as though the answer stood nearby.

Leah clasped her hands in front of her. "Well. Okay. But, Granny's too stubborn to—" She lowered her lashes where spatters of moisture dotted the edges. "—die."

Mia covered her mouth. "No."

"We're guessing." I gulped. "It could be anyone."

Leah rolled her eyes, tears sprinkling her cheeks. "And just *anyone* would make you worried, right?"

Sniffling, Mia stuttered. "But-but, I love Granny." She wiped her nose on her coat sleeve.

Leah and I formed a ring around Mia, shushing her.

A shadow darkened the door entrance. "I was on my way when your papa called." Granny-Too reached for us. My sisters and I fell into her arms. We sobbed on her like three blubbering babies. "Oh, my goodness, it's okay now. Let's pray for Granny."

Leah choked out. "She's not dead?"

"No, no. Her heart did become irregular. Doctors got it pumping normally." Granny-Too bowed her head and spoke in a hushed voice to the Lord.

We sniffled with her murmured words. At the end, we said the name which calmed. "In Jesus. Amen."

Granny-Too scooted next to Mia on the sofa, her face smudged with pink blotches. "We thought we'd lost you all." She tsked her tongue. "Your poor mama and daddy."

My sisters' expressions drooped. I bowed my head.

Leah bent forward, sobbing into her hands. We patted her until the tears dried. "I talked us into going with Granny. It sounded like fun, until we were driving down the road." She hiccupped.

Lifting a damp strand of hair from Leah's chin, I tucked it behind her ear. "And, I couldn't imagine Granny traveling alone." This was part truth.

Nodding, Mia stood. "I wanted to see Papa and you, Granny-Too. Later I got scared."

"I'm grateful my girls are okay." Granny-Too swiped at her own damp cheeks.

I should have hid her car keys.

"Yeah, Kari, you should have." Leah smirked.

"I said that out loud?"

Leah nodded.

"We didn't know about the storm." Mia shrugged. "Honest."

Feeling extra bold and a bit angry, I sat up straight. "I should have locked Granny in her house."

"Yeah." Leah giggled. "If she tried to escape, I would have locked her in her room."

Mia shook her head. "That's not nice, girls."

Now Granny-Too smiled. She gathered Mia into another embrace. "Of course no one would have kept Granny against her will, honey." But, her shoulders shook in a silent chuckle.

Leah and I exchanged a knowing look. Granny-Too had a great sense of humor.

During a quiet moment, Granny-Too opened her purse. "Mia and Leah, get everyone drinks and snacks at the vending machine." She gave Leah the cash.

Mia frowned. "How'd you know we'd want more goodies?"

With a glint in her eyes, she leaned forward. "Granny's make it their business to know these things." She settled her back against the sofa. "Later, I'll take my girls home with me and cook your favorite meal."

We shouted, "Chicken and dumplings."

"Shhh." Granny-Too tapped her upturned lips. "You guessed on the first try." She flapped her hand at my sisters. "Now, scoot."

"Come on, squirt." Leah grabbed Mia's hand.

As the girls left, Granny-Too patted the seat next to her. "Sweet pea?" I sat, always willing to snuggle with Granny-Too. "I'm so grateful my girls are safe." Her thumb stroked my cheek.

I thought of the old angel. Should I tell Granny-Too? "I saw an angel. At a rest stop."

Granny-Too's brow rose. "You did?"

"Yes. She told us to make a decision together. Jesus would want us to, she said, like she knew him personally."

"What were you trying to decide?" She caressed my jaw.

"Whether or not I should drive." I shuddered. "I was so scared."

Kissing me on the forehead, Granny-Too said in a dreamy tone of voice, "It all worked out, didn't it."

As I shut my eyes, I laid my head on her teeny mound of a belly. *Safe.* Always.

~*~

My eyes flew open, haunted by the reality of my dream when I couldn't breathe under the snow bank. Granny-Too's boney lap brought me to the present.

The book she read, one of my favorites, seemed to cause Granny-Too's stomach to jiggle in a chuckle. My lips parted in a grin at the pictures in *Green Eggs and Ham*. I petted the tiny sag of skin on Granny-Too's under arm.

She raised the book high in the air. Her eyes dancing. "Did you sleep well, Rosy?"

"Yes, ma'am." Twisting my knuckles on my closed lids, I raised to sit. "Where are the girls?"

"They brought you a cocoa and left." She closed the book. "They found a new friend. A patient named Tara Jane."

Reaching arms over my head, I stretched. "Really?"

"They're in Tara's room telling her about their adventures this week."

"That could take hours." I pointed at a full cup of cocoa. "Is this mine?"

"Yes, but it's surely cold."

I sipped from the cup, not caring. At least it wasn't stale. It slid down thick and rich. The cocoa tasted almost as yummy as what I made at home. "Why's Tara Jane here?" I placed the half-full cup on the coffee table in front of us, opened a snack pack, and placed a cracker on my tongue. I sucked on it until it melted to mush.

"She fractured her leg from a skiing accident during her spring break. The way the girls told it, Tara had extensive surgery."

I drank the rest of my cocoa. "Ouch. Sounds painful." I angled my head. "You haven't heard about Granny?"

"No, sweetheart." Her lashes fluttered. "Now that you're awake, I'll go find out any news."

"I'm coming with you." I scooped up my trash and placed it in a waste basket.

After we checked on Leah and Mia, we headed for the emergency room. The slap of our shoes echoed off the polished floors. Turning right, the sign above the double doors read EMERGENCY. Granny-Too squeezed my shoulder. "I'll be gone for only a few minutes."

"Okay." People walked by, some smiling, some red-eyed with mouths fixed into a frown. A nurse pushed an older lady in a wheelchair. I waved. They nodded.

What was keeping Granny-Too?

My heels flush with the wall, I squatted. The cocoa upset my stomach. I needed peppermint tea. Sighing, I massaged my middle and hoped for a quiet burp. The emergency doors swished open, but a guy in blue hospital clothes hurried on by. I crossed my arms on my knees and rested my cheek there.

"What are you doing, Kari Rose?" Red veins scatter-shot within the whites of Papa's blue eyes.

"Is Granny okay?" I slid up the wall to stand.

"You know it." He hooked his arm around my neck and scrubbed the top of my head with his knuckles. "They're getting a room ready for her."

He let me wiggle from his iron grip.

"She didn't eat too well at the lodge?" A line formed between Papa's brows.

"None of us did. We had to use what was in the food barrels and eat smaller amounts toward the end."

Walking on ahead of me, he took long strides. "Your granny-too will stay with Granny as they transport her."

I skipped ahead and walked backwards in front of him. "Where are we going?"

"Since we can't go home yet, I thought we'd eat in the cafeteria." He made a right and stopped. "What's on the menu? Do you know?"

"Not sure." Standing next to him, I scratched at a tickle in my ear. "I thought by now I'd be at your house."

"Me, too, Kari." He pulled his phone from his coat pocket, and a glove fell on the floor. I handed it to him. "I need to check in with your mom. Let her know we'll be here for a while."

At the mention of my mother, a band of muscles tightened across my chest.

We entered the waiting room, and Papa made the call. The edges of his mouth curved upward. "Hey, where are you?" He nodded. "Good, good." He listened again. "Oh, sure."

Papa pushed the phone near my face. I took a backward step.

"Someone wants to talk to you."

My fingers reached for the phone. They froze in mid-air. How much trouble could I be in? What should I say?

If Mom is furious? I'll be as popular as a fly in a bowl of ice-cream.

29

See In The Mirror Dimly

I imagined taking the fly out of my mouth. "Mom?"

She's crying.

Then Mom's crying became distant.

"Kari Rose?" Daddy sighed. "Thank goodness you girls are safe."

Tears smarted at the bridge of my nose. "I can't wait to hug you guys." I pinched the pain with a thumb and forefinger. "Will you be here soon?"

"Moments ago, we past the entrance for the town of Williams. We'll be at the hospital in less than two hours." A pause. "Kari, your mother's too upset right now to talk."

I pondered the meaning behind *upset*. As in relieved upset? Angry upset? *Grounding me until I'm an old woman like Granny?* If this went bad, I'd never get my own cell phone.

Dad cleared his throat. "Tomorrow, we'll talk about you girls taking this trip. Let's concentrate on Granny and also on us getting there."

"Yes." I gulped, not sure if I could hold back the tears for one more second. "Tell Mom I love her and miss her. You, too, Daddy."

"Sure, honey. We love you, and we'll see you in no time."

I cut off our reception and handed over Papa's cell. Oh, how I hoped my parents would go easy on us.

Will Mom remember what she'd ask of me?

If only they knew what we went through. I had to tell someone, and Papa was right there. "Papa, I was so scared at the lodge. Leah got trapped in the Cadillac and could have frozen to death. Then, I fell in a snowbank and couldn't breathe, but Derrick saved us." Papa's cool blue eyes became shiny. "Leah was brave, though, much braver than me. She can tell you her bear story."

His brows drew closer together. "I take it the outcome was good." He hugged me to him. "When we didn't know where you were, I almost cried." Papa's voice cracked.

Eager to reassure my tough-cop Papa, I shook my head. I placed an ear on his chest. His heart thumped strong.

~*~

My sisters found us. Together we went to the cafeteria and ate a meal of creamed bisque vegetable soup and crisp-fried chicken. Afterward, we waited outside the emergency room. Papa checked to see if Granny had been moved.

Like a drooping soufflé, I sagged against the wall. "I spoke to Dad."

Mia stared at me wide-eyed. Leah craned her neck. "You did?"

"Yep." I nibbled at a hangnail. "Mom didn't talk to me. Too upset, Dad said."

"Oh, brother." Leah lowered her gaze. "We really did it this time."

"Did what?" Mia's mouth went slack. "We didn't lie, or tear up anything, or be mean to anyone." She sucked on a corner of her lip. "You think they'll ground us?"

Cocking my brow, I thought of how to explain this to a seven-year-old. "What we did was bigger than being in trouble for fighting with one another, not cleaning our rooms, or sassing Mom and Dad."

"We don't have anything to compare it with." Leah picked at a pimple on her chin and winced. "Ow."

"We're good girls." Mia tapped her cheek and grinned. "You think they'll give us a break?"

Leah and I giggled. It felt so good to laugh. I tweaked Mia's nose. "The things you say, Mia Babe."

The emergency room door opened. Granny-Too dug in her purse looking for something and walked past. "Oops. There you are." She joined us at the wall. "I have good news. The nurse is about to transfer Granny to a room." Granny-Too hugged her purse.

Leah stabbed her index fingers in the air. "Oh, yea, Granny, you go, Granny."

Tilting her head, Granny-Too's eyes glimmered. "Now we can think about taking you home with me."

Mia and I slapped high fives.

~*~

Less than two hours later, Granny's chest rattled. Nurses moved her into the intensive care unit. The doctor's diagnosis kicked me in the heart. Pneumonia.

When Mom and Dad arrived, we sisters cried as we huddled around them. I was so shocked at the news about Granny. I couldn't find the words to express my feelings. Surely, we didn't come all this way north for our granny to, to, to …

I coughed on a sob.

"I missed you, Mama and daddy." Mia wiped a finger across her runny nose.

Leah nodded. "Me, too."

I sniffled.

"We were scared." Mia trembled. "And cold." Mom and Dad hugged us tighter.

Papa stepped into the hall from Granny's doorway and waved everyone inside. "We're going to pray."

As a family, we gathered around Granny's bed. We sniffed, cried, and blew our noses. When Mia's time came to pray, she blubbered. "Please, God … need … Granny."

At Leah's turn, her voice faltered. "Lord—I've been mean to my granny. Please make her better, so I can tell her I'm—sorry." Shoulders heaving, Leah cried.

I hugged her around the neck, keeping her close. When it was my turn to pray, I bawled.

With prayer time over, Papa took a backward step. "I think everyone should check into the motel down the block." Mom quietly sobbed in a corner. "It's been a long day." Papa reached for my mom and cradled her in his arms. "I'll stay here."

Everyone nodded in agreement. Except for me. "I'm not leaving." I decided I should stay. I was the oldest child, grandchild, and great-grandchild. As the one who learned how to drive on a freeway when Granny couldn't. She trusted me while I didn't trust myself. She said at the lodge, I was the great-grandchild who was always there for her.

And—I gave my word to Mom on the day she dropped us off at Granny's. Unfortunately, it included a trip of delusion. *I'll keep my word now.*

Stepping closer, Mom placed her palms on my cheeks and kissed between my brows. Her tears got me with their sprinkles. I grabbed Mom. I didn't want to let her go, and hoped, hoped, hoped, she'd understand. With my embrace would she remember? Why I'd done what I'd done through to this moment?

With everyone gone, Papa and I got permission from the nurse to sit in Granny's room. We were both so glad we didn't have to wait down the hall in the waiting room. I became giddy with relief and caught myself grinning. Papa scooted a chair closer to Granny's bedside and settled into it. He leaned back and intertwined his fingers over his eyes.

When Papa snored, I felt doubly glad I stayed. What if Granny took an even worse turn and no one noticed?

Across from Papa, I moved my chair next to Granny. My tears leaked in streams along my cheeks, and I prayed. God might heal instead of take. He could do anything. Sighing, I hung onto those peaceful thoughts, while the nurse came in and out throughout the night.

I awoke to a raspy voice near my ear. "I'm hungry."

Lifting my cheek from the bed, I peered at the person who spoke. "Granny!" I giggle-cried. "You're not dead."

30

Faith, Hope, Love Abide

"Of course I'm not dead." Faded eyes glared. "But, I will if I don't get some food."

Thank You, Lord!

"What?" Papa jumped. "What's wrong here?" His frown softened. "Mom. You're awake." He fidgeted with the call buzzer. "I'll get help."

"You tell that nurse, a gnaw in my belly woke me." Granny lifted her head off the pillow. "Land's sake. A body could starve in this dern place."

Moving to pour Granny some water, I pressed on my teeth. I had to think before I spoke. She could still be extra fragile. "We won't let that happen, Granny." I held the cup for her.

Done after a couple of sips, Granny licked her lips. "Thank you, Kari Rose."

"Well, look who's awake." The nurse walked into the room. "How are you feeling, Adele?"

I read the nurse's name tag. *Olivia.*

"Hungry." Granny's blue eyes became slits. "And I need something for my chapped lips."

Olivia took Granny's vital signs. "We'll start you off with Jell-O." When Olivia finished checking Granny's oxygen level and blood pressure, she grinned. "Good, good, all looks amazing." Olivia patted Granny's shoulder. "Your breathing is much better, Adele. The medication is working." She left, but stuck her head into the open doorway. "I'll return with a snack and some lip gloss."

"A measly treat is better than nothing." Granny waved her arm and let it fall. "Could you make it cherry?"

Olivia winked. "I'll see what I can scrounge up."

"No, no, we've been scrounging for food too many days now. Just get me the cherry." When the nurse left, Granny closed her eyes. "I'm beat." She sighed. "What an ordeal." Soon, she became still. Her breathing came in more even waves.

I smiled at Papa, and his lips creased upward. Minutes later, Olivia carried in a tray of red Jell-O, a spoon, napkin, and lip gloss. She set the tray on Granny's moveable table top and left.

"You should go into the waiting room and stretch out, Kari." Papa stuck a thumb toward the door. "Ask for a blanket."

I glanced at the wall clock. "I can't believe it's already five in the morning." I moved to Granny's bed and dipped my pinky into the gloss. "Think I will." Gently, I spread the gloss on her sore lips. Granny never woke. "There now," I whispered. On my way out, I hugged Papa. I searched for a nurse to borrow the bedding.

With a weave-designed blanket and a pillow, I stretched across the small sofa in the quiet room. Just before I fell asleep, I thanked God again for helping Granny to keep breathing.

~*~

A wisp of air tickled my forehead. I slapped at the annoyance.

"Yoo-hoo, wake up sleepyhead." I opened my eyes. Mia's face peered at me, upside down. Her breath moved across my lashes.

Covering my head, I moaned. "Stop!"

She shook me, and I growled. "I said—" Peeking out at my surroundings, strangers watched us. I snatched off the blanket, grabbed the pillow, and stomped from the room.

Light footsteps scurried. "Golly, Kari, you're mean."

I stopped and wagged my head. "Golly, Mia, you're mean for waking me." I rolled my eyes at the ceiling and continued down the hall. "Honestly."

Mia yanked the thin blanket off my shoulders. It fell to the floor. "Did you hear about Granny?"

My feet came to a lightning bolt halt.

31

The Greatest Of These Is Love

"Oh." I leaned against the corridor wall. "Is she—gone?"

"No, silly girl." Mia grinned as if she were the first one to deliver the good news. "She's all better."

I thought to shake her but good. Instead, I clutched the pillow. "Don't scare me like this, Mia."

Her grin wobbled. "I didn't mean to."

"I know." Sighing, I bent to her eye level. "Hopefully, Granny will get to come home today."

"You mean to Papa and Granny-Too's?"

"Sure." I yawned really loud. "It doesn't matter we haven't been to their new place. It'll still be home."

Mia pulled on my hand. "Come on, everybody's waiting."

In my sleep-deprived state, I grew certain we were headed in the wrong direction. "Not this way."

"Yes." She tugged harder.

I followed her. Too exhausted to argue.

~*~

Granny's room buzzed with conversation. Papa and Granny-Too stood at one corner. Mom and Dad waited in another. The head of Granny's bed raised, Leah's shoulder rested next to hers.

"Leah, you and Granny look like you're plotting mischief." I winked at my sister as I past. Hugging Mom and Dad, I wanted to apologize. Honestly, I didn't feel regretful. *I kept my word to Mom.*

Granny cleared her throat. "We need to talk."

When I faced Granny, Mom cupped my arms.

Granny-Too stood next to me, kissed my cheek, and held my hand. "Sleep well, Pumpkin?" I nodded.

With a slight tremor, Granny clutched the cup Leah guided to her lips. She pulled it away when she finished. "I want to clear the air about what happened." Her calm expression glided over each one of us.

My muscles stiffened. Granny-Too squeezed my fingers. Leah shuffled her feet and blinked hard.

Granny raised her gnarled hand and wagged it. "This whole affair was my doing." Moisture gathered at the corners of her wrinkled lids. "I only considered myself. What I wanted, not what was best for the girls." She wheezed, and the room grew quiet. "Girls." She motioned for Mia and I. We joined Leah. "Will you forgive this old lady?"

"I'm not angry at you." Mia hugged Granny's arm. "Honest."

Standing with Leah on the other side of Granny's bed, I patted Granny's knuckles where her hand lay across her stomach. "We're not angry, either."

"No." Leah shook her head. "I'm not at all. Anymore."

This undid Granny. Her shoulders shook with sobs. The rest of the family drew closer and comforted her with words of

255

love. She sniffed on the last of her tears and stared at my mom. "Bethany Maria, I need your assurance the girls won't be punished for my wrongdoing."

Dad and Mom locked eyes. One of my mom's brows rose. "Okay, Granny. There's no need for us to discipline them." She pointed at me. "Although, I can't help being disappointed in my eldest."

My heart beat double time.

Leah squealed. "Mama!"

I'd been studying Granny's IV needle connected to her vein. "I felt torn, Mom." Her face blurred from my tears. "I should have taken charge for Leah and Mia's sake, but—" one glance at Mom. I gave up. "I'm sorry." *I truly am.*

Mom blinked. "For which offense are you sorriest, Kari Rose?"

Batting my lashes, I looked at Papa. His chin dipped. I winced. "For driving without a permit?"

"You think?" Mom fake-smiled like she did when angry. "That was not a smart decision, young lady. You could have caused a serious accident."

Fresh tears stung behind my nose. *I knew it.* Mom wouldn't let this go.

"Enough, Beth." My dad touched Mom's cheek. "Kari understands."

Granny leaned forward, piercing my mom with a triple-wrinkled frown. "You've got to know, Beth, Kari drives very well."

I swiped at the wet smears on my face. "Thanks to Papa."

"What?" He squinted. "Oh, now I remember. The times I let you drive my pickup in your pasture." He bobbed his head. "Good thing I gave you the driving lessons."

Dad gathered me into a hug. From behind, Mom circled her arms round us both. My sorrow in disappointing them festered. Beneath it all, though, it still seemed unfair.

I have to say something.

Even if they still thought I'd done wrong. I spoke in a quiet voice, above a whisper. "Mama, don't you remember before you left us at Granny's? You told me to take care of her. That she wasn't *really* in charge."

My dad let out a grunt of surprise. Mom's arms tightened and slacked from around us. "Oh, Kari. I did forget."

I faced my mom. "I would have had to hide her car keys for this trip to never happen."

Mom gave me a sad smile. "You're right, of course."

Across the room, someone coughed. My eyes wavered over my dad's shoulder. Papa nodded. I returned the gesture.

"Granny." Mia crossed her arms on the rail of Granny's hospital bed. "When are you going to finish your story about you and Grand?"

Smiling, Granny placed an index finger on her chin. "Oh, yeah, where was I?"

I wiggled from my parents' embrace. Leah and I hurried back to Granny's bedside and leaned near her elbow. Leah rested her hands at her jaws. "You told Grand to visit you at your house *after* your dad got home."

257

"Yeah, Granny." With the pads of my fingers, I smoothed over the wrinkles on her arm. "Grand must have been so brave. He wanted to *meet* your dad."

Right then, Granny stared at the ceiling. "James was one of a kind and knew how to handle the likes of me."

Sighing, I wondered if Harry would be my one of a kind.

Jean Ann Williams, the eldest in a large family, enjoys digging into her fascinating childhood to create stories. Having written over three hundred articles for children and adults, *Road Trip of Delusion* is her second book for young readers. A member of American Christian Fiction Writers, she writes regularly at *Putting on the New* blog, *Book Fun Magazine*, and her own *Real Stories for Real Girls* website. Jean Ann and her husband live on one acre in Southern Oregon where they raise a garden, keep goats, and hug their chickens. Her favorite sports are hiking through the woods and practicing archery. When grandchildren visit, Jean Ann plays Scrabble with them. Sometimes they allow Nana to win.

Acknowledgements

My online critique group who gave suggestions in the bright beginnings of this book: Siri Weber Feeney, Lynn Becker, Terry Pierce, Dawn Baertlein, and Rebecca Langston-George.

To Nina Newton, of *Ruby Magazine*, you are always willing to help me with the many tasks I'm not gifted in. Thank you! Your fantastic designs make me smile. I call you friend.

My editors, Leslie McKee and Nina Newton, you ladies catch the problems in my work which would interrupt the readers and fling them out of the story. I appreciate you both.

Thank you, Lee Carver, author of *Katie's Quest*, for your formatting expertise.

I'm so glad someone recommended Barbara Oden who did an amazing copy edit and proof of this book.

To a wonderful illustrator, Carley Rose Herlihy: I enjoy your work and can't wait to see what you create for the next book cover.

Beta readers, Dan Evangelho and Sommer Rose Livingstone, for your encouragement and suggestions.

Cousin Deanna Lomker, I appreciate your expertise for the medical scenes in this book.

Atmospheric scientist Molly Smith for advising me on weather and assuring me a blizzard is indeed possible in Northern California in April like the one which happened in 1880.

To our family snowplow guy, Denton Scott. Thank you for giving me a ride in your snowplow.

My granddaughters, Morgan Ann, Lynsey Michaela, and Carley Rose, and my husband's mother, Wanda Williams. Each of you inspired me.

Now, I'll share the story behind this story. I told my recently widowed mother-in-law we would drive down to pick her up when she was ready to stay in our home. She commented she just might get in her car and drive all the way to Oregon. I glanced at my granddaughters and said to Mom, "Well, you better bring my granddaughters with you." Because of this conversation, *Road Trip of Delusion* took root, I watered it, and God gave the increase.

And last but not least and in praise of well-seasoned love, to couples everywhere who commit to love each other until death do they part.

~ Jean Ann Williams

In loving memory of James and Wanda Williams
They finished raising me

To my husband of 46 years. Thank you, Jim, for your support in my publishing endeavors. Our heavenly Father, Who loves and nurtures me daily, even though I'm unworthy. His Son and Holy Spirit Who walk with me on my spiritual journey.

If you enjoyed this book, please register for my newsletter in order to receive information on my new releases at jeanannwilliamsauthor.com. Also, I'd like it if you were to share your opinion of *Road Trip of Delusion* by leaving a quick, honest review at Amazon and Good Reads. If you've read my first book, *Just Claire*, by *Clean Reads*, I hope ClaireLee's story sticks with you for a long time to come.

Thank you, and may God's blessings shine upon you!

A sneak peek of *Season of the Fawns,* releasing fall 2018.

1

COUSIN VALE~I SHALL NOT WANT

Vale shifted her Jeep, a CJ7, into first gear and stopped for a rusty, bullet-ridden stop sign. She checked the watch fastened on her freckled wrist. "I hope he didn't have a bad night." After his climbing accident two months ago on Watch Tower Mountain, her cousin, Caleb, suffered with monster headaches caused from his fall and head injury.

She rolled into Caleb's weed-invested driveway and halted next to his pickup. The swinging bridge their grandfather, Papa, had built welcomed her. She grabbed a weaved-basket off the passenger's seat filled with Caleb's favorite foods. Her cowboy boots hit the ground with a thud. Vale breathed deeply the smells of an autumn day, dried leaves and grasses beneath a blue sky. She threw the Jeep keys in the air. The sun reflected off the metal as they soared over the roll bar and plopped on the driver's seat.

Perfect toss.

As Vale readjusted her grip on the basket, she couldn't wait to talk with Caleb about next week. They would celebrate their twentieth birthdays. *No longer teenagers.*

Her foot twisted sideways on pine cones, and Vale whirled her arm to gain her balance. "When is he ever going to rake Papa's walkway?" Swinging her free arm in a hurried pace, she reached the wooden bridge. She steadied herself with one hand on the taut, rusty logging cable Papa used to attach the railing.

With the sway of the bridge, her memories flowed. She was a little girl again at her grandparents' cottage. As Vale's boot met with solid ground, the past swaddled her like a quilt, the cottage solid and inviting.

She stomped up the porch steps and stood before Papa's rough-hewed wood door. The knob wouldn't budge. "Hey, Caleb, open up." She peeked through the door's crisscross window panes. Clothes were scattered across the floor, sofa, and even over Jimmy Bird's now vacant cage. *Even birds don't live forever.*

She tapped on the glass with her short fingernails. "Hey, Cuz, I made your favorite Pastrami on a French roll." She raised her voice. "With extra mustard and Ma's pickled cucs."

Vale set their lunch on the redwood floorboards. She walked over the bridge and retrieved her keys. Back at the door, she stuck in the key and twisted. The door groaned open with a push. The air inside smelled musty and wise—like her grandparents. Deceased now, they left an ache in Vale's heart.

She propped the piggy door stopper against the kick plate, one of dozens of pigs from Grandma Nana's collections. Vale slid the basket on in with the side of her boot and frowned. "Gross. Caleb." She smelled more than wisdom as she walked through the middle of the living area. *Since when is Caleb messy?*

Vale's once tidy cousin now lived in clutter, cobwebs, and rotting food. The word *slob* came to mind. It would be too harsh of a word for someone who had been meticulous. She paved a trail with her boots, forcing clothes and a few to-go containers through the cottage Nana had left to Caleb.

"Caleb?" Vale pressed her ear to a closed door. "Are you ready in there? Did you remember our picnic?" Twisting the glass knob, she shoved against the warped door and into Grandma's old sewing room. Closed shutters over the bay window let in slants of light. The large sofa Caleb used as a bed filled the room, bare of sheets and blankets. Vale's brows waggled in a worry-wart dance. She stepped over his sawdust-covered jeans and opened an adjoining door to their grandparents' bedroom.

Caleb—Vale rushed to a mattress on the floor. His head and shoulders had slumped off the bed. She pressed fingers into his neck to feel for a pulse. Finding a heart rhythm, she sighed in relief. After Vale lugged him onto his pillow, she nudged his shoulder. "Caleb, wake up." She touched his cool cheek and with the other hand fished her cell phone from the pocket of her western riding skirt. She punched buttons and waited.

"911. What is your emergency?"

"My cousin needs an ambulance. 2020 Rifle Creek Road, fifteen minutes past Forest Glen Retirement Center in Glenway."

Twenty minutes later, the operator still had Vale on the phone as she instructed Vale to keep a check on Caleb's pulse. As Vale gave another pulse report to the operator, she broke off in mid-sentence with the sound of sirens. "They're here," and Vale disconnected the call with the 911 operator. The sobs she controlled now boiled over like cowboy coffee on a blazing campfire. The medical team moved in with one swoop, and Vale leaned against the wall a few feet away. They assessed

Caleb's condition. After what seemed like an eternity, the team carried her cousin on a gurney to the ambulance.

In her Jeep, Vale followed the ambulance to the hospital in Griffins Pass. Once they drove through Glenway and onto the freeway, she gained control of her shakes. She pressed the name on her cell and a woman said, "Hello."

"Ma!" Vale's voice broke. She veered off toward the shoulder but swerved back into her lane.

Rodell Cutter, Vale's mother, replied. "What's going on, baby?"

"I'm okay, but it's Caleb." She nodded with her ear to the phone at her mother's question. "Yes, he's on the way to the hospital. I found him unconscious."

Vale's mother gasped. "What happened?"

Tears blurred her vision, and she blinked. "I'm not sure, but the ambulance guy grabbed a bottle of sleeping pills from the top of Nana's old dresser."

"Oh, dear Lord." Rodell spoke in a near whisper. "I hope he didn't do this on purpose."

Vale yelled, "Don't say that just because of Papa."

"You're right, I'm sorry. Maybe it's something else, and he was taking his pills correctly." Rodell sighed. "I'll meet you at the hospital."

"Okay, Mama." Vale clicked off her phone and tossed it to the passenger seat.

Curvy roads down one of the mountain passes became a hair-pin and required her full attention. The last time she begged God for help was when Caleb fell on the mountain. "Dear, Lord, please keep him alive." She trusted God heard her words.

Vale's foot was like lead on the gas pedal as she came upon a straight stretch of road. Ahead of her, the ambulance continued to flash its lights. Caleb seemed far and away. *Could it be forever?*

It took the fourth mountain pass, and entering the valley to calm her. The landscape spread before her with vivid green firs accented with red Madrones.

After thirty miles of driving, she took the exit leading to Griffins Pass. Six traffic lights stood between her and the hospital. By now, Vale was sure her mother paced with anxious steps in the emergency room.

She frowned as she remembered her mother's comment—the thought ripped like a buck knife. *Was Papa's death really not an accident?* He'd been on various medications for different ailments, including narcolepsy. A year ago, Papa stopped his medications all at once the day before Thanksgiving and died from a Grand Mal Seizure.

Vale geared down, slowing to enter the ER parking lot. She pulled the CJ7 into a narrow space, cut the engine, and leaped from the seat. Slipping her keys in her corduroy pocket, she patted the other where her wallet was safely nestled. At the automatic doors, she stalled to wait for them to open. Running inside, she stopped as if she'd hit a wall. *Where's Ma?* She held her hands near her chin as if in prayer and searched the crowded lobby.

Rodell hunched over a water fountain, her bowed legs bent, and splashed water on her flushed cheeks. *Ma's crying?* Very few times had Vale seen Rodell Cutter gush with emotion—happy, sad, or otherwise.

Wiping her hands on the back pockets of her boot-cut work jeans, Vale's mom swiveled to face her. The two women met in the middle of the room where Vale launched into her mother's arms. She sniffed. "How soon until we hear?"

"I checked in with the receptionist." Rodell brushed Vale's wild, auburn curls from her face. "Honey, they have to stabilize him first."

With Rodell a half a foot taller, Vale craned her neck. "Stabilize?"

"Yes. I'm sure Caleb's in bad shape, *if* he indeed took too many sleeping pills."

Vale clenched her fingers.

Rodell grabbed Vale's fist and pulled her toward the French Brothers coffee hut. "I'll buy us something to drink."

Vale relaxed her hand within her mother's.

Hot drinks in hand, they found a quiet table. Vale blinked in concentration between sips of mocha. "Ma, Caleb hasn't been doing well ever since he fell on Watch Tower Mountain."

Rodell shook her head. "No, he hasn't."

"I pray our yearly birthday trip will change things for him." Vale swallowed another mouthful of the rich liquid. "You know, perk him up."

"We'll see." Rodell set down her cup. "You may have to cancel your trip."

"It's not for a whole week." Vale leaned forward with a jerk, sloshing mocha over the rim of the thick paper cup. "I'll nurse Caleb back to health before then. You just watch."

"Now, Vale. Don't start."

"Ma." She pursed her lips. "He can't miss our yearly. This would be like giving in to his troubles, and Caleb's not a quitter." A knot formed in her throat, and she swallowed it along with another gulp of her drink.

"I hope you're right about Caleb." Rodell squeezed her daughter's arm. "People can be pushed to their limits, Lord knows."

There's this again. She means Papa.

The receptionist called from behind her counter, "Mrs. Cutter?"

Vale shot forward from her chair. "Is Caleb ready?"

Rodell came around the table, circled an arm around Vale's shoulders, and slowed her walk to a normal pace toward the lady.

The receptionist smiled. "I'll show you to Mr. Unger's cubicle." She pointed. "Meet me at the double doors to your right."

Rodell reached for Vale's hand, and Vale hung on.

***

A nurse stood outside the closed curtain.

"I'm Caleb's cousin, Vale, and this is my mother, Rodell."

"I'm Siri." The nurse looked from one to the other. "You're the closest of kin?"

Vale nodded. "My mother raised him, because his folks died when he was a baby."

The nurse raised her brows. "Caleb had a close call with his sleeping pills."

"Was it intentional?"

Vale glared at her mother, and Rodell's lips trembled from her own question.

"The few amount of pills we pumped from his stomach? It's hard to tell."

"So it's possible it was an accident?" Vale winced, hoping, hoping.

Siri rested the clipboard with Caleb's information against her chest. "He took enough to consider this an overdose, even if it was accidental."

Rodell clasped her hands and twisted her fingers. "You're saying he could have thought more than the prescribed dose would be better?"

"I wouldn't know, ma'am, but the doctor will talk to Caleb soon."

Vale's spine became cold as ice. "I need to see him."

"Remember, he's sore and exhausted." Siri touched Vale's arm. "He probably won't feel like talking."

Vale moved closer to the curtain. "Thank you, ma'am." She locked eyes with Ma. "May I go in first?" Rodell nodded, and Vale separated the drape with a swish along the metal rod. She breathed in deep and forced a pleasant expression upon her face. For Caleb.

29674074R00168

Made in the USA
San Bernardino, CA
17 March 2019